“Despite your dire v
wouldn’t work toget
feeling that you’re not so sure that still
rings true.”

“Andrew—”

“Before you deny what I know as facts, hear me out. I propose a trial.”

Her mouth dropped open. “A what?”

“When our assignments are over, let’s schedule some time together. Uninterrupted time to get to know each other better. Without work getting in the way.”

“Andrew, I—”

He took her hand, turned it over and kissed the pulse point of her wrist. Instead of releasing it, he held her hand captive, caressing her fingers with the pad of his thumb.

“Don’t think. Feel, Alexa.”

At the moment, Alexa could barely breathe. She stared at Andrew stroking her hand as if she had just grown the appendage out of thin air.

“That’s a good sign.”

Alexa felt warm and tingly all over. “What is?”

Andrew leaned in closer. “The fact that I’m not on my knees in a headlock right now.”

Dear Reader,

Alexa King has been living in my head for quite some time now, demanding that her story be told. I'm elated to finally bring her journey to light in *The Bodyguard's Deadly Mission*. This story centers on overcoming personal tragedy, conquering obstacles in life and allowing yourself to trust again after your heart has been broken.

Alexa and Andrew are intense, passionate and laser-focused apart. But together, they are a powerful force of nature! I wanted their relationship to slowly grow and develop as the story unfolded because each of them had reasons for guarding their heart and trust takes time.

I love to travel, so I'm always going to work exciting new destinations into my stories. I had fun researching Chamonix, France, and the fun winter sport of skijoring! Thanks so much for reading! I hope my characters are memorable for you and that you end up rooting for them to find lasting happiness as much as I do!

Lisa Dodson

THE BODYGUARD'S DEADLY MISSION

Lisa Dodson

ISBN-13: 978-1-335-59393-1

The Bodyguard's Deadly Mission

For questions and comments about the quality of this book, please contact us at CustomerService@Harlequin.com.

Harlequin Enterprises ULC
22 Adelaide St. West, 41st Floor
Toronto, Ontario M5H 4E3, Canada
www.Harlequin.com

Printed in U.S.A.

Lisa Dodson is a nationally bestselling author and an Amazon #1 bestselling author of over nineteen novels in multiple genres. Lisa writes positive, realistic characters that she hopes readers can connect with while enjoying her novels. Lisa works as a business development manager at a technology consulting firm, is the mother of two adult children and a Maltipoo, Brinkley, and lives in Raleigh, North Carolina.

Books by Lisa Dodson

Six Days to Live
The Bodyguard's Deadly Mission

Visit the Author Profile page at Harlequin.com for more titles.

To my niece and brilliant forensic scientist, Jillian Lewis.
Thank you for the invaluable insight!

To the Alexa Kings and Brendas in the world.
Embrace your power!

Chapter 1

Alexa King dropped the yellow rose she was carrying on the wicker casket. Unfortunately, mourners weren't allowed to stay and watch the casket be lowered into the ground, so the memorial service for her best friend, Tanya Singleton, was officially over.

Walking over to the row of white fold-up chairs near the grave site, Alexa knelt in front of Tanya's mother, Viola Singleton, and took her hand. Tall and athletic in build, Viola was deep in her grief, but it did little to minimize her timeless beauty. Her cream-colored dress with the blouson sleeves was cinched at the waist with a wide tan leather belt. Her curly brown shoulder-length hair was adorned with a single white lily. Viola looked like she was ready to enjoy a picnic in the grassy meadow as opposed to laying her only child to rest. Alexa knew that would be exactly how Tanya would have wanted it.

"You were such a joy to my daughter. She would have loved all you've done to honor her today."

Alexa struggled to get the words out over the lump in her throat. "She was my best friend, and I loved her dearly."

"I know, honey. Thank you for driving all the way here. I know Pittsburgh isn't exactly around the corner from Washington, DC, but this place fits Tanya." Her mother sniffled and dabbed her eyes with her handkerchief. "The environmentally friendly burial was fitting. Thank you for finding it."

Hugging Viola tightly, she said, "You're welcome. And you're right. She would've loved this place." Alexa kissed her cheek before moving off and letting others pay their respects.

The burial site was on the other side of a meadow. Some

people with health issues took advantage of the caretaker's golf cart while most attendees walked.

When she reached the other side of the field, Jake and Margot Stanton King took turns hugging their daughter. Alexa and her parents were all wearing black suits and dark sunglasses. Each had a lapel pin of a gold crown with diamonds. It was a family trademark passed down to each male heir and family for generations.

"How are you, darling?"

Alexa lowered her sunglasses. "My heart is broken, Mom."

Her mother touched her shoulder. "I know, honey. We're so sorry."

"Lex, why don't you come back home with us? Take a few days to rest up and recuperate?"

"I can't, Dad. I have to finish packing up Tanya's apartment."

Her mother frowned. "Alexa, isn't there someone else who can do it?"

"No, Mom. I volunteered. The Singletons have enough on their plate back home with Tanya's brother still in the hospital recovering from surgery."

"I'm sorry he had to miss the funeral."

"We all are, Mom, but there was no way he was well enough to travel."

"Any word from Byron?"

Alexa's hands bunched into fists at her side. "No, and if he knows what's good for him, he'll stay away."

Jake frowned. "It seems strange that he's just disappeared without a trace."

"Well, after the police cleared him of any wrongdoing and the district attorney rejected the case, he decided to make himself scarce."

Margot rested her hand on Alexa's shoulder. "Honey, we know how you feel, but there's no proof."

"I've got plenty of text messages about their arguments and his temper, Mom."

"You know that Tanya never called the police on him, nor did she file a report. He also doesn't have a documented history of violence against his girlfriend. So even if you could produce the text messages, they'd never hold up against cross-examination. The defense will say you could've sent those messages from Tanya's phone."

Alexa blanched. "That's not true."

"It doesn't need to be true, Alexa. All it needs to do is introduce doubt to a jury about their authenticity."

That gave Alexa pause. "He can't get away with this. I don't care what it takes. I'll find a way to ensure Tanya's death wasn't in vain."

"You will be careful," her father warned. "I don't want you getting in over your head, Alexa. Suppose it wasn't an accident? Who knows what Byron could do if he felt cornered. The last thing we need is you to voice your theories on this publicly."

"If there is anything more to find, you let the police handle it," her mother cautioned.

When Alexa didn't readily agree, her father said, "Alexa."

"Okay, I hear you. I won't do anything on my own. I promise."

Her parents relaxed.

"I want you to take some time off work, Alexa."

"Dad, I'm fine."

"You've been working nonstop since she died, Alexa. You need some time to rest and regroup."

"No, I don't. I've got it under control."

Her father looked skeptical but agreed. "Okay, but you take it if you need it."

"I will," she promised.

Alexa's father, a retired intelligence officer for the Defense Intelligence Agency, cofounded J.M. King & Associates with his wife. Her mother headed up the legal side at the risk management firm in Washington, DC. After college graduation, Alexa went to work there and rose in the ranks to senior cyber threat intelligence analyst. A third-generation corporate lawyer, Margot wanted her daughter to follow in her footsteps and those of her mother and grandmother, but Alexa chose her father's profession.

"I have to go." She kissed both parents. "I promised Tanya's landlord I'd be over in the morning with the movers. Most of her belongings will be donated to local missions and charities."

Jake squeezed her hand. "That's wonderful, sweetheart. Let us know if you need anything."

After their goodbyes, Alexa headed for the parking lot while her parents went to say goodbye to Tanya's family. She had almost reached her convertible Volkswagen Beetle when someone called her name. Recognizing the voice, she kept walking.

"Alexa, wait." The man beckoned. When she ignored him, he ran and jumped in front of her. "Please," Byron Monroe said, holding up his hands. "I just want to talk to you for a minute."

She stepped back. "We have nothing to say to each other. How dare you even be here," she hissed.

"I have every right to be here," he said indignantly. "Tanya was my girlfriend."

"Every right, huh? Is that why you're slinking around and weren't at the grave site?"

He shifted on his feet. His hands shoved into the pockets of his navy blue slacks. "I didn't want to upset the family."

She took in his haphazard suit and unshaven face. "Get out of my way, Byron."

When she went to step around him, Byron blocked her path.

"You must know I would never hurt Tanya—I loved her. We were going to get married. So why would I do her harm?"

"Spare me. That's the garbage you told yourself and my

friend, but I'm not buying it." Alexa's expression turned menacing as she jabbed her index finger at his chest.

"I don't know what you're talking about."

"Tanya's death may have been labeled an accident, but we both know differently, don't we?" Alexa pressed, ignoring her parents' warnings. "She finally decides to leave you, and suddenly, she has an accident, trips down a flight of concrete steps, puts herself in a coma and eventually dies from her injuries?" She scoffed. "I don't think so."

Byron wiped his hand across his jaw in agitation. "I won't lie, we were arguing, and she tried to leave. I attempted to grab her arm, but she snatched it away from me, lost her balance and fell backward. It was an accident, Alexa—I swear."

She eyed him with contempt. "I'm not buying that. Save the innocent act for someone who doesn't know your history of losing your temper and taking it out on my best friend. I can't prove it now, but the truth will come out, Byron Monroe. When it does, I'll see that you pay for your crime, and I promise you that I won't stop until you're under the jail."

All pretense at civility was gone. When Byron leaned over, he was so close to Alexa that she smelled his cologne and breath, a cross between stale smoke, cheap liquor and cherry cough drops. She almost gagged.

Knowing that his proximity was an intimidation tactic, Alexa stood her ground.

"Regardless of what you think, I loved Tanya. I didn't kill her, and if I were you, I wouldn't continue digging up imaginary dirt—it's not wise."

"Is that a threat?"

A hint of a smile curled on his lips. Then, standing to his full height, he said, "Merely a warning from a concerned friend."

"We've never been friends. I tolerated you in my life because of Tanya. Nothing more."

"Everything okay over here?" a man called out.

They both turned in his direction.

"Yes, thank you," Alexa said sweetly before turning to Byron.

"If you think I'm going to cower in fear and let this drop, you don't know me."

Alexa shoved past him and strode to her car. Using the remote to unlock the door, she slid inside and started the car. When she looked up after starting the vehicle, Byron was gone. Taking a moment, she composed herself.

"The nerve of him." Her heart was racing, and her hands shook with suppressed fury and grief. "I will not be intimidated by you, Byron," she vowed.

Her thoughts drifted back to her last conversation with Tanya. It was, of course, about an argument with Byron. She could tell her friend wasn't telling her the whole story. But just as Tanya began to open up, Alexa got called into an important meeting at work.

I'm sorry, Tanya, I'm late for a meeting.

Okay, but you'll call me back?

Yes, I promise.

Alexa had been swamped the rest of the day and into the evening. She'd missed several calls and text messages, two from Tanya. It was almost two o'clock in the morning when Alexa dragged herself through the front door of her condo. Kicking off her shoes, she padded across the room to the couch, where she collapsed in an exhausted heap. She realized almost fifteen minutes later that she'd never called Tanya back.

It's too late to call now. I'll do it first thing in the morning. It's Saturday, and we'll have plenty of time to catch up, she'd promised herself.

Alexa tried to call and text several times the next day but never reached Tanya. When she finally did get a call, it wasn't one she'd ever expected to receive. Instead, it was a police officer calling to inform her that her friend had had an accident and that she should get to the hospital. They had called Alexa because they couldn't reach Tanya's next of kin, and Alexa was listed as her emergency contact.

Hours later, Alexa's world wobbled on its axis at discovering that Tanya was in Intensive Care in a coma with severe head trauma. The prognosis wasn't good, and even worse, the only person with her at the time of the accident was her on-again, off-again boyfriend, Byron.

Flipping through Tanya's phone, police had discovered a text message that Tanya drafted but never got to send. Chills shot across Alexa's body when she could finally read it herself.

You're right. People don't change, and Byron certainly isn't going to. So I finally broke up with him. But, of course, he insists that he'll win me back. Tanya was in the middle of saying that it would never happen when the text stopped, incomplete.

A horn honk jolted Alexa back to the present. Startled, she saw a car go by with two people waving goodbye.

Resting her head on the steering wheel, Alexa closed her eyes. "I failed you," she whispered into the quiet. "I'm sorry, Tanya."

During the five-hour drive back to Washington, DC, Alexa pondered her conversation with Byron. It made her skin crawl.

Just because I can't prove you're guilty doesn't mean you're innocent.

She disliked Byron with a vengeance and only tolerated his presence because of Tanya. He had never been worthy of her friend's love, and she liked him even less after noticing his mean streak. But Tanya had loved him and defended him regardless. To her peril.

The thought was like a dagger plunged straight into her chest. Fresh tears flowed, causing her vision to blur. Alexa angrily wiped them away with the back of her hand.

The pain closed in around Alexa. It gnawed at her, overtaking her waking hours and invading her sleep. It was the second time in her life that she had lost a friend to a violent encounter—first Shelley Porter, now Tanya. The guilt was so intense it was almost incapacitating.

On the other hand, the fact that Shelley hadn't died was a blessing, but it was bittersweet because her family had covertly blamed Alexa for the encounter in the park. Like she had control over some vagrant man trying to rob them in broad daylight.

Then, as the days turned into weeks and Shelley still hadn't recovered mentally, her mother, Carol Porter, showed up on the Kings' doorstep and accused Alexa of causing the whole incident and not protecting her daughter. Alexa denied any wrongdoing, and her parents had defended her against their neighbor's accusations.

"Mrs. Porter was right. I should forget about having close friends. I'm like a magnet for disaster." She gripped the steering wheel so tight that her fingers went numb.

Initially, Alexa felt certain the rift with Shelley would mend, but it had only grown. Eventually, the Porters packed up and moved without warning. The severed friendship with Shelley broke Alexa's heart, but losing Tanya to another violent act had exposed the deep wound festering inside. She was the common denominator, and if it weren't for their association with her, Shelley would be free from mental torment, and Tanya would be alive.

Tentacles of ice felt like they had snaked out and surrounded Alexa's heart, making it impossible for Alexa to deny the truth any longer.

"This was my fault."

Chapter 2

It was almost seven o'clock by the time she arrived at her condo on the Southwest Waterfront. After taking a shower, Alexa put on a pair of lounging pajamas and ordered takeout. While waiting, she sat on the couch and jotted down the action plan for the next day. She wasn't looking forward to being in charge of packing up Tanya's apartment, but she had promised Tanya's parents she would handle it.

Lighting a few candles, Alexa sat down for a quiet meal but moved the steak salad around in the mango wood salad bowl with the Moroccan blue-tiled inlay. It was a gift from her cousin, Zane King, and one of her favorites. Unfortunately, her appetite was as absent as a good night's sleep these days.

The cell phone ringing startled Alexa. Upon seeing the caller's name, she didn't bother with salutations when she picked up.

"I wish you were here with me."

"If it weren't traveling for work, you know I would be," her cousin replied. "I know today had to be rough for you."

"Yes, it was. I've realized that I don't need to have close friends."

"What? Lex, what are you talking about?"

"Bad things eventually happen to people that I love."

"First of all, that's merely a coincidence. Besides, I'm your best friend, and I'm still here."

"Yeah, but for how long, Zane?" she cried. "Plus, you're family. Maybe you all are immune."

"Lex, that's grief and fear talking. These are mere flukes, that's all. You aren't a magnet for danger. It's unfortunate, but sometimes bad things happen to good people. It's not your fault."

When she remained quiet, Zane said, "Quit ignoring me."

"I hear you, Z."

"You say you do, but do you believe it?"

"I had a run-in with Byron," she said, changing the subject.

"What? Why?"

"He didn't take too kindly to me ignoring him and refused to leave until he had convinced me of his innocence. I told him I didn't buy his act for a second and that I'd find a way to make him pay for Tanya's death."

"Easy, cousin. Don't underestimate that man. He could be dangerous."

"I know, but I'm not about to let him get away with anything, Zane. Tanya is gone because of his violent nature."

"We don't know that for sure."

Her eyebrows shot upward. "Zane—"

"Wait, hear me out before you jump all over me. Look, I agree with you, Alexa. Byron Monroe is bad news. I'm merely suggesting that you tread lightly. We can't prove that Tanya's death wasn't an accident, and you can't convict anyone of murder due to a feeling."

"Quit worrying. I promised Mom and Dad that I would be careful and will."

Zane audibly sighed. "Good. Hey, I've got to run. I've got an early meeting. Keep me posted on how things are going, okay?"

"I will," Alexa agreed before hanging up.

It had been three weeks since the funeral and clearing out of Tanya's apartment. The more days ticked by, the worse Alexa became. Sleep was a foreign concept. She practically lived at work and survived on bottled water and protein bars. But the one thing that provided Alexa with a modicum of peace was laps in the condo's swimming pool. It was the only time when her mind was at ease. It was her coping mechanism.

One night after work, Alexa was about to go swimming when her father called.

"Hey, Dad," she said as she maneuvered into her suit. "What's up?"

"We have to talk, honey."

Two things tipped her off this would not be a social call—her father's gruff voice and the fact that he placed her on speakerphone. Not having time for beating around the bush, Alexa jumped right in.

"Okay, what do you two need to discuss?"

"You, Lex," her mother replied. "We're worried about you."

"I don't know why."

"Then allow me to clarify," her father replied. "You haven't been home for a family dinner in forever, you're working a minimum of fifty hours a week, and from what I hear, you look like you haven't slept in ages. I won't even mention the mini meltdown you had at work."

Alexa was shocked, but that quickly drifted into anger. "What, are you keeping tabs on me? I don't need anyone trying to micromanage me, Dad."

"Alexa, that's not what your father is doing, and you know it. You're merely deflecting because everything he's said is true."

"It may be true, but I can handle myself."

"I should've insisted on this weeks ago." Her father sighed. "Alexa, you need to take a leave of absence and get yourself together."

"Dad, that's crazy. I don't need—"

"You know what we're dealing with at work. I need you operating at one hundred percent, Alexa."

"I haven't dropped one ball nor had a decline in my performance."

"Yet," he countered. "Something could happen at any time. That's not a risk I'm willing to take from any employee—especially not my daughter."

When they ended the call, Alexa was livid. Snatching up her bag, she slammed out of her condo and strode toward the elevator. Jamming her finger on the down button, Alexa paced in circles while waiting.

"I can't believe he benched me. Like I can't handle myself," she snapped, and took the steps down to the fitness center instead. She pushed the door open and almost slammed it off its hinges. Yanking off her clothes, Alexa tossed them on a lounge chair and dived into the cool water.

Swimming laps, Alexa lost count of how many revolutions she did. She continued until all the hurt, anger, guilt, pain and sadness had left her body, and her muscles ached with exertion.

Hovering weightless in the water, Alexa let her mind go blank and floated. Nothing mattered except the comforting silence and the next breath. Not just to sustain her life but to honor Tanya's.

When Alexa emerged from the water thirty minutes later, her skin was wrinkled like a prune, but she felt rejuvenated and lighter than she had in weeks.

"Dad was right. I'm in no shape to continue like nothing is wrong." Alexa hoisted herself out of the pool. "It's time to stop moving through life and reacting to things that happen. From now on, I have to get proactive," she said with conviction. "Everyone has a God-given talent. It's time I found mine."

Alexa stood at her parents' front door, her finger hovering over the doorbell.

"Once I do this, there's no going back," she said aloud.

Alexa had spent the last three weeks at the Serenity Wellness Center in San Jose, Costa Rica. It was a pristine white compound in the middle of a lush rainforest. It had exceeded her expectations. At the retreat, Alexa had spent the entire stay surrounded by professionals dedicated to creating a safe, welcoming environment that encouraged their guests to restore their minds, bodies and souls.

There, Alexa met Dr. Marena Dash-McKendrick, a biochemist from North Carolina. They gelled instantly and promised each other to keep in touch.

Another incredible outcome of her time at Serenity was that Alexa had discovered her purpose. It was the reason why she had come straight from the airport to her parents' without delay. Now that she had a direction, she was eager to begin her new life.

Alexa greeted her parents and eagerly discussed her trip. She answered questions and gave them gifts she had purchased on one of the group outings to town.

Now she sat perched on the edge of her favorite leather armchair in her father's office doing her best to summon the courage to jump into the abyss without a parachute.

Alexa laid out her plan in detail because Margot and Jake King were laser-focused when it came to setting the groundwork and laying out all the facts.

Once done with her well-thought-out argument, what concerned Alexa the most was that her parents just sat there staring at her in utter silence. Both were on the couch across from her with their hands folded in their laps.

After more painful seconds, Alexa felt compelled to demolish the silence.

"Dad, I know how it sounds, but I'm not crazy."

Jake leaned forward, his elbows resting just above his knees. "I didn't say you were, sweetheart."

"Well, I was thinking it," Margot snapped before turning to her daughter. "You want to be a bodyguard? Alexa, this is insane, not to mention dangerous."

"Not just a bodyguard. I did the research," she added. "I'll be a close protection officer."

Margot shook her head. "Oh, great, that's even riskier."

"I know, Mom, but it's what I want to do—what I have to do."

"Is it? Alexa, I know you feel guilty about losing Tanya, but you can't continue blaming yourself."

"It's not just about her, Mom. It's about protecting the Brendas in the world."

Margot glanced between her daughter and husband and then threw her hands up. "Am I supposed to know what that means?"

"Brenda was a woman at the retreat. She was in a horrible relationship that almost turned violent. It got to the point where she said she didn't even recognize herself anymore. There were so many similarities between her and Tanya." Alexa's voice trembled. "Family and friends begged her to leave him, but it wasn't until he threatened to kill her that Brenda found the courage to leave.

"It took a lot for her to tell her story. The counselor said that was why she founded Serenity. She felt that everyone needed the chance to open up. To release the pain holding them hostage and stealing their voice. To transform themselves no matter their circumstances. To heal. That's when I knew what my calling had to be."

"Alexa, there must be a better way to devote yourself to a cause that doesn't include peril. Why not volunteer at a shelter, or start a nonprofit? There are a million ways you can make a difference without risking your safety."

Jake turned to his wife. "Can you give us a minute, love?"

"Only if you plan on talking some sense into our daughter."

He squeezed her hand. "Please, Margot."

Nodding, she turned and strode out of the room, slamming the door behind her.

"I know Mom is upset, but I'm not changing my mind about this, Dad."

Her father stood and walked over to his desk. "I can see that, Lex. But what I need to know is if you have thought this through." He sat on the edge of the table and crossed his arms.

"I mean good and thoroughly through, Alexa. This isn't an easy path you're choosing. It's dangerous, and to become an expert, you'll have to know a great deal about many subjects. This profession is… We're talking life-and-death, but also risk assessment and mitigation, tactical, combat, movement safety—"

"Dad, we work in risk and threat assessment now. I know this job has much to learn, and I'll need specialized training."

"There's so much more to it than that, Lex. First, you'll be putting yourself in harm's way to protect someone else." Jake studied his daughter. "Do you understand the gravity of that choice? Hundreds of things could go wrong for each one that goes right in the field. Are those odds you can live with?"

Chapter 3

Alexa stood resolute in front of her father's desk. "I'm not changing my mind, Dad. I want to be an executive protection specialist to protect women who can't protect themselves. It's what I want to do. It's what I *have* to do."

Jake pinched the bridge of his nose. His stern expression echoed the gravity of his only child's decision.

"If you're sure, Alexa, and you're one hundred percent committed—"

"I am."

He shook his head. "I guess I shouldn't be surprised. When you were at the university library, you almost made that Peeping Tom eat a book on constitutional law when he got fresh with your dorm mate."

"Well, he needed to study that book anyway," she pointed out.

Unable to help himself, Jake chuckled. "Okay, Alexa. If you're dead set on this path, all my resources will be at your disposal. I have an old friend who runs a training academy with his son and a few other buddies who can help. They each have decades of experience, so you'll have the best training available."

She visibly relaxed. "Thank you, Dad. And I'm sorry about leaving you short one senior analyst."

"Don't worry about it, honey. I'll make all the arrangements."

She rushed to hug her father. "Thank you."

He returned the embrace. "The only thanks I need is you to be safe, sweetheart." He glanced into her eyes. "Do you hear me?"

"Yes," she said tearfully.

He kissed her cheek. "Good. Now I have to talk to your mother. Which isn't going to be easy." He sighed heavily.

"No, this is my decision, Dad. I'll be the one to talk to Mom."

Alexa found her mother outside by the pool in her favorite chaise longue. As was her habit, she sat by her mother's feet at its end.

The lights were on in the pool and around the perimeter. They both sat transfixed as the nighttime shadows and the shimmering blue water vied for dominance.

"I know you're worried."

"That would be an understatement," her mother murmured, never looking up. "Alexa, this is dangerous. Anything could happen."

"I know, Mom. But I can't ignore this anymore. It's eating away at my soul. I wasn't there for Shelley or Tanya. Not when it mattered. I want to help other women feel protected and safe, at least when they're in my care."

Margot turned to face her daughter. Alexa saw that she had been crying. There was also undisguised anguish in her eyes. Her mother's pain tore at her heart.

"Why is this your cross to bear, Alexa? All this guilt is misplaced. What happened to Shelley was an unforeseen event caused by a desperate man's ill-considered actions. Tanya also had a choice to make, and she made it. To her detriment. You aren't to blame for either incident."

"Mom, I'm not trying to hurt either of you—"

"I get it. You have to follow your heart. Your tenacity is something I've always admired about you, Alexa. You've always been a fighter and willing to help anyone that needed it. And as worried as I am, I know you'll do well. You're my daughter, after all."

That garnered a smile from Alexa. "I learned everything I know from my mother."

"Not everything," Margot chuckled before reaching for

Alexa's hand. "Whenever you're obstinate and set in your ways, you remind me of your father."

She leaned in and hugged her mother tightly. "I love you, Mom."

"I love you, my darling daughter. I couldn't be prouder of the woman you've become. Promise me that you'll be careful and return in one piece."

"I'll do my best."

When she got home, the first thing Alexa did was call Zane and bring him up to speed on her decision.

"I couldn't be happier for you. When do you leave?"

"What?" Alexa lay back on her bed and crossed one leg over the other. "I thought you'd try to talk me out of it, too."

"For what? It wouldn't make a difference anyway. I'm nowhere near as persuasive in arguing as your parents, so why waste my time swimming upstream?"

Alexa couldn't fault her cousin's reasoning. Not when it was true.

She went upstairs and began brushing her teeth and prepping for bed.

"You realize you're putting a damper on my social calendar, don't you? How am I supposed to hang out with my best friend if she's in— Where are you going again?"

"Colorado." She paused while rinsing her mouth. "Dad said that his buddy James Riker Sr. and his son own a facility in Pagosa Springs."

"Uh-huh. For how long?"

"Twelve weeks."

"You can't be serious," Zane complained. "Three months, Lex? That's insane."

"It's going to take time. There's so much I have to learn. Functional movement, first aid, several martial arts disciplines, defensive and offensive evasive maneuvers—"

"While that all sounds very impressive, I'm still going to miss you."

"I'll miss you, too."

"I can't believe that Uncle Jake is arranging all of this. Who doesn't he know?"

"Seriously," Alexa agreed. "I must admit to being surprised myself. I knew Dad had a lot of connections and old military buddies, but I never knew how extensive the list was until now."

"I'm sure his contacts will be helpful later," Zane reasoned. "Count your lucky stars. You're getting the VIP treatment."

"Zane, I don't want anyone going easy on me because I'm Jake King's daughter. I plan on earning my place on my own merits."

"I hear what you're saying, but don't be crazy. It's a highly competitive world you're about to enter. You'll need all the help you can get."

"That's true."

"Lex, I'm proud of you. You're daring to envision a whole new life for yourself. You'll be making a difference in the world. Don't get me wrong, you were excellent in cybersecurity, but I'd always felt that was Uncle Jake's choice for your life and not your own."

"I loved my job, Zane. I'm not leaving because I'm unhappy with it. I'm going because I believe this will be more rewarding for me."

"I'm sure it will, Alexa. I can't wait to hear about how it's going."

"I promise to keep you in the loop on my progress."

"You'd better."

After hanging up, Alexa set her cell phone on the nightstand. Then, staring at the ceiling, she placed her arms behind her head. This was such a significant change in her life. She was excited, but she was terrified, too. Failure wasn't an option. She would go all in, and she would complete the program.

"Well, Tanya. Neither of us saw this coming."

* * *

In the late afternoon, Alexa arrived at the Phalanx Training Academy in Pagosa Springs, Colorado. It was a seven-hour flight from Washington, DC, with a layover in Denver and an hour's ride from the Durango Regional Airport to the southwestern town. The academy had hired a driver to pick her up, for which she was grateful since it allowed her to stretch out after the long flight.

Upon sign-in, a young woman escorted her to James Riker's office.

When they entered, he was engrossed in paperwork.

"Ah, you must be Alexa King."

"Yes, I am."

James came around his desk and hugged her, which caught Alexa off guard.

"It's a pleasure to meet you finally. You can't imagine how your father goes on and on about you. I tell you, Jake would talk a dead man to death if you let him." He winked.

"I'm afraid Dad doesn't talk much about his military buddies other than they're his brothers for life."

"That we are. And don't you mind us old dogs. Once we get settled somewhere, we seldom visit each other, no matter how much we talk about it."

Alexa laughed. He reminded her a lot of her father. They were tall, muscular, good-looking men with infectious smiles, rich brown skin and salt-and-pepper hair that was cut close.

James took Alexa's luggage and ushered her outside to a nearby Jeep.

"Come on, let's get you settled, then I'll show you around. You'll meet my son, JJ, later. He's in the middle of teaching a class. Normally, we have a full house, but our summer session isn't as busy. He teaches several free classes if time permits. Come on, I'll give you a tour."

Alexa barely got in an "okay" before James was on to the next topic. She listened to him provide background on the academy while they drove. He reminded her of her father in many ways, just more talkative.

"We have about three hundred acres total, with a few lakes, the national forest nearby and spectacular views of the San Juan Mountains."

"It's beautiful here but kind of remote."

"That's by design," he replied. "At Phalanx, we teach many courses in ninety days. Executive protection officers put their life on the line for their principal." He turned to her. "That's the person that you're protecting. Depending on the contract, that may not be your actual client."

"I understand."

"Anyway, you must know the job's practical, functional and technical aspects. They must become instinctual, Alexa. Our reputation is without reproach because we hire the best instructors in the field, surpassing what other companies teach their students and offering continuing education to our graduates."

"I've read up on your company. You all have an impeccable track record, Mr. Riker."

"Please, call me James, or Jim."

"Okay. I wanted to say thank you for taking me on as a student on short notice."

"When your father called, I admit I was surprised by his request."

"Why? Because I'm a woman?"

"No, the number of women in executive protection is rising. It's because close protection isn't for everyone, Alexa. It takes a unique person to handle the job. It's dangerous work and solitary, with extended hours, not many holidays off or visits home."

Finally, he turned and pinned her with a stare. "You need to ask yourself if this is what you want to do in life and be clear on your answer."

"I understand."

"I don't know that you do, Alexa. I'm asking if you are

willing to turn your life upside down for this program. Are you willing to put your mind and body through pain, discomfort and being pushed to the limit of what you think you can handle? This program is more than just learning new skills and carrying a weapon. It's about mind over matter. Realizing that you can do things you never thought you'd be able to do, being responsible for another human being's safety and well-being. And most importantly, ask yourself if you're willing to take a bullet for your principal if it comes down to that? Are you willing to lay down your life to protect someone else, Alexa?"

Chapter 4

After their talk, James drove Alexa to her lodgings. They pulled down a dirt road, the only one Alexa had seen for some time. It led to a circular drive and a small log cabin surrounded by trees. The red cedar home had a red tin roof with modest landscaping.

"This isn't too remote for you, is it?"

Alexa jumped down from the Jeep and looked around. The mountain vista was majestic, with not one wrong view from any direction.

James pointed toward the back of the cabin. "There's a lake just a few minutes' walk down that path. It's well-stocked, so there are a few poles and a tackle box in the shed if you're an angler. There's also an ATV. You know how to drive one of those, don't you?"

"Yes, I do."

"Great. We're having dinner at our place tonight if you're up to it?"

"Oh, yes, of course. Thank you."

"It'll be after JJ's last class. The ATV's out back. You can ride up to my office at about seven."

"Thanks, I'll see you then," Alexa replied, escorting him out.

Alexa gazed around the log cabin. It was an open floor plan with many windows to let in the natural light. The living room had a fireplace made from river rock. A well-worn maple-brown leather couch with two big pillows with an Aztec design was right across from it. A coffee table and two chairs with a side table completed the space. The decor was homey and welcoming. The wood dining room table had six chairs and was right under the window, giving guests a magnificent view of the mountains. Photographs of

Native Americans were displayed proudly on the beamed walls in color and black-and-white.

Expecting the kitchen to be understated, Alexa was pleasantly surprised to find it was high-end and well furnished. The countertops were black-green granite with white and gold veins across the surface. A stainless-steel KitchenAid gas stove with five burners took up one side of the kitchen with the built-in microwave and oven nearby. In addition, there was a coffee machine, an air fryer and a slow cooker.

She ran her hand over the beverage brewing system before peeking into the metal drawer underneath that housed apple cider, coffee and tea pods.

"I can't wait to use you," she said dreamily.

The stainless-steel farmhouse kitchen sink was under the window.

"Eye candy. Just what I need while I'm doing dishes."

Next, she headed to the bathroom and gasped when she saw a large corner Jacuzzi tub in the same river rock as the fireplace. Half the wall behind it was glass. There was a separate shower, double sinks and a toilet area.

The cabin had two bedrooms that were similar in size on opposite sides of the house. Both had en suite bathrooms, a sliding door leading to a wraparound porch, window seats and huge walk-in closets.

Going back to the other bedroom, Alexa unpacked and took a shower. The hot water beating her back like a drum solo felt heavenly on her tired muscles.

Alexa chose jean shorts and a short-sleeve T-shirt to wear for dinner.

She glanced at her watch. She still had two hours before dinner. "Good a time as any to look around."

She shoved the phone in her pocket and went to retrieve the quad keys. Alexa had always been good with geography, so she confidently followed the path and her instincts to return to the main building. When she passed a break room, she spotted a refrigerator case with drinks and healthy snacks. Thirsty, Alexa retrieved an iced tea and continued down the hallway.

Rounding a corner, Alexa was about to enter James's office but stopped short at hearing raised voices.

"Since when is Phalanx a vacation destination?"

"What are you talking about?"

"Dad, I saw Jake King's note about doing him a favor and getting his daughter enrolled."

"JJ, he was talking about—"

"So, Alexa King has nothing better to do than disrupt our lives by signing up for our program she'll drop out of after two days? Can't we give her a tour and a T-shirt and be done with it? These weekend warrior wannabes are a waste of time and space."

"Don't be rude, JJ," his father snapped. "Alexa isn't here to take up space. Jake was very clear on his daughter's intentions. He assured me that she would take our training seriously, and I believe him."

"Well, I don't. We haven't had a woman complete our training program since…in forever," James Andrew Riker Jr. finished abruptly. "She could get hurt or, worse, cause someone else to be injured while she's out proving to herself that she can cut it."

"Nonsense," James dismissed. "I've met her. You haven't. She's serious about being here and deserves a chance to prove herself. So she stays. End of story. And the favor you mentioned that Jake asked me for was to *not* treat Alexa any differently than anyone else. She must earn her spot here. If she doesn't he expects her to get cut just like any other student."

His son crossed his arms. "I say you're making a big mistake. I read her application. It's obvious that Daddy gives her whatever she wants. She works for his company, went to the best schools and was a military brat."

"So were you," James pointed out.

JJ's expression darkened. "She's nothing like me, and I'm not going easy on her just because. It may be a moot point anyway. Mark my words, she'll wash out within a week and go crawling back to her fancy condo in Washington, DC."

Alexa reared back as though she had been stung by a bee. Her chest rose and fell with the pent-up energy she held in check. It was all she could do not to barge into James's office and demand his obnoxious and rude son retract every haughty accusation he'd slung her way.

Angry didn't scratch the surface of how she felt. *How dare he!*

She had no clue what she'd done to deserve this man's venom, but Alexa was determined to shove her diploma under his sanctimonious nose when she graduated.

Hearing both voices coming closer, Alexa rushed down the corridor. Unsure where to go next, she was about to head outside when another sound caught her attention. Following the noise, Alexa opened the door and went into a studio. There were several older adults in a circle on the mat. They were sparring, so she hung back not to be intrusive.

An instructor was teaching them an evasive technique. The man was wearing a protective face mask along with protective gear. His voice was calm and encouraging as he explained the moves to the students and studied their movements as they practiced.

Spotting a row of bleachers in the corner, Alexa took a seat. The man seemed kind and patient as each person had a turn.

"There seem to be some trainers here that can be professional and courteous. Shocking," Alexa snarked.

When a buzzer rang, the man announced that the class was over. The group thanked him and dissipated as another man entered from a side door and strode onto the mat. Alexa observed him with curiosity.

After patting a few people on the back, the teacher walked over to where the newcomer was standing. He was also wearing a protective helmet over his face. Some participants filed out of the room, saying their hellos to Alexa as they passed.

A woman stopped in front of Alexa. "Are you joining our class?"

"She's not old enough," a man said patiently from behind. "This is a senior citizens' self-defense class," he explained. "She doesn't look like she has an AARP card yet."

"That's true," Alexa chuckled. "I'm here for another training program, I just heard the commotion and came in to check it out."

"What do you think it'll be today?" one of the seniors asked his buddy before sitting down on the bench next to Alexa. "Sticks or swords?"

His friend shrugged. "Beats me, but it's always good. My money's on Andrew."

"Oh, great. More of that invisible money you love to bet with."

A loud crash caught her attention. Glancing up, she saw the two fighting with long sticks.

A woman nudged Alexa. "Looks like it's bōjutsu."

"What?"

"It's Japanese for staff technique. It's a type of stick fighting."

The woman had to speak loudly because the instructors were going full throttle, and the noise was deafening. Fixated, Alexa watched in awe as one man used his pole to sweep the other's feet from under him. There were several passes before they threw down the sticks and started grappling. When the man on the bottom finally tapped out, his opponent helped him up. Taking off their masks, they slapped each other on the back before walking over to join the crowd.

Alexa noted that both men were tall, and very attractive. One looked like an older, heavier version of the actor Scott Eastwood. The new guy was Black, had a muscular physique, arresting brown eyes, a mole on his cheek just under his right eye, and a scar from his bottom lip to his chin. Alexa found herself wondering how he got it. She guessed that he was either military or a former serviceman by how he carried himself. Either way, he was swoon-worthy, and she would have had to be incapacitated not to have an immediate response to his physical attraction.

She tried not to stare, but at this point, Alexa felt it would've been easier to outrun a bear while drenched in honey.

Eventually, the man's gaze connected with hers from across the room. When it did, his demeanor shifted so fast it caught Alexa off guard.

Unprepared for his outward hostility, she choked on her tea, dissolved into a fit of coughing, and then spilled her drink down the front of her clothing. She yelped as the cold liquid met her skin.

Everyone in the room turned and stared. Including the man she was just gawking at.

Though struggling to breathe, Alexa stood there dumbfounded. From the hostile way he was staring at her, and the similarity in looks, this guy had to be James's son.

Chapter 5

Mortified, she bounded out of the room and down the hallway to the break room. Grabbing some paper towels, Alexa wet them and vigorously dabbed at the front of her shirt.

What a jerk, she mused. *One minute he's smiling, and the next he's glaring like I spit in his coffee.*

"You must be Alexa King."

Alexa whirled around to find the rude man in question standing inside the doorway with his arms crossed. Despite just having had a rigorous workout, he was as relaxed as she was flustered. A towel was draped over his neck, with sweat still glistening on his face.

Well, if he thinks he's going to intimidate me, he's in for a disappointment, she said to herself. *He may be cute, but that doesn't give him a pass to be ill-mannered.*

Giving up on the shirt, Alexa threw the mound of wet paper in the trash and turned to face him like she was going into battle.

"And you must be James Riker Jr. Or should I call you JJ?"

"Andrew is fine. It's my middle name. Outside of family, no one calls me that."

He pushed off from the wall and came forward. He extended his hand. "It's a pleasure to meet you, Miss King."

Her arms stayed at her side. "I find that hard to believe given your behavior earlier," she replied with a calm she didn't feel.

That gave him pause. He lowered his hand. "Have we met?"

He may look like his father, but it was obvious he had not inherited James's easygoing nature.

"No, we haven't. Which is the reason why you dragging my name through the mud to your father was baffling."

For the first time, Andrew looked uncomfortable. "My apologies. I didn't mean for anyone to overhear."

"Interesting that you apologized for being overheard, and not what you said. Look, I don't know what your problem is, or why you've painted me with a broad brush. Frankly, I don't care. I'm not easily intimidated, Mr. Riker. Nor do I cower on command. I'm here to gain what's up there," she said, pointing to his head. "Not your approval."

"Fair enough. But I admit that I'm surprised to find you at Phalanx, Miss King. Based on your application, you don't seem the type that's interested in this kind of career."

"It would appear that you have a certain image in your mind of who I am, and what I would or wouldn't do. I can't imagine what's caused this fixation."

"Fixation?" Andrew laughed heartily. "I certainly wouldn't call it that. No, you just remind me of someone I know. She talked a good game, but in the end, she didn't have what it took for this line of work. My guess is neither will you."

"Ah. Biased and closed-minded." Her smile was as sweet as cotton candy. "Why should I be surprised based on your rudeness."

He returned the smile. Not in the least ruffled by her put-down. "Good to know. I see we're off to a great start."

"Thanks to you."

Before he could say more, Alexa turned on her heel and strode out of the room.

Andrew stood there a few moments, feeling like he'd just been dismissed. He had to admit that he was surprised that Alexa overheard his discussion with his dad. That was unexpected, and he chided himself for losing his temper at work. It was unprofessional and never should have happened. But he had seen her picture, and it had sparked a memory that wouldn't let go.

Alexa King was sure of herself. That much was obvious. And clearly, she wasn't overly sensitive because she had gotten angry instead of dissolving into tears. Andrew appreciated her spunk, but from the moment he read through her application and saw her picture, Alexa had rubbed him the wrong way. She reminded him of someone he would have preferred never to think about again. Despite that, meeting Alexa for the first time was startling. Andrew was surprised by her beauty and how she carried herself. Her photo had not done her justice.

Alexa was taller than most women he had met, with long, wavy hair that framed her face. There was a faint scar on her left cheek that made him wonder at the cause. Alexa had dimples and bright, welcoming eyes.

Not exactly welcoming, he corrected himself. Her gaze when he caught up with her in the break room was as brittle as frozen metal. Andrew could've kicked himself for stirring up this beehive. "Why did you have to look like *her*?" he groaned. Maybe Alexa would do them both a favor and quit by the week's end. *That would put us both out of our misery*, he reasoned. A man could hope.

Alexa gritted her teeth. She was so angry at Andrew Riker that she couldn't think straight. She had returned to the cabin and pondered not going to the welcome dinner, but Alexa had given her word. And once given, she never rescinded it.

Decision made, Alexa changed into a pair of brown linen trousers, a plain white oxford shirt that was open at the neck and a pair of black block-heeled sandals.

Dainty gold earrings with a matching necklace completed the semidressy look. Next, she swept her hair up into a high bun. If she was going into battle with Andrew Riker, she wanted to look good doing it.

Confident and relaxed, she headed out. Not wanting to arrive windblown, and with bugs stuck in various places, she took her time driving the all-terrain vehicle.

The Riker residence was a combination of wood and stone. Alexa marveled at its natural beauty and how large it was. She figured that it was at least six thousand square feet. A wraparound porch on the front, several rocking chairs and a two-seater swing allowed for plenty of conversation while admiring the mountainous views. By the time she parked the ATV and was heading up the steps to the porch, Andrew was already on the top step waiting.

"Welcome, Miss King. I hope you're hungry. Dad has never mastered just cooking for a small group, so there's a lot."

Confused by his congenial behavior, Alexa made an effort to reciprocate. "Thank you. And yes, I am."

"Mom died two years ago," Andrew explained. "I was hoping that Dad would take more time off, but he did the opposite. Instead, he threw himself into work and hasn't come up for air yet."

"I'm sorry to hear about your mother."

"Thanks." Andrew motioned toward the front door. "It's been rough, but we've done our best to be there for each other."

"I, um, have to ask. What's with the complete turnaround? Earlier you were—"

"Rude? Horrible? Loud and wrong?"

"Keep going, I'll stop you when I disagree."

He chuckled. "I deserve that."

An awkward silence crept into their conversation. Alexa struggled for something to say. "Do you have any siblings?"

"No, I'm an only child."

"Me, too," Alexa confessed. "You know when it's hardest to bear?"

"Holidays?"

"Yep. That's when I miss having brothers and sisters. Though I don't mind being spoiled," she joked.

Andrew stared at her for a moment. His expression darkened slightly, but it was enough for Alexa to notice.

"There you two are," James yelled from the kitchen. "I was beginning to think the guys and I would have to eat this super-scrumptious meal ourselves."

The lighthearted moment restored, Andrew looked heavenward. "He loves to brag about his cooking like some seasoned pitmaster. He just started grilling and smoking meats last year."

They went into the kitchen and greeted Andrew's father.

"I hope you two are hungry. Got enough to feed a bear."

Glancing at Alexa, Andrew mouthed the words *I told you* before saying, "Can't wait. It smells amazing in here."

The meal stretched out on the granite countertops was massive. There were six side dishes: smoked brisket, chicken and sausages, corn on the cob, potato salad, coleslaw and yeast rolls.

"Dad?" Andrew said in shock. "What in the world? You said a little something."

"Well, I got to grilling, and the grilling bug bit me, so I kept adding more stuff. Finally, I decided I'd better invite everybody." He grinned.

A woman came into the kitchen carrying an armful of folded napkins and a tablecloth. "You know how he gets once there's a burr under his saddle."

Alexa had to hide her smile as the older woman nudged past James to get several trivets from a drawer.

"Esther, this is Alexa. Alexa, this is my housekeeper and boss, Esther." James winked.

"Nice to meet you, Alexa, and don't mind him," she said, inclining her head toward James. Esther turned and handed the linens to Andrew. "Would you take care of the table while I finish up in the kitchen?"

"I'll help you," Alexa replied, and followed him into the dining room.

They worked as a team to set the table.

"Your housekeeper seems like she's time enough for the two of you."

"Esther is wonderful," Andrew agreed. "She has us toeing the line for sure. She's been with our family for decades and is like a second mother to me."

"Do you normally have students here for dinner?"

"We have a big dinner on the first night. We feel it's important that the students should get to know each other. You all will be working as a team for the next ninety days."

"Oh, I'm surprised you're not hoping I drop out long before that."

Slightly embarrassed at her guessing his thoughts, he said, "Being in the protection business isn't about being a lone wolf. It's about teamwork. Your team has to trust you, and it's the same for you. There are many moving parts, Alexa. Each must function independently but also as part of the whole. That's how you keep your principal, team and yourself safe."

"That makes sense."

When they were done, she followed Andrew back into the kitchen to help bring out the food.

James and Andrew were at ease entertaining and being cordial to their guests. Including Alexa there were twelve students, a lead trainer and several instructors who came to dinner. It was a loud, laughter-filled affair. The dinner was buffet style, so some were seated at the dining table, while others grabbed spots in the family room.

Being the only female student at dinner didn't intimidate or bother Alexa. Instead, she worked the room, introducing herself to each classmate, sizing them up as she went. Most were cordial and welcoming, but there were a few of the guys who weren't overly thrilled that she was there. One of them, Tate Bannon, was overtly hostile.

"You can't be serious," he said when she introduced herself. "You really think you're cut out for executive protection?" He practically laughed in her face.

"That's what I'm here to find out," she said, looking him straight in the eye. "This is a marathon, not a sprint, Bannon. And I plan to cross the finish line just like everyone else here."

"Wanna bet?" he remarked under his breath.

Alexa moved off before she said something to Tate that she would regret.

She wasn't about to make it easy for Andrew Riker to dismiss her. For whatever reason, both had assumed she wasn't cut out for the job. Which meant that she would do whatever it took to prove them wrong. *Loud and wrong,* she added for good measure.

Later that night, Andrew sat on the wooden swing on the back porch. He was absentmindedly swaying the rocker with the heel of his foot.

His thoughts drifted to Alexa. Despite their rocky start, Andrew tried to make up for his bad behavior earlier that day. He was engaging, sought her out on several occasions to ensure she was enjoying the party and offered to drive her home in his Jeep so she wouldn't have to drive the ATV at night, but she had declined, assuring him that she would be fine.

"Glad to see you've mended fences with Alexa."

He turned to see his father coming through the screen door. James leaned on one of the porch's support beams and observed his son.

"I wouldn't exactly call it that."

"One thing you'd better call it is finished," his father warned. "There's enough to worry about with the training and coursework. I need everyone focused and with a clear head, so no one gets hurt—that includes you, Andrew."

Whenever his father called him Andrew, he meant business.

"I know," he responded. "Business is business, Dad. I'm not about to jeopardize that for any reason."

"Good. Then keep whatever hang-up you've got about Alexa to yourself. I don't want it affecting your work, or her learning."

"It's not a hang-up," Andrew countered. "But come on, Dad. Don't tell me you don't see the resemblance."

"What I *see* is you stirring up trouble where there is none. And that's not something we can afford."

After a few moments, Esther joined them on the porch.

"It's a beautiful night," she breathed.

"Yes, it is," James replied, stepping away from the railing. "How about a stroll? Something tells me that my son here could use some alone time."

Andrew knew his father was right. He would do his job and train Alexa just like any other student. If she decided it was too much to handle and quit, that would be one less potential crisis later.

Chapter 6

The next few weeks were grueling for Alexa. She loved every minute. After the preliminary introductory coursework, filling out a guard card application and other required documents, they watched videos on executive protection, legalities and government policies. From there it was straight into hands-on and practical applications. An entire world opened up before Alexa, and she embraced it wholeheartedly.

That afternoon's sessions were all about strength, agility and endurance. Their instructor drilled them on functional movements to help improve flexibility and speed.

Alexa's muscles were sore when they were finished, but she kept it to herself since no one complained about their workout.

One of her classmates waved. "See you tomorrow, Amazon."

Alexa waved back. Everyone in class had a nickname, and Alexa's was Amazon. She was hoping it would wear off after a few days, but no such luck. It had stuck, so she embraced it. Upon reaching the cabin, the first thing she did was run a hot bath. Scouring the linen closet, Alexa almost whooped for joy when she found another box of Epsom salts. While the water was running, she called her parents to catch up.

"I was beginning to think you'd forgotten our telephone number," Jake teased.

"I'm sorry, Dad. It's been hectic this week. And we had functional movements and hand-to-hand combat training all afternoon. I'm spent."

"Did you have Dixon?"

"Yes." She grimaced and instinctively massaged her arm.

"He's a machine. He's going to put you through your paces, Lex."

"I can see that," she grumbled. "I'm running an Epsom salt bath as we speak. It's the third one this week."

Her father laughed. "Get used to it, Booba. There'll be plenty more in your immediate future."

She grinned at hearing the nickname that only he used. "I know, Dad. Gotta take the bad with the good, right?"

"You got it, kiddo."

"Speaking of much-needed pain relief, I have to run. My tub is almost full. Say hi to Mom for me. I'm sorry I missed her."

Jake chuckled. "She will be, too, sweetheart. And take it easy. You're the only daughter we've got."

"Don't worry. I plan to return in one piece."

A week later, Andrew was in his office working on a lesson plan when his father came in and sat down.

"Hey, Dad. What's up?"

"Just wanted to check in and see how things are going with Alexa?"

Leaning back in his chair, Andrew crossed his arms. "She's doing great. Her firearms instructor said she's at the top of the class and is an excellent marksman." He caught himself. "Markswoman. She's inside the eight rings every time. She's got the aptitude for mastering the fundamentals, and Alexa is acing all her written exams and holding her own in the simulations."

James nodded. "But?"

Andrew frowned. "But something is holding Alexa back. The mechanics are there, but the passion isn't. Her focus is split, and that keeps her from giving it her all. From being in the zone, you know?"

"Does that have anything to do with Tate Bannon? From what I've seen, he enjoys giving her a hard time. A few of them do."

"I don't think so. Alexa seems like she can handle it. She can give as good as she gets."

"Still, keep an eye on that," his father warned. "Competition and ribbing go with the territory, but I want to make sure that's all it is. This is no place for bullies."

"Understood."

His father got up. "Whatever is going on with her, you'll have to find it, JJ, because we're getting to the drop-off point, and Alexa needs to make it over the hump, or she's done. And I'd hate to tell Jake King that his daughter washed out of the program at this stage in the game."

Andrew tapped his pen absentmindedly on his desk. "I know."

That afternoon, the students were taken a few miles away to a practice center. The group was split into two teams for tactical maneuvers. Their assignment was to find the hostage in an abandoned building and get them to safety while eliminating any threat. Everyone was required to wear tactical gear, but they would be using practice ammunition. Alexa's team was first up. Headsets allowed them to keep in contact as they fanned out. The building was dark and musty, and visibility was poor, so Alexa stuck to the walls as she made her way across the space toward the steps.

"Watch your backs," their instructor cautioned. "Anything could be a potential threat."

Alexa made her way up the stairs. Her heart was hammering inside her chest, and she felt the sweat gathering at the nape of her neck. The gear was heavy and the heat stifling. She took a few deep breaths to calm herself before proceeding to the second floor.

The sounds of gunfire and yelling erupted in the silence. Glancing over at her partner, he motioned for them to get moving. Following his lead, Alexa hurried up the stairs. At the top, she melted into the wall and followed it down the corridor. Her eyes were burning from the perspiration that ran off her forehead. She took a second to swipe it away before they were under fire.

Dropping down to make herself small, Alexa's partner

spun around to return fire before yelling, "Move," over his shoulder.

She was running down the hall now with him right on her heels. Alexa entered the first door she saw and barely had time to duck as something whizzed past her head.

Crouching down, Alexa saw two figures in the far corner.

"Help me, please," a woman cried out.

Alexa raised her weapon. "Let her go," she demanded.

A man had one arm around her neck while the other was holding a pistol straight at Alexa. "I don't think so. Drop your weapon, or she's dead."

Dozens of scenarios rushed through Alexa's brain as she struggled to keep her wits about her. Adrenaline coursed through her body, causing her to feel nauseous, but she ignored it.

"Do you have a clear shot?"

"Negative," her partner replied.

Before she could react, the kidnapper opened fire before dragging the hostage out a rear door. Alexa hit the floor before returning fire. She heard her partner yell, "I'm hit!"

Alexa turned around and saw that her teammate had a huge bright yellow spot on his chest.

She rushed after the kidnapper.

"Wait," her partner called after her. "Shouldn't we wait for backup?"

Alexa pulled him farther into the room and slammed the door. Grabbing a turned-over chair, she wedged it under the doorknob. "There's no time. We're not losing this exercise. You're fine," she said, checking her ammo. "Stay put. I'll go."

It was eerily quiet as Alexa ascended the stairs in front of her. The radio chatter in her ear confirmed that there was only a handful of students from both teams still left in the maneuver.

Crouched low, Alexa cautiously opened the door and proceeded into the room. Boxes and junk were everywhere. The rest of the area was cast in shadows, with only one window providing light. Recalling her training, she stuck close to the wall as she moved.

Someone jumped out from behind a box with a gun pointed at Alexa. She fired without hesitation. As she ran past, another assailant grabbed her from behind. Her rifle fell to the floor. Alexa barely dodged a blow to the gut. She took a swing, but it was deflected, and before she could recover, the man snaked an arm around her neck and tried to pull Alexa off her feet.

"Give up," the man growled in her ear. "You're not cut out for this. Just admit it."

"Not happening," she gasped, trying to break his hold.

"One day you'll be in over your head and cost someone their life, King. And you'll be powerless to stop it."

That got under Alexa's skin. She paused for a split second, but it was enough.

Her opponent flipped her, and she landed hard on her back, knocking the wind out of her. Alexa turned on her stomach. Slow to get up, she mumbled something.

"I can't hear you," he taunted. "Do you give up?"

Spinning around, there was a pistol in Alexa's hand. She fired at point-blank range. A yellow paint splatter surfaced across the man's middle section before he hit the ground with a groan.

"I said, not today."

Retrieving her rifle, she spotted the target running toward a narrow plank, pulling the hostage behind him. Alexa raced across the space, and when everyone was clear, she launched herself at the man and victim, knocking them both off-balance. With the assailant effectively separated from the woman, Alexa jumped to her feet ready to engage the man when the crack of a pistol shot rang out. She felt the bullet connect with her chest a second before the force of impact knocked her backward and sent her crashing into a stack of crates.

Chapter 7

"Alexa? Alexa, can you hear me?"

She felt something tugging at her and a cacophony of sounds overhead. Alexa tried again to drag herself out of oblivion and back to consciousness, but it was useless.

"She's out again," the facility's doctor confirmed.

"How did this happen?" Andrew snapped.

Before anyone could answer, he continued his rant.

"Someone better tell me how in the world someone's gun had live ammo," he yelled as he paced. "We're supposed to have safety protocols in place to ensure that nothing like this ever happens. Alexa could've been killed."

Several of the instructors were hovering just inside the treatment room in the infirmary. Each looked incredibly worried, and nervous.

"We have our team looking into it," one of them replied, his face a mask of concern. "It was clearly an accident."

"An accident I can't explain," another man chimed in. "I double-checked all the equipment last night before locking up."

"Obviously, something was overlooked."

Everyone turned at the irate voice behind them.

The men scattered as Andrew's father rushed in and went straight to the hospital bed. He peered down at Alexa and then at the doctor treating her.

"How is she?"

"She'll feel like she got run over by a dump truck and likely have one heck of a bruise, but she'll live."

"I want a report on my desk in an hour—including a statement from the student who shot her."

Andrew didn't bother looking up to see if his employees acknowledged his command. The two teachers nodded to no one in particular before rushing out of the room.

Andrew sank into the chair next to Alexa's bed. He ran a hand over his face.

"This could have been so much worse, Dad."

"I know, JJ." He clapped Andrew on the back. "We'll get to the bottom of this."

"She could be out for a while," the doctor informed them. "I can call you when she comes to."

"You go ahead," Andrew told his father. "I'm going to stay."

James took Alexa's hand and squeezed it. "Okay. Let me know the moment you hear something."

"Roger that."

It was almost midnight before Alexa came to. Andrew was leaning back in the chair asleep with his arms crossed and legs stretched out in front of him. His eyes snapped open when he heard Alexa moan.

"What happened?" she asked. Her voice sounded like tires rolling over gravel.

"You had an accident," he confirmed. "Hang on a second."

He hopped up and went to get the doctor. They both returned less than a minute later. Andrew hovered while he examined Alexa and asked her a few questions.

"I'll give you something for the pain," he said as he injected her with medicine. "It will also help you sleep."

Alexa's worried gaze connected with Andrew. "I don't remember anything."

"Don't worry. Try to rest, Alexa. I'm sure it'll come back to you soon."

Her eyes drifted shut and seconds later she was asleep.

"You should call it a night, Andrew. She'll be out until morning."

He nodded and headed for the door. "I'll be back first thing."

Andrew glanced over his shoulder at Alexa. His expression was grim as he watched her chest rise and fall several times before he left.

Walking the short distance back to the house, he was grateful when he arrived to find it quiet and everyone gone to bed.

Silently, Andrew climbed the steps to the second floor. He was careful not to make noise as he headed to his bedroom. He was exhausted and had a pounding headache. The last thing he felt up to was a lengthy conversation with his father.

Aside from the clock on his nightstand, the room was pitch-black. The darkness was soothing to his head, so he moved around without light. Kicking off his shoes, Andrew stripped and dumped his clothes in the hamper just inside the bathroom before turning on the water for a shower. He placed a towel on the bronze hook on the wall outside of the shower and climbed in.

He welcomed the pounding hot water beating into his tired muscles.

While he soaped up, Andrew replayed the events of the day. He couldn't wrap his head around how a gun containing real ammo was used in one of their training exercises. In the history of their school something like this had never happened before.

If Alexa had not been wearing a bulletproof vest for precaution, she would have died.

That thought flooded him with anger, which was quickly replaced with remorse when he recalled his treatment of her when she had first arrived.

Andrew turned the water off and stepped out of the shower. As he dried off, his mind ran through various scenarios of how such a momentous mistake could have happened.

What if it wasn't a mistake? What if Alexa's accident was intentional?

Still moving around in the dark, Andrew retrieved a pair

of pajamas from his dresser and put them on. When he was done, he settled into bed.

After a few minutes of trying to go to sleep, Andrew rolled onto his back and placed his arms behind his head. He pondered several of his students who hadn't warmed to Alexa and had on occasion given her flak.

Tate Bannon was at the top of this list. It was no secret that he didn't want Alexa in the program and had even gotten into an argument with her after she bested him sparring during a martial arts class.

That thought made his jaw clench. If one of his students had purposely endangered another student's life, it would be grounds for expulsion. And Andrew wouldn't hesitate to nail whoever was responsible's butt to the proverbial wall. He wasn't about to risk Phalanx's reputation on a student's prejudices, no matter who it was.

Later that morning, Alexa was sitting up in bed when the doctor came in.

"And how are you feeling, Miss King?"

"Like an elephant sat on my chest all night."

With a smile, he examined his patient and then scribbled a few notes into her chart.

"I want you to take it easy for a day or two. And no physical exertion until you're feeling better."

"Thank you for taking good care of me."

"My pleasure, Miss King." His blue eyes twinkled as he wrote her discharge orders. "Try not to get yourself shot again, okay?"

"Believe me, it's the furthest thing from my mind, Doc."

"Glad to hear it," Andrew replied as he strolled into the room.

The doctor repeated her discharge instructions and then excused himself. Andrew observed Alexa, who was attempting to put on her shoes.

"Here, let me help."

He rushed over and helped tie up the laces.

"Thank you, for the change of clothes," she replied congenially.

"You're welcome. Though I admit I thought you were going to challenge me and say that you could put on your shoes yourself."

"I would have, but I'm too tired."

Alexa tried to sound lighthearted, but it came out sounding like she was exhausted.

"Let's get you up," Andrew replied, helping her to stand.

Alexa gritted her teeth against the soreness in her chest.

After helping her into his Jeep, Andrew hurried around the side and jumped in.

A man watched the sport utility vehicle drive down the dusty path toward Alexa's cabin. Retrieving the cigarette from his lips, he dropped it on the ground and stamped it beneath his boot.

"Close call, Miss King. Next time, you won't be so lucky."

Alexa had fallen asleep a few minutes after Andrew helped her to bed. When she woke up, the sun had almost set. She blinked a few times and cautiously raised herself up on the pillows strategically placed behind her head.

"Take it easy," Andrew said, popping up from his chair and rushing over.

"I'm fine," she replied after making a bit of an adjustment. She sighed with relief because it had not hurt as much as she had anticipated.

Esther came in an hour later.

"Changing of the guard," she announced before setting the tote bag she was carrying on the bench at the foot of Alexa's bed.

"I've got cards, movies and magazines in case you get bored."

"Esther, I'll be fine tonight. There's really no need to stay."

"Nonsense," the older woman dismissed. "The doctor

told you to rest, and that's what we're going to ensure that you do. Now, how about one of my homemade lemon bars?"

Andrew leaned over Esther and retrieved a sugary treat. He took a bite and sighed blissfully. "These are the best, Esther. You ladies have a good night. I'll check in first thing in the morning."

Ensuring the house was locked up tight before he left, Andrew drove back to his office to retrieve the requested report. He was sitting at his desk with his feet up, poring over the document, when his father came in and sat down. "Anything of import?"

"No. Velasquez confirms that all the weapons had dummy ammo when he transported them to the building."

"Then who secured them once they arrived?"

"Roberts did, but admitted there was a window of about fifteen minutes when he was instructing the class that his eyes weren't on the equipment."

James frowned. "So we've got nothing."

"Not yet. But I'm not about to let this go until we find our culprit. My gut tells me someone was deliberately targeting Alexa."

"How? No one knew who would get each weapon."

"That's not exactly true. The gear was all separated out by the time the students arrived. We started the maneuvers shortly after that."

"So it couldn't have been a student because they were all accounted for and receiving instructions," his father reasoned.

"We only had two teams there for manuevers, but other training sessions were going on that day. Anyone could've had access during those fifteen minutes where the weapons were unattended."

"I don't like this one bit. We need to find this guy, Andrew, before anything else happens. Alexa shouldn't be fearing for her safety."

"I'll get to the bottom of this, Dad. Rest assured, this won't happen again."

Chapter 8

"A perfect way to start the weekend," Andrew said as he set his helmet on the seat of his ATV and walked over.

"I thought so," Alexa replied.

"How'd baton training go?"

Her face lit up. "Loved it. They had me sparring against Big Mouth. I took great pleasure in sweeping his legs from under him—again."

Andrew laughed at the thought of Tate Bannon being bested again by Alexa. Getting behind her, he pushed the swing. He expected Alexa to protest, but when she didn't, he continued.

"I haven't been on a swing since middle school."

"Just like riding a bike," Andrew countered.

"I suppose you're right."

He pushed Alexa higher and higher until she laughed so hard she started hiccuping.

"Get me down," she yelled between gasps of air.

"Not until you say the magic word."

"Embussing."

"Nope."

"Cover fire?"

"Not even close."

"Chase car?"

It was Andrew's turn to laugh heartily. "You're terrible at this game."

"Andrew, please let me off."

Immediately, he took hold of the swing and began slowing her forward momentum until she came to a complete stop.

Alexa placed her feet on the ground, and Andrew extended his hand. She put her fingers in his firm grasp. When she stood up, she pitched forward into Andrew's chest. He wrapped an arm around her waist to keep her steady.

"Are you okay?"

"Yes, sorry about that," she said when she could steady herself. "Got a bit dizzy. So, what was the magic word? Please?"

"No," he said with a devilish grin. "It was Andrew."

"Andrew," she repeated slowly.

Gazing into his eyes, Alexa stood rooted to her spot, which meant there were mere inches between them. Andrew's arms were still wrapped around her waist. It hadn't dawned on him yet to remove them. Instead, the blush that inched up her neck and splotched its way across her face had him riveted.

He stared at her intently. His hands caressed her back before he moved one hand up to catch a wisp of her hair blowing across her face. Andrew twirled it between his thumb and index finger before placing it behind her ear and resting his hand on the side of her cheek.

"You scared me to death. Do you know I've barely thought about anything else but you since the accident?"

Alexa peered up at him. Whatever she expected Andrew to say, this wasn't it. Nor was the expression on his face that made her skin tingle.

"That wasn't my intention," she whispered once she could speak.

"Mine, either," Andrew said absentmindedly as his fingers outlined the curve of her face. "Yet here we are."

For a moment, Alexa gave in to the fascinating tingling she felt unfurling inside of her and leaned into his touch. When his gaze moved to her lips and his head lowered, Alexa closed her eyes in anticipation of a kiss she hadn't dreamt of wanting until this moment.

"Andrew."

A noise behind them broke the spell.

Alexa's eyes flew open. The shock of what had almost happened was enough to bring her back to her senses.

"Andrew, I'm sorry. I shouldn't have… This can't happen," she blurted out before backing out of his arms with such force she almost toppled over. "I had no right to lead you on like that. I'm—"

Andrew reached out to steady her before returning his arms to his sides. "Married?"

Alexa's face scrunched up in question. "No."

"Oh, you have a boyfriend."

"No," she repeated. "I'm not seeing anyone. I just can't get involved with anyone. I don't do relationships. It's dangerous to be near me."

His eyebrows shot up in surprise. "What?"

"I'm sorry, I didn't mean to be precipitous. What I should have said was—"

"I got it," Andrew cut her off. "Strictly professional. I shouldn't have tried to kiss you. The last thing I want to do is make things awkward between us."

For a moment, his expression was unreadable, but eventually, it returned to neutral and he offered up a reassuring smile.

Alexa wasn't making sense to him right now, but he understood that she had drawn a line between them, and he would respect it.

Though there was some chemistry there, Andrew had learned from past disasters that all endings weren't happy. It was a lesson that almost cost him everything and not one he would ever repeat. Not even for Alexa.

"Thank you," she said before putting some space between them. "That was fun."

"You're welcome." It took Andrew a moment to remember why he'd come over in the first place.

"Fishing," he finally blurted out. "How about going fishing with me? There's a stream not too far from the house."

"Sounds good. How about you get the equipment, and I'll be back in a few?"

"Sure," Andrew agreed.

Waving, Alexa disappeared into the house. She hurried to the bathroom and doused her face in cold water.

"What was that?" she said, staring at herself in the mirror. "You can't afford distractions, King—of any kind."

There was no doubt that Andrew Riker was good-looking with an enigmatic air about him, but that was no reason for Alexa to get off track. She didn't have time for playful banter or harmless flirting. She was there to learn her trade and that was it. *So how is fishing work-related?* Alexa asked herself.

"Good point," she said aloud. Brushing her hair, Alexa secured it into a bun at the top of her head. She retrieved a sun visor from the closet in her bedroom and then rushed outside to meet Andrew.

Alexa carried the fishing poles while Andrew took the tackle box and a bucket. He had tried to bring everything, but she refused.

"Do you have to do everything yourself? You know it's okay to get help sometimes, right?"

"I was raised to be self-sufficient," she replied. "My parents thought it was important to rely on your abilities to get things done. So I had my first job at six."

He looked surprised. "Doing what, a lemonade stand?"

"No, a cleaning business."

He arched an eyebrow. "Are you serious?"

"Yes. My friends would pay me to help them clean up their rooms."

Andrew shook his head. "Somehow, I can see that."

Reaching the stream, they set up and then searched for worms.

"These lakes are stocked with catfish, panfish, perch and bass, so we should stand a fighting chance of catching something for dinner."

"This is the perfect time to come," Andrew said after

they'd cast a few times with no luck. "Early morning or late evening is ideal."

As if to prove his point, Alexa got a hit.

"I've got a bite," she said eagerly. She waited until the third hit before reeling it in.

"That's a decent-sized yellow perch," Andrew remarked before dropping it into the water-filled bucket.

They chatted as they fished, and by the time the sun started setting, Alexa was bragging about her superior fishing skills as they packed up and returned to the cabin.

"Uh-huh. How about you save that boasting for when it's time to clean fish?"

"Please," she scoffed. "I slay at that, too."

Andrew burst out laughing. "The, uh, fish slayer?"

She joined in. "Now, doesn't that have a ring to it?"

Working together, it didn't take long to clean and prep all the fish for frying.

At dinner, Andrew took a bite and smiled. "This is delicious. You did a great job on the fish. Is there anything you can't do?" he teased.

"I'm not too good at relationships," Alexa replied, but clammed up. She was surprised that she had even said it aloud.

There was an awkward silence where the statement drifted in the air like an airplane circling the runway.

"Why not?" Andrew asked before he could think better of it.

Alexa was quiet so long that he looked up.

"It's a long story that I'd rather not go into tonight," she finally answered. "Suffice it to say, I've been known to have trust issues."

"You've been hurt before?"

"You could say that. I had a best friend that was in a toxic relationship. I saw firsthand how deadly the consequences can be. It's not something I'd ever want to experience."

Andrew's eyebrow rose at that. "Alexa, not every relationship is like the one you described. Look at your parents. They're still married. You've got a decent blueprint for relationships that do turn out well," he reasoned.

"True, but I've never known that kind of happiness. The boyfriends I've had were few and nothing memorable. It's better if I'm alone because at the end of the day, I'm just not willing to risk it."

He glanced over. "Risk what?"

"My heart."

"Well, in this line of work, you miss all those important get-togethers with your significant other. Like birthdays, anniversaries, holidays. It's hard on relationships."

"As I said, I'm not interested in a love life."

"Then you'd be the first woman I've ever encountered that wasn't."

Alexa cut her eyes at him. "I always say what I mean. I never lie. You think every woman is just waiting around to get swept off her feet by a man?" Before he could answer, she continued. "Well, not me. I'm good."

Andrew digested that information. Alexa may not lie, but something was lurking under the surface that she wasn't sharing, affecting her performance. *Don't worry, Alexa*, he said to himself. *Whatever it is, I'm going to find it.*

"Are you okay?"

He glanced up. "Yeah, why?"

"You have this intense look on your face."

"It's nothing, just an issue at work that I'm trying to solve."

"I'm sure you'll work it out. You seem to be resourceful."

Andrew grinned. "Careful, Lexi, that sounds pretty close to a compliment."

She paused. That was the first time he'd called her by a nickname.

Alexa made a face. "Oh, so we're friends now?"

He sat back and regarded Alexa. "I thought you weren't good at relationships?"

"I meant the romantic kind, and you know it."

Andrew stood and began clearing the dishes from the table. Alexa followed suit.

"Well, now that we have that cleared up," he teased as he placed the dishes in the dishwasher while Alexa put the rest of the food away.

Suddenly, he stopped and turned around.

"Yes, Alexa. I'd like it if we were friends." Andrew leaned closer. "That doesn't mean I will take it easy on you."

"The thought hadn't crossed my mind," she shot back before resuming her task. After a few minutes of working in companionable silence, she glanced at Andrew over her shoulder. "Besides, I'd be disappointed if you did."

Chapter 9

Alexa was slammed back into the wall, and her opponent brought his arm to her neck.

"Get your back stabilized, Alexa. Break the hold before he chokes you out," her instructor cautioned. "And don't try to pry his arm away with your hand. You won't win just trying to go strength against strength."

Using the palm of her hand, Alexa struck the man she was fighting against in the face, but he didn't budge, so she did it again.

"If he doesn't drop his arm, what do you do? Come on, think. The average person is unconscious from lack of oxygen in six seconds."

She immediately used her fingers to simulate an eye gouge, took her other hand, shoved his arm away from her neck, wrapped it around his face, and pushed him up against the wall before following up with a knee kick to his middle.

In the following exercise, Alexa went for a strike, but it was blocked, and she was thrown to the mat so hard that it took her a moment to recover.

"You okay, Amazon?" her classmate laughed. "You gotta learn to take a punch."

"Knock it off, Bannon," her instructor warned before pulling Alexa aside.

"King, you're not concentrating. Try it again. This time, think about how you're going to take out a hostile that's bigger and taller than you. Sometimes an obvious response may not be the best—you need to improvise."

"Got it." Alexa returned to her place on the mat. This time she evaded Tate's frontal attack and responded with a combination of hits before taking him down to the mat and following up with a blow to the gut and the jaw.

She jumped to her feet. "You're right," she said, breathing heavily as her opponent slowly got up. "I gotta learn how to take a punch."

"Good job," a few of her fellow students remarked as she walked by.

"Okay, class. Hit the showers and report back in an hour. Your tactical mobility instructor will meet you out front."

Alexa left the training room and hurried to her ATV. The last thing she wanted was to have a classmate stop her for a chat. The instructors were sticklers for time, and anyone late usually got called on the carpet for tardiness.

At the cabin, Alexa went straight to the kitchen cabinet and retrieved a bottle of ibuprofen. It was hard to open the bottle because her hand was slightly shaking from exertion. It took some effort, but she got the bottle open, took two pills, then a swig of water from her bottle. Finally, she took a minute to sit on the couch and regroup.

When her cell phone rang, Alexa glanced at the table.

"You're lucky you're this close," she said tiredly before reaching for it.

"Hey, Lex," Zane said when she answered. "I haven't heard from you in a while and thought I'd check in to see how it's going?"

She leaned back and closed her eyes. "It's going. I'm just not sure in which direction yet."

"You sound horrible. Uncle Jake and Aunt Margot said they haven't heard from you in over a week, and before that, it was only ten minutes."

"I know. We've had a lot of work to do, Zane. There are only a few weeks until the course is over. So the pace has been pretty intense."

"Lex, are you sure this is still what you want?"

"Yes—one hundred percent. Training is insane, but I've never doubted that this is what I want to do with my life."

"Okay, just checking. I'd be a horrible cousin and best

friend if I didn't ask, right?" He chuckled. "So, is there anyone you want to take to the mat yet?"

"Not on your life. I'm here for business, not to fill my social calendar. But there's one superhot commando teaching us tactical and combat training and—"

"Wait, did you say superhot? Sounds like you're mixing a bit of fun and pleasure with all that business. I'm surprised at you, Lex. I didn't know you had it in you," Zane joked.

"What? No, it's not that at all. We're not— Nothing is going on. I meant cute in the loose sense of the word."

"Nice try, but I know you better than that, cousin. You meant it exactly as you said it."

"Since you *know* me, you know that nothing will come of it. I'm merely pointing out the obvious. Andrew is good-looking and knows his stuff."

"Alexa, you know it's possible to talk and chew gum simultaneously, right?"

"Not for me. I have a plan, Zane. After I graduate, I'll learn the ropes, build up my experience and eventually open an agency of my own. The dating game doesn't factor into my plan."

"I hear you chirping, Big Bird," he teased. "But life has a way of throwing curveballs we didn't expect. You should know that more than anyone."

She thought of Tanya and felt guilty for being so busy that she hadn't thought of her friend sooner. She was one of the main reasons she was there.

"Thanks for calling, Zane, but I have to go. I still have to shower and get ready for the next session."

"Okay, but call your parents sometimes, please. Of course they'd never say it, but they miss you, Lex. A lot."

"I miss them, too, and I will. Thanks for calling, Zane. It's good to hear your voice."

"Likewise, kiddo."

Alexa hit the shower when she hung up. She still had

thirty minutes left when she finished, so she took a quick twenty-minute nap. It wasn't much, but it helped her refocus.

Defensive and tactical driving were two of Alexa's favorite classes. Unfortunately, the instructor announced that today's training was at a different facility, so a shuttle drove the group to a closed course.

"Your job will take you worldwide, so we don't want to assume that you'll only be driving in urban areas," their instructor reasoned. "For example, you may protect principals in Europe, where driving conditions may not be as congested as in the United States. Some maneuvers you'll learn, like a J-turn, barricade breach and pendulum turn, better known as a Scandinavian flick, will come in handy."

The drivers had radios in their helmets for close contact with their instructor.

"What we're going to practice in this turn is front and rear weight transfer and side slides. This maneuver is perfect if you find yourself on the wrong side of the road and need to bring your vehicle under control. You will be using both feet. The left for braking, and the right for the throttle to help shift the car's weight. With practice and calm, you'll be able to do this on multiple road surfaces and at speed."

After discussing the fundamentals, the instructor said, "King, you're up."

"Yes, sir."

Alexa got into the vehicle, secured her seat belt and took off. She executed the pendulum turn and skidded sideways around the curve without error. Alexa felt excitement as the car handled as she'd expected.

"Well done, Miss King. Try it again—faster."

This time, Alexa went through the course at a greater speed. Her face was a mask of concentration while she maneuvered the car through the turns. As she was coming out of a turn, Alexa went to hit the brake. The pedal went all the way to the floorboard.

Alexa tried it again, and it occurred a second time.

"My brakes are out," she said calmly into her headset.

"Don't panic," her instructor replied. "I need you to carefully engage the emergency brake."

"That doesn't work, either," Alexa confirmed after following his instructions.

Downshifting to a lower gear, she was coming up fast on the next turn. Alexa hugged the outside lane not just to shave off some speed, but to keep the car from sliding or rolling.

"You need to cut more speed," her instructor advised.

Easing the two right tires off the road and onto the shoulder slowed the car down even more. The car careened off the road and down an embankment, but it did not flip over. Eventually, the vehicle rolled to a complete stop. Her hand was shaking so bad that it took a few moments before she could put the car in gear and shut the engine off.

"Well done, King," her instructor said in her ear. "Hang tight. We're sending help to come get you. We'll tow the car back so that we can check her out to see what happened."

"Roger that." Alexa heaved a sigh of relief. Her hands shook as she removed her helmet. "It's going to be okay," she told herself several times while she tried to fight back tears.

Upon returning back to Phalanx, the class was invited to a picnic and given the weekend off from studies since Monday testing would commence. Alexa was still shook up by the incident and decided that she needed some time to compose herself. Back at her cabin, Alexa pondered whether she would go to the picnic.

It was a harrowing experience, but she did not want to appear antisocial or as though she was still spooked from the incident at the driving course.

Alexa was putting the finishing touches on her outfit

when she heard a knock at her front door. When she opened it, she was surprised to find Andrew on the other side.

For the first time since she arrived, Alexa was wearing a sundress. It stopped at her knees and showed off her shapely brown legs. She was wearing platform sandals, and her hair was still wet from the shower and slicked back in a high ponytail. The natural curls cascaded behind her, stopping just above her shoulders.

He stared at her for a few moments before saying, "Are you okay?"

Oblivious to the shift in the air, Alexa stepped aside and let Andrew enter.

"Would you like some iced tea? Or I've got lemonade?"

She would have walked by, but Andrew took her by the shoulders and turned her to face him. His expression was a mask of concern.

"Are. You. Okay?"

She took a moment to study Andrew's face. His eyes were wide, and his face was taut with worry. She could feel every point where his fingers connected with her arms.

Her stoic expression slipped. "No. Not really."

The words were coerced from inside Alexa as fluidly as a snake being propelled out of a basket by a snake charmer.

Before she could elaborate, Andrew swept her into a hug. After a moment's hesitation, Alexa relaxed into the embrace and held on tight.

"It's okay," he said softly. "You did everything right."

The tears fell faster than she could stop them. "I'm sorry. I'm here bawling like a baby."

"Shh," he soothed. "You're entitled."

Andrew swiped the tears from her cheeks with his thumbs. Before he could stop himself, he leaned down and kissed her.

Chapter 10

Though his face was mere inches away, Alexa was shocked when Andrew's lips touched hers in a tentative kiss. Shock soon gave way to a rush of desire so unexpected and powerful that Alexa had to hold on to him for support.

The caress grew more intense by the second, making Alexa oblivious to anything but the warm feel of Andrew's lips moving possessively against her own.

This can't be happening, she chided. *This is too dangerous, and you need to stop.*

She heard the warning in her head and knew that no good could come of it, but at that moment in time, Alexa was oblivious to anything but the feel of Andrew's body. The scent he wore was the perfect blend of sexy, spicy and woodsy. Its distinct notes overloaded her olfactory receptors, making it hard to concentrate on anything but Andrew Riker and the sensations he evoked.

Somewhere in the distance, Alexa detected a ringing sound. For a moment, she thought it was her own ears, but eventually realized it was her cell phone.

It could have gone on ringing for an eternity for all she cared, but it was enough of a distraction to yank them both out of the haze of yearning they were caught up in.

Alexa came down as sharp as an elevator lurching to a stop. It was jarring.

"I'm…I'm sorry," she said, trying to find her bearings.

"No, I'm at fault. I promised I wouldn't cross a line and I did."

His breath sounded so ragged that it gave Alexa a start.

"We both got caught up in a moment," she murmured.

"You had a harrowing experience, Alexa, that would've upset anyone."

She smoothed her dress and tried not to focus on her shaky hands.

"Yes, but it's part of the job. I should learn how to handle the unexpected better than this."

A sheer look of discomfort passed across Andrew's face. He ran a hand over his jaw and cleared his throat. "It wasn't an accident."

She stared at him. "What?"

"The brakes on the car you were driving didn't just go out on their own. It was sabotage."

"But why? Who would've done something like this?"

With his faculties back under control, Andrew focused on the imminent danger from the attacks on Alexa as opposed to the way that brief interlude had made him feel.

"I don't know, but I promise you that we'll find out. Until then, it's probably prudent to suspend your training. I don't want any more accidents. Thus far, you haven't been seriously injured. I don't want to keep putting you in scenarios that will push the envelope."

She nodded and began thinking over run-ins that she had encountered with different classmates. There had only been three of them, but which one was responsible?

"Please stop doing that."

Startled, Alexa glanced up at Andrew. "Doing what?"

"When you're hyper-focused on something, you bite your lip. It's distracting."

Her mouth dropped open. She had not known that. By the intense way he was staring at her, it was a habit Andrew was trying his best to ignore.

"We should go."

"Sure, I'll just get my purse."

She hurried into the bedroom to retrieve her pocketbook from a chair. When she returned, the front door was open and Andrew was waiting on the porch. He held the door open as she stepped through it. Locking it behind her, Alexa dropped the key into her purse and followed him down the steps.

"Your dress is pretty."

"Thank you. I threw it in at the last minute. I wasn't sure if I'd even have an opportunity to wear it."

"You'll make quite an impression on the guys."

"Hardly. Most of them don't even notice me. Which is just fine," she added quickly. "I like being just one of the guys."

Andrew's step faltered. He waited to see if she was kidding, but Alexa looked like she believed what she'd just said. So, as crazy as it sounded, he decided not to point out that there was no way any man considered Alexa just one of the guys. Especially him.

Walking around to the driver's side, Andrew had to take a minute to compose himself. Alexa was wreaking unexpected havoc on his system. Was she oblivious to her effect on him and several other students at Phalanx? Everyone respected Alexa in class, but even Andrew noticed a few appreciative glances as she walked into a room. He caught a few men staring too long and gave them a look.

Not that he was trying to stake a claim or anything. They were just friends, and though he was attracted to Alexa, he would never take it further than that kiss. It shouldn't have happened in the first place. The last thing anyone needed while learning extensive training was distractions. Everyone's head had to be in the game. Mind-wandering could get someone injured or worse.

Besides, Alexa had made it clear that she wasn't open to a relationship. And as much as he had enjoyed that kiss, she was right. He wasn't up for getting his heart battered and ripped to shreds again, either.

Just friends. Yeah, I hear you, Alexa. Andrew smiled back. *A wise decision for both of us. Let's pray it lasts.*

"So, tell me some things about you that I don't know."

"Really?"

"How else is our friendship supposed to grow?" he countered.

After eating at the picnic, they decided to take a walk down to the lake. They had strolled in companionable silence before Andrew posed the question.

She glanced over at him. "Fair enough. I worked as a senior cyber threat analyst for my parents' company. I loved my job. I enjoy a wide range of movies, music and books. Except for horror movies—I never could get into them."

"Let me guess. You sleep with the light on after watching?"

"Uh, I so do," she laughed. "I enjoy being out in nature—always have. My favorite food is nachos, and sweets are my go-to food when I'm stressed."

She stopped walking. Andrew halted and turned around. "What's wrong?"

"I've had two worst days in my life. The first was when my best friend, Tanya, died a few months ago. The second day was at a park in Great Falls, Virginia. I was a teenager at the time. My friend Shelley and I got attacked while hiking on a trail."

Andrew's expression turned somber. "I'm so sorry, Alexa. I can't imagine how you must've felt in both situations."

She stared off into the distance. "It took a long time for me to come to terms with losing them. They were my best friends."

Andrew placed a hand on her shoulder. "You're still not over them, Alexa."

Their gazes locked. Sadness waded in the depths of her eyes, replacing the happiness that occupied them only moments before. She absentmindedly ran a finger along the scar on her cheek.

"No, I guess I'm not. But I try not to let the pain of losing my best friends engulf me. Instead, I try to focus on ensuring that Tanya's death and my lost friendship with Shelley weren't in vain."

He stepped closer. "Alexa—"

"Let's not," she cut him off. "I don't want to get melancholy and spoil this amazing day."

Her body language was a clear sign that those walls of protection were back up, so Andrew didn't push. Instead, he placed her hand on his forearm and guided her down the path.

"What you need right now is a distraction."

She beamed with excitement. "Then lead the way."

It had been ages since Alexa had enjoyed herself this much. Andrew had taken them to the other side of the lake with a paddleboat. As they moved around on the water, he told her a stockpile of funny stories that kept her laughing. It was hard to feel down around him, and she appreciated getting to know him better.

"You know, after Shelley and Tanya, I didn't think I'd meet anyone again. Now I've got two great friends in my life. You and Marena. It makes me..." She stopped suddenly.

"What were you going to say?"

"It makes me less hurt over the two I lost."

Reaching out, Andrew grabbed her hand and squeezed. "Alexa, you aren't alone. I'm here if you need me—anytime."

Andrew knew it was true the moment he said it. He may not be able to connect with anyone again on a romantic level, but he could offer Alexa friendship. That was safe and predictable, and wouldn't break his heart. He was also recovering from a relationship that had left him in pieces. For Alexa, it was violence and grief that kept her at arm's length. For him, it was an overambitious ex-girlfriend who loved power, connections and prestige more than him.

"Thanks, I appreciate that." She closed her eyes and released a breath. "This day was exactly what I needed. You must read minds, too."

Andrew shrugged as he continued pedaling. "What can I say? It's a gift."

The two sat in silence for a long time and enjoyed their surroundings. Andrew studied Alexa when she was soaking up the sun. Then, as if sensing his scrutiny, she opened her eyes.

Watching her sunbathe brought back a similar outing. It started out as a wonderful day but had turned into a huge blowup faster than a summer rainstorm in Florida. Just thinking about his ex-girlfriend instead of the great time he was having with Alexa made him feel out of sorts.

She touched his arm. "Are you okay?"

He shook himself out of the memory. "Yeah, I'm fine. I guess it's time we headed back."

"Oh. Yes, of course." Alexa helped him paddle back to the other side of the lake.

On the way back to the cabin, Alexa tried not to ask about Andrew's sudden mood change while they drove home. He turned on music, but she remained quiet other than asking about an occasional song.

When he pulled around the circle in front of her cabin, Alexa unbuckled her seat belt and turned.

"Andrew, is everything okay?"

"Yes, of course. I'm sorry, Alexa. I was just thinking about some work I must complete tomorrow."

"Tomorrow's Sunday. I thought you were off the entire weekend?"

"That was the plan," he replied. "Until I remembered some tests I have to grade and post."

"Okay."

Before she could say anything else, Andrew jumped out and walked around to her side. He opened it and helped her out.

"Thank you."

"My pleasure." He followed her up the steps.

"I had a wonderful time today," she said after unlocking the door.

"I'm glad you enjoyed it."

She shifted from one foot to the other. Finally, she said, "Have a good night."

"You, too, Alexa."

Andrew watched her walk in and didn't move until she'd shut the door.

By the time she peeked out of the window, he was already in the Jeep and pulling off.

"What was that about?" she wondered aloud.

Chapter 11

Jake King was in his study reading when his cell phone rang. Glancing at the screen, he set his book down and grabbed the phone.

"Alexa." He sighed with relief. "Are you okay, sweetheart?"

Alexa settled back onto the pillows. Hearing her father's voice caused a rush of emotion. She forced herself not to cry. "Just fine, Dad."

Standing, Jake moved to the couch. He sank into the buttery soft leather cushions, his legs stretched in front of him.

"Andrew said it'll be nose to the grindstone until graduation."

"Are you talking about JJ Riker?"

"Yes, everyone but James calls him Andrew."

"Got it," her father chuckled. "He seems like a very accomplished young man."

"He is, Dad. He's very knowledgeable on a lot of subjects. He's smart and very caring."

Grinning, Jake reclined farther into the plush cushions. His gaze traveled to his bookcase, where there were pictures of his daughter in various stages of her life. His favorite was one with the three of them after falling into a mound of leaves they had just raked. He missed his daughter's light, carefree nature. Listening to her talk in such an animated way provided a glimpse of the old Alexa. It warmed his heart.

"Sounds like you two have hit it off."

"We have. The Rikers have been wonderful hosts."

"Glad to hear it," her father said approvingly before leaning forward so his elbows rested on his thighs. "So, when were you planning to tell me about the accidents?"

There was a long pause. So long that Jake said, "Before you deny it, I should mention that James called me to tell me about both training incidents."

"He shouldn't have done that."

"Lex, it's obvious from the sounds of it that you weren't planning to tell us."

Alexa got up out of bed and started pacing. "That's because there's nothing to tell, yet. The Rikers are investigating what happened."

"Booba, I can—"

"No, Dad. You've done enough—and I mean that in a good way. There haven't been any incidents in the last week. Plus, I can handle myself."

Before her father could respond, Alexa heard a commotion and then her mother's voice in her ear. "We know you won't let anyone push you around, Alexa."

After ending the call with her parents, Alexa was too wound up to sleep. She decided to go for a walk outside. Changing into a pair of shorts, a T-shirt and sneakers, Alexa left out the back door. The landscaping and floodlights provided some illumination as she walked down the path toward the old wooden swing.

Alexa could hear crickets and the occasional woodland creature as she continued her stroll. The last thing she wanted was her father intervening to discover who was behind the attempts to scare her.

Was that all it was? she pondered. *Some person with a bone to pick? How is that even possible? I don't know anyone here.*

Sitting on the plank, Alexa pushed off so that she could gently sway to and fro. She thought back to the last time she was out there with Andrew.

Closing her eyes, she recalled their playful banter and the heightened awareness of him.

"He's a complication you just don't need," she whispered aloud.

Suddenly, Alexa stopped in her tracks. The hair on the back of her neck shot up and she had an uneasy feeling that she was being watched.

Turning to the left and then right, she attempted to hear anything that might give her a clue what was out there.

What if it was a bear? Or some other dangerous animal? Alexa was defenseless against that kind of attack. Her eye caught something at the base of the tree anchoring the swing. She stared at it for several seconds. There were several cigarette butts scattered on the ground.

That's when she heard the distinct sound of movement to her right.

"Who's there?" she yelled.

Silence.

It was too dark to make out a target, and with no weapon, she didn't stick around to investigate. Alexa jumped off the swing and took off running in one motion. Air filled her lungs and fear propelled her forward. Not once did Alexa slow down or look over her shoulder. Only when there was a door safely between her and the outside did she look back. There was nothing there.

Locking the door, she rushed to the front door and checked the bolt. Next, she checked each window latch. Everything was secure. Arming the alarm, Alexa should have felt safer, but she didn't. She was still plenty freaked out.

She glanced at the clock on the mantel. It was one thirty in the morning. She thought about calling Andrew. She knew he would come, but she didn't want to disturb him. For now, she was safe and in no danger.

Going into the kitchen, Alexa made herself a cup of tea, hoping it would calm her nerves. She was still in fight-or-flight mode and felt jittery.

She sat on the couch and tucked her legs under her. There was no way sleep was coming anytime soon.

* * *

"What were you thinking? You should've called me, Alexa." Andrew knelt and examined the used cigarettes littering the ground. He used a plastic baggie to scoop them up. Turning it inside out, he secured the bag and placed it into his pocket.

"I don't care what time it was, you should've let me know what happened."

"I was fine," she countered stubbornly. "There was no reason to wake you in the middle of the night. I made it back to the house, everything was locked up tight and I turned the alarm on. Nobody was getting inside."

"Unless they wanted to," he pointed out before striding off toward the house.

Alexa fell into step beside him. "Okay, next time, I promise to contact you the moment something strange happens."

"There won't *be* a next time," he ground out. "Whoever the culprit was did a pretty good job of hiding his tracks. Until now. Your coming outside was unexpected. It startled him, so he took off to avoid being discovered but left these." He patted his pocket. "There will be mucosal cells on the tips of his cigarettes. I have a friend at the FBI that works in the lab. He'll get these analyzed. If your assailant is in the CODIS database, my buddy will find him."

"CODIS?"

"It's the FBI's Combined DNA System, which is a DNA database. It has multiple tiers, criminal, federal, local and international, that can be accessed to track anyone who has been entered into the system. If he's a student of ours, he doesn't have a criminal background, or he wouldn't have been accepted. So what we're looking for is anyone who has a reason to have their DNA samples in the database. Likely a state or federal employee."

"Will that take long?"

"Likely a few days. Depending on how many tiers have to be searched. In the meantime, you're coming back to the main house with me. It's not safe for you to be out here by yourself until we have the culprit."

"Andrew, is that necessary? I have the alarm, and I'll be careful."

"We're not taking any chances, Alexa. This could've gone differently last night. I'm not about to give him an opportunity to come at you a third time. Let's go pack your gear and get going."

Realizing he wouldn't be swayed, Alexa nodded and went to pack her belongings. When they arrived at the house, James and Esther were on the front porch.

"Everything taken care of?" James asked his son.

"Yes, the house is secure, and the alarm is on."

"I'm sorry to impose," Alexa began.

"Don't be silly," James replied. "We are here to ensure that our students are safe. We take that responsibility seriously, Alexa."

She nodded. "Thank you for your hospitality."

"Of course," Esther replied, taking Alexa by the arm. "Come on inside and let me show you to your room."

Andrew hung back with his father.

"How soon can we get the results?"

"I called in a few favors to get it rushed, but it depends. It could take a few days or a week or so. I'm driving into Pagosa Springs shortly, where my contact will be waiting. He'll get the samples to my friend at the FBI."

James held the door while Andrew took in Alexa's luggage.

"I want a lid kept on this. I won't risk Phalanx's reputation on some crazy with a personal grudge against one of our clients."

"I'll handle it," Andrew said tersely. He moved off to take the bags upstairs, but James stopped him.

"Hey, what's going on?"

"Nothing."

James stepped into his son's path, crossed his arms and waited. "Andrew."

Blowing out a harsh breath, he dropped the bags he was carrying.

"This shouldn't have happened. I let myself get sidetracked. If I'd followed protocol like I should have, I'd have continued the investigation after the first incident. Now we almost had a third occurrence. Alexa could've been accosted, or worse. This is unacceptable, and I'm not just talking about for our company's reputation. She could've been killed, Dad."

"I agree. How did you let yourself get sidetracked?"

Andrew frowned. "What?"

"You mentioned that you let yourself get sidetracked. How?"

He ran a hand over his stubbled jaw. "By Alexa. I've been spending time with her lately and—"

"And that's a bad thing?"

"Yes," Andrew countered. "If I'd been doing my job instead of getting to know her better, we may have caught this guy by now."

"Do you have a Magic 8 Ball or something?" James chuckled.

"I'm serious, Dad. I should've stuck with my original instinct and just stayed clear of Alexa King. She's all over the place, and I still get the feeling that she's holding something back. If she's not one hundred percent committed to this career it could cost someone their life. Plus, you'd think her reminding me of Olee would be enough of a warning. I should've listened to my gut and steered clear of her."

A gasp overhead drew both men's gazes upward. Alexa and Esther were standing in the interior balcony. Holding on to the rail, Alexa's face was flushed red with embarrassment. Realizing that she'd been discovered, she excused herself and rushed down the hall. Seconds later, the bedroom door slammed. Esther tsked and shook her head before following Alexa.

James scowled at his son. "And what does your gut say now?"

Andrew closed his eyes and shook his head. "That I've just made a monumental mistake."

Chapter 12

For the next week, Alexa and her classmates didn't have time to come up for air. Instead, it was nonstop training and testing for the group. For her, the days began to blur together. She hadn't seen Andrew at all outside of his teaching capacity. He had attempted to knock on her door and apologize afterward, but she ignored him.

After a few days it had become weird. Alexa decided to confront him about what she had overheard, but he was gone by the time she got up, and not home by the time she went to bed. James and Esther had done their best to compensate for Andrew's absence and were model hosts. Alexa let it go. She was under a lot of stress getting ready for finals, and the last thing she wanted to do was increase the weirdness between her and Andrew.

In hindsight, Alexa would later recall that things being just weird would've been a cakewalk compared to the full-blown disaster that was about to occur.

After class, she went looking for Andrew.

"He left a while ago," James told her when she poked her head into his office. "Had a burr under his saddle about something. Try the sparring room. JJ usually goes there when he needs to blow off steam."

"Okay, thanks."

"My pleasure, kiddo."

Alexa found Andrew in the studio practicing on the Wing Chun dummy. The wooden athletic instrument cultivated fighting skills and chi in Chinese martial arts training.

Not wanting to interrupt him, she sat at the back of the room and watched.

It was some time before he stopped and said, "What's up, Alexa?"

Surprised, she said, "Sorry, I didn't mean to disturb you."

"I saw you when you came in."

Alexa thought Andrew must have used peripheral vision since he hadn't looked up once since she'd arrived.

She got up and walked over to the edge of the mat.

"Don't you think it's time we cleared the air?"

"What are you talking about?"

"About what I overheard and how absent you've been since then."

"I've been busy. This is the last week of the program, so it's been hectic."

"Yeah, you mentioned that before. I just wanted to let you know that it was never my intention to cause problems for you. I don't know who Olee is, but clearly whoever she is, being compared to her wasn't a compliment."

Andrew stepped away from the testing equipment and faced Alexa. He opened his mouth to say something but then stopped.

"What?"

"Nothing."

"Andrew, I know something's up. Even your dad said something's on your mind, and you're distracted. Please, just tell me what it is."

"Why do you want to be an executive protection officer?"

Her eyebrows shot upward. "What do you mean? I thought I'd already answered that. I want to help protect people. Especially women."

"I know what you said. I just question your motivation."

Alexa frowned. "What, you think I'm lying?"

"That's not what I'm saying," he countered. "You said you want to help women. So why not volunteer or work with already established organizations back home? In comparison, being someone's bodyguard and protecting someone's life with your own seems excessive."

"I want to help women in danger, whether from a person, a hostile situation due to work, or external forces."

"That's the *what*, Alexa, not the *why*."

She blew out a breath in frustration. "I don't know what you want from me, Andrew."

"The truth."

"You got it."

Without warning, Andrew grabbed her and spun her around so that his arm was around her neck. Caught off guard, Alexa struggled against him.

"You're the only one keeping me from getting to your principal and doing whatever I want. So what are you going to do to stop me?"

Immediately, Alexa used a jujitsu defense to break his rear choke hold. She tucked her head slightly, grabbed his arm, and pulled down heavily on it before wrapping her leg behind the calf of his leg. Then, she dropped her base and spun one hundred and eighty degrees before pushing against her blocked leg, causing Andrew to lose balance and hit the floor. In seconds he was up and coming after her again.

He tried to swing at her, but she blocked his arm and pushed it away from her face.

Alexa backed up to give herself some distance. She was baffled as to why he was forcing this fight, and she was getting angrier by the minute.

"Andrew, what are you doing?"

"Why, Alexa?" he asked as he moved to take her down again. "Tell me what's really at the heart of it?"

She evaded his takedown and countered with a blow to his midsection. Andrew doubled over. Sweat was dripping from his forehead now.

Alexa was getting angry at him. He could see it in her stance, in the way her chest heaved with exertion and by her expression. Behind the confusion at what prompted the altercation, she was mad. Good. It's the reaction that he was after. Irate people were more concerned with being irritated than hiding the truth.

"I don't know—"

"You're lying," he snapped before coming after her again and again.

"I told you that I don't lie," Alexa snapped back.

Andrew had gotten under her skin in a way that no one had before. Alexa's eyebrows scrunched together in concentration as she looked for weaknesses in his attack. Her nostrils flared from the anger rushing throughout her body. "Then tell me."

This time, it was he who was on the defensive as Alexa tried to back him into a corner. But her triumph was short-lived because Andrew countered the maneuver and knocked her off-balance. Alexa crashed to the floor. Her body protested in pain, but anger was a powerful strength booster. She was back on her feet in seconds ready to lunge at him again.

"What are you hiding, Alexa?"

The question caught her unawares, and was just the push he needed to cause her to erupt.

"I couldn't protect them," she yelled. Her face contorted with rage. "I couldn't stop us from being attacked at the park. Is that what you want to hear? Fine, I wasn't strong enough."

Frustrated, Alexa threw a punch at Andrew, but he used his hand to push her fist slightly past so that she missed the mark. She tried again, but he rotated his body to avoid the hit, countered and knocked her to the floor. She let out a howl of frustration. Next, he set up a mount.

"You said 'us.'"

"No, I didn't."

"Yes, you did. You said 'I couldn't stop *us* from being attacked.' This isn't just about your best friends, Alexa. Your decision to be a CPO is also about *your* need to feel safe and in control."

Setting up a guard using her forearm, Alexa placed her

other hand across her wrist to keep him from moving higher up her frame. "No, it's not," she gasped, struggling.

"It is. The man in the park took something from you, didn't he? Your innocence? Your feeling of safety and security? Losing Tanya took something from you, too. You've spent all this time trying to get it back. Trying to make yourself whole again, but deep down, you're the one needing protection—aren't you?"

"You don't know anything about it," she roared. Grabbing his hips, Alexa used the force of an upward thrust to launch Andrew off to the side before rolling out of his grasp and vaulting to her feet.

"Shelley's whole life has changed. She's a shell of the person she once was. And Tanya shouldn't have died. She'd be alive today if it weren't for her abusive boyfriend."

"How is that your fault?"

"I begged her to leave him, but she didn't listen until it was too late. So spare me your sympathy, because you have no idea how I feel—what I lost."

Andrew stood. "I do," he shot back. "I know what it's like to lose someone you loved and be helpless to stop it. I've felt the pain and guilt eating you from the inside out. It's all-consuming, and you'd do anything not to feel it—to be able to escape."

Andrew's voice broke. "Alexa, you have to let the baggage go." He placed his hands on both shoulders to keep her in place. She tried to pull away, but he held tight.

"Let me go."

"It's affecting your focus, and that's not good for you or your clients. You can't let anything distract you in the field. If you let your emotions lead, you'll make a mistake that can get you both killed." Andrew dipped his head so that they could make eye contact. "Do you *hear* me?"

"That won't happen because I'll never let my feelings jeopardize a mission."

"You can't say that," he countered. "One day, an enemy may discover who you care about and exploit that."

"Not if I've stopped caring."

Andrew stared at her a moment. "What does that mean?"

"Aside from my family, the people I love tend to sever contact or die, so now it's easier not to let anyone into my heart anymore."

"And you think you can just turn off your emotions?" Andrew said incredulously. "Alexa, that's not sustainable."

Exhausted from the sparring, she leaned over to try and catch her breath. Tears flowed down her face, making her gaze blurry. She blinked several times to clear her vision but eventually wiped her hand across her face as if the tears were an annoyance. "Loving people is a liability I can't afford," she said tiredly.

He loosened his hold but didn't let her go. Instead, he pulled her into his arms.

Alexa tried not to cry more, but it was pointless. She was too overwhelmed, so the tears just flowed.

"While I may not agree with your logic, I get it, Alexa."

"Who was it?" she finally murmured into his shirt a few minutes later. "The person you lost?"

His eyebrow arched in surprise. Olee came to mind, but he tamped that memory back down where it belonged. That betrayal was too raw to voice. "One of my buddies in the field," he whispered. "He was my best friend and was killed in the line of duty. I wasn't there when he died."

She raised her head to look at him. "I'm sorry, Drew."

He nodded. "It took me a very long time to get past it. Past the anger and the guilt over losing him."

"Of being spared?"

"Yes."

"I know how that feels."

He smiled. "Did you just call me Drew?"

"Yeah, I guess I did. Do you mind?"

"No. Can I call you Lexi?"

She scrunched her face up. "If you must."

Andrew laughed. "Does anyone else call you that?"

"No."

"Then I must."

She burst out laughing. He soon followed suit.

Suddenly, Andrew sobered.

"Alexa, I'm sorry about what I said last week. It wasn't about you. Well, not completely. I was feeling out of sorts because of what happened. It caused me to remember another time when I was in a situation where I didn't feel in control of what was happening around me. Let's just say I learned a painful lesson that I don't ever want to repeat."

"Thank you," she murmured.

Andrew's thumb brushed away the tears under one eye. "You're welcome."

"Are you ever going to tell me what happened with this mysterious woman from your past?"

Andrew looked like he'd just been sucker punched. "How did you—"

"You may not have provided details, but it's written all over your face."

"Maybe someday," he reluctantly admitted. "But not now."

"This," she said, waving her hand around the mat, "was you trying to find my Achilles' heel, wasn't it?"

He nodded. "The scab had to be removed so that the wound you're still carrying can heal."

Alexa inched closer. "Thank you."

Standing on her tiptoes, she pressed her lips against Andrew's mouth without warning. It took a moment before his arms wrapped around her waist to hold her tight.

A purr of contentment drifted out of her mouth before she grasped his shoulders like she was drowning and Andrew was the only life preserver for miles.

Eventually, Alexa pushed against his chest, and Andrew released her immediately. It was so sudden that the momentum propelled her backward. He reached out to stop her from falling.

"I'm sorry. I shouldn't have kissed you like that," she squeaked, moving away. "That's not exactly the kiss that friends give each other."

"Depends on the friends," he teased.

"Andrew, I don't want to complicate things. We're friends. We need to stay that way. Anything else would just get awkward."

His expression turned incredulous. "Kind of late to put that horse back in the barn, don't you think?"

Chapter 13

"We have to," she replied. "I just poured my heart out to you about why I don't do relationships. I'm sorry."

She hurried across the mat.

"Alexa, wait," he called out.

She turned but remained where she was. "Thanks again for helping me, Andrew. And I want you to know that I heard you."

He observed her from across the distance.

"I meant every word, Lexi," he replied. "Including the unspoken ones laced in that kiss."

She rushed out of the room and didn't look back. It was hard for Alexa to think of anything on the ride home except the feel of Andrew's mouth covering hers in a kiss that ignited every dormant area of her body like an accelerant. Now Alexa felt like she was blazing out of control.

"What were you thinking?" she accused herself. "This is a disaster."

The move was reckless and crazy, yet at that moment, it was impossible not to do what she had been fantasizing about for a long time. The wonder of kissing Andrew had overridden all her carefully erected boundaries and common sense.

Parking the ATV, Alexa went inside and headed straight for the shower. As the hot water pounded against her back, she realized why she needed to forget Andrew Riker's mischievous smile and smoldering eyes.

"Because no good can come of it," she scolded, but then her thoughts of the kiss they shared caused Alexa to switch the hot water to cold.

Desperate for a voice of reason, Alexa called her cousin when she was finished.

"Hallelujah. It's about time," he said after hearing the account of what happened.

"Zane, this is no time to joke."

"You thought I was? Lex, what's the big deal? You like him, and clearly, the feeling is reciprocated, so why not see where it goes?"

"I'll tell you where it's going," she groaned. "Straight into a bona fide disaster."

Sitting on the bed, Alexa spun around until she was lying on her back with her legs stretched out on the headboard. "I'm not about to see that happen. I need Andrew in my life."

"You're telling me."

"As a friend," Alexa clarified. "He's important to me, Zane. I can't risk losing that."

"You realize you're overthinking this, right? By a lot."

"I'm being cautious."

"No, you're being crazy. You haven't talked like this about a man in eons."

"That's because work is my life."

"It's not your life, Alexa. It's your camouflage."

She turned right side up in the bed. "What is that supposed to mean?"

"You're hiding in plain sight, cousin, under the guise of socializing and spending time with people, but in truth, you're scared to have anyone get too close to you because you're afraid of what that kind of closeness could mean if things go pear-shaped."

"Zane, that's not true. I'm friends with Marena, and everything is going just fine."

"We both know that's because she lives in North Carolina, far away enough to keep her at arm's length. It's safe."

An uncomfortable silence descended on the telephone line.

"You may be mad at me for what I've said, but you know that all of it is true. I love you too much not to point out that you're self-sabotaging your life, Alexa. Our hearts aren't designed to be encased in plexiglass for fear of being broken. That's not how life works. Risking pain and heartache comes with the territory. It's time you came back to the land of the living because you can't spend your entire adult life waiting for the other shoe to drop."

After hanging up, Alexa recounted the conversations with Andrew and Zane. She didn't feel like she was self-sabotaging. In her mind, it was self-preservation. It was time for her to fess up about why she didn't let anyone new in too far past her defenses. It was simple. Her heart couldn't take another break regardless of Zane's statement about living without the plexiglass. After having two best friends ripped from her life, she wasn't strong enough to have it happen again.

So if that meant living the life of a hermit and only experiencing life on the periphery, one step below loving someone, then so be it. No one would end up hurt, damaged or dead. "I'm fine with those odds," she said before propping her arms behind her head and staring into the dark. Thoughts of what Tanya would say to that drifted into her mind.

Lex, quit pretending to live and live.

The expression on Tanya's face and the intonation in her voice played out in her head.

"Oh, Tanya," she cried softly into the soundless room. "I miss you. If ever I needed your advice about what to do, it's now, because I'm scared to death."

"You wanted to see me, sir?"

Andrew and his father glanced up as one of their students entered the office.

"Yes, Jeffries. Take a seat."

James grabbed the folder sitting on his desk. Not one to mince words, he got straight to the point.

"You're expelled, Mr. Jeffries."

The young man's eyebrows shot upward. "Excuse me?"

"This can't be a surprise," Andrew replied in a clipped tone. "You were behind the attacks on Miss King. Are you going to make us go over the evidence?"

He shifted in his chair. "What evidence? I haven't done anything that warrants you kicking me out."

James opened the folder and retrieved a document. He tossed it across the desk.

"We retrieved all the shell casings from the training exercises. Each student has color-coded ammo so that we can track their fire patterns and how well they did in the assignment. Your count was off by two rounds. Which, subsequently, was the number of live rounds fired at Alexa. In your statement, you said that you were nowhere near Alexa during any of the exercises that day, but surveillance cameras show you and Miss King engaged in hand-to-hand combat prior to your shooting her in the chest. She struck you in the face, after which your blood splattered onto her tactical gear. We had the sample analyzed, and you are a match."

His gaze shifted from Andrew to his father. "That was an accident," Jeffries stammered. "You can't be suggesting that I would purposefully try to harm her?"

"I'm not suggesting anything," James said curtly. "I'm flat-out saying you did it. We can't place you at the scene when her brakes failed, but it was you outside of her cabin smoking the cigarettes that you so carelessly left."

"So? I was merely watching her. That's not a crime," he shot back.

"Stalking is an escalated crime. And the DNA left on the cigarettes also points to you, Mr. Jeffries. Add the training incident, and it's enough to have you arrested and charged," Andrew informed him.

Edgar shot to his feet. "I wasn't trying to harm her," he repeated. "I was only trying to scare her. I wanted to prove that she'd crack under pressure. She doesn't deserve to be here, and everyone knows you all gave her preferential treatment. Just ask Tate and a few of the other guys. After a few mishaps the plan was she'd quit and prove my point."

Andrew glared at him. "Then you're as stupid as you are careless. Alexa is highly qualified and earned her spot—you just lost yours."

Two police officers entered the room to take him into custody. When he saw the cops, he tried to make a run for it, but didn't get far. Andrew anticipated his resistance and grabbed him.

"You can't do this," Edgar yelled, trying to break free. "My father has connections—"

"So do we," Andrew countered before shoving him in the direction of the two officers. "Get him out of here."

Edgar's face was contorted with rage as he fought against the police officers. The vein in his forehead bulged against his skin as he was dragged out of the room.

After the three men left, Andrew sank into an armchair. He pinched the bridge of his nose. "Glad that's over."

"Me, too," his father agreed. "Now Alexa is safe from that nitwit's schemes."

Three days later, the Phalanx students graduated. Everyone was dressed to impress in dark suits for the ceremony and could barely contain their excitement. Hearing her name, Alexa got her certificate and shook hands with James, Andrew and the instructors. It was their last night at the training academy, so the Rikers threw a party. Alexa stayed for about an hour but decided to call it quits. She said her goodbyes and was headed out when Andrew called her name.

"Leaving so soon?" he asked when he reached her side.

"Yes," she told him. "I'm headed back to the cabin to pack."

"Then allow me to give you a ride."

"No, thanks. It's a beautiful night out, so I'll walk."

Without another word, Andrew fell into step beside her.

It was dark out, so he retrieved a flashlight from his car. While they walked, Alexa gazed at the starry sky. "I'll miss it here."

"Me, too."

She looked surprised. "You're leaving?"

"I've taken a consulting job in Dubai. I'll be gone for a few months."

A frown wrinkled her forehead. "Oh. Well, I wish you all the best, Andrew."

"Thanks. You, too."

Alexa stopped suddenly and faced him. "I want you to know that I appreciate everything you and James have done for me. This has been the most amazing time of my life, Andrew. I'm a better, stronger person because of you."

"We just laid the foundation, Alexa. The motivation and raw talent were already there."

Shaking her head, she resumed walking. "Can't you take a compliment?"

"I'm just saying that you did a fantastic job."

"Drew."

"Okay, okay," he laughed. "Thank you."

By the time they reached the door, they were laughing and joking like old friends.

She unlocked the door and turned to Andrew. "Would you like to come in?"

He stepped forward until he was mere inches away. "I would, but I think I'd better go."

They stood rooted to their spots for a few moments staring at each other. They were so close that their breaths mingled. Finally, it was Alexa clearing her throat that severed the connection.

"Well, I'd better go in before we get attacked by mosquitoes." She hugged him. "Thanks for everything, Andrew."

He held her tight for a moment before letting her go. "My pleasure, Lexi."

Andrew searched her face a moment, committing it to

memory before he leaned down and kissed her. It was meant to be a light, quick action, but it quickly morphed into something hotter than he had expected.

Alexa's arms slipped around his neck, prompting Andrew to back her up against the side of the cabin and deepen the kiss.

Moments later, their embrace ended as abruptly as it began. He released Alexa.

"I'm sorry. I should not have done that."

"It's okay," she said quickly. "No harm done."

The sudden loss of shared body heat made Alexa shiver. She rubbed her arms to warm up. Everything in her screamed out to stop him. To not walk away without coming to an agreement, but Alexa ignored her own longing. Her stomach was tied up in a ball of knots over the decision. Feeling a sudden emptiness, she forced herself to back away. "Take care of yourself, Andrew."

He lingered for a moment, but then stepped back, too. His face showed his resignation. "You do the same."

She watched him head back down the path before turning and going inside. After she shut the door, Alexa leaned against it. Her heart was racing, and her lips tingled from their explosive kiss. She missed him already. "I have to walk away," she said aloud. "It's better this way because if anything happened to you, Andrew Riker, I might not survive it."

Chapter 14

Three years later...

Alexa placed her SIG Sauer P365 handgun in its holster and slid the navy blue suit jacket over her white blouse. After fastening the buttons, she retrieved a dragonfly lapel pin from her jewelry box. Its wings were gold, and the body was garnet. She secured it to her lapel and then put on diamond stud earrings before sweeping her hair up in a chignon bun at the base of her neck.

Picking up a pair of glasses from her nightstand, she put them on and headed downstairs.

Before she had reached the bottom of the steps, her cell phone rang.

"Alexa King?...Yes, I'm heading out now."

She hung up the phone, grabbed her luggage and purse, and left.

There was a black Mercedes S-Class sedan waiting for her at the curb. When she reached the bottom step, a woman had exited the passenger seat and opened the back door.

"Thanks, Miranda."

"You're welcome, Miss King."

"Good morning, Valerie."

"Good morning, Miss King," her driver replied.

Her assistant handed her a gold folder.

"Is everything in order, Miranda?"

"Yes, ma'am. Your gear is in the trunk, the advance team has scouted out the route and car two is in place. Everything is green."

"Good. And how was your date?"

Miranda blushed. "It was great! Things are going along

well. His name is Apollo Hayes. He's tall, handsome and so attentive. I can't wait for you to meet him!"

Alexa's assistant was a stunning petite Hispanic woman. At five foot four, she stood below Alexa's shoulders. Miranda had long black hair and brilliant brown eyes and dimples. Her family was from Houston, Texas, and they were very proud of her moving to Washington, DC, and landing her dream job. Miranda was passionate about learning the ropes and working her way up the ladder at Dragonfly International. Her goal was to eventually become a close protection officer, and she relished the opportunity to learn and work under Alexa. To her, her boss was strong and smart, and cared about everyone around her. She looked up to her and was inspired by Alexa's strong work ethic.

"I'm glad you had a good time. Bring Apollo by the office sometime. I'd love to meet him," Alexa replied before she turned her attention to a file she needed to review.

Alexa's condo was a quick drive to the Salamander hotel on the Southwest Waterfront to pick up their principal.

When they arrived, Valerie pulled up to the front of the hotel. Alexa got out and walked into the opulent lobby. Spotting her CP officer, Dyan Grayson, standing to the side while her principal checked out, Alexa walked over to her operative.

Dyan was one of Alexa's good friends. They met when Alexa was just starting out. Both had worked at the same firm while on assignment and had hit it off. Dyan was five foot eleven, and had a strong, muscular physique. She had smooth, dark brown skin and vivid gray eyes. Most people who saw her became mesmerized. They often mistook her for a model. Which Dyan would graciously deny and keep moving. Occasionally, she would wear contact lenses in the field to allow her to blend into the background when needed.

As serious about exercising and weight training as she was about protecting her clients, Dyan was always training.

When Alexa decided to start her own agency, she instantly gave her notice as well, telling Alexa that it wasn't even a question of if she were coming to work for her.

"How is everything, Dyan?"

"Uneventful night, Miss King. The principal had an early dinner, worked until about eleven thirty and then called it a night."

Alexa nodded. "I'll see you on the plane."

"Yes, Miss King," she replied before her team walked past Alexa and left.

Dyan was a regimented person and never called Alexa by her first name when they were in mixed company. Alexa knew she wasn't going to budge on that, so she did not try to dissuade her.

A woman in a red pantsuit turned around. When she saw Alexa, she smiled.

"Thank goodness you're here, darling. Dyan is nice, but she never lets me have any fun."

"Good morning, Mrs. Crawley. I'll be sure and speak with her as soon as we're wheels-up."

As they walked to the car, Alexa had to smile. Veronica Crawley was an heiress to a large private equity firm in Zurich, Switzerland. She was one of Alexa's top clients.

She guided her principal out of the door and into the Mercedes.

"I hope you've packed evening wear, Alexa. I've been invited to several parties while in Chamonix."

"Of course, Mrs. Crawley."

"Good. It will be good to get back to Beauté Majestueuse."

"Yes, ma'am, it will."

The chalet Beauté Majestueuse was one of her client's residences. It was in the luxurious resort area of Chamonix-Mont-Blanc at the junction of France, Switzerland and Italy. A gift from her late father, the seven-thousand-square-foot villa with six bedrooms and seven bathrooms boasted picturesque views of the Alps.

Alexa watched the scenery whiz by on the way to Washington National Airport, also known as Ronald Reagan Washington National Airport. She glanced at her watch. Unfortunately, Alexa would not get a chance to let her parents know she would be on an assignment out of the country. Typically, they preferred a phone call instead of texting if she traveled, but Alexa was pressed for time, so she typed out a message on her cell phone.

A few seconds later, her father responded with a frown emoticon. Since she and Shelley got accosted years ago, her parents' protectiveness was expected. When she pointed out that she was in her thirties now, her mother replied that she failed to see the relevance of that argument because she would always be her daughter.

Alexa wondered if her grandmother acted like her mother but refrained from asking. She didn't have time for one of her mother's lengthy rants.

When they arrived at the airport, Alexa thanked her driver before her team of close protection officers headed to Mrs. Crawley's private jet. Their client received numerous death threats and required around-the-clock detail when she traveled. As a result, several bodyguards and close protection agents worked directly for Crawley's company. Still, Veronica preferred that her immediate detail be all women, so Alexa and her team were on point with the others as secondary protection.

Once they were wheels-up, Alexa and her associates reviewed their operations plan. It listed everyone's assigned roles. For example, the drivers, surveillance officers and personal escort section all played a role in protecting Veronica. Alexa was the primary protection officer, also called PPO, and once she was satisfied that everyone was up to speed on all the plans, safe houses, maps and multiple routes reviewed, she allowed her team to take a break and relax for the remainder of the flight.

"What's troubling you?"

Glancing up, she saw Dyan take a seat across from her chair.

"Nothing. Why?"

Dyan secured her seat belt and then relaxed into the plush leather.

"You look a little edgier than usual."

Alexa shrugged. "I don't know why. I'm fine."

"You know Clive likes you."

"Say what?" Tilting her head to the left, Alexa briefly observed him. He was one of her client's main bodyguards. He was a mountain in a single-breasted suit.

"No, I didn't know that," she said dismissively. She did, but she wasn't about to tell Dyan that. Ever the romantic, her colleague would try to read more into it than there was. As far as Alexa was concerned, Clive was efficient, professional, he knew his stuff, and he could keep a cool head in a crisis. She wasn't interested in him for anything more than that, so personal details about him were irrelevant.

The look Dyan gave her said she didn't believe her. Alexa shrugged, almost as if Dyan had voiced her opinion aloud.

"I'm going to get some sleep," she announced, stretching her legs and getting comfortable.

"You just don't want me plying you with questions about Clive," Dyan mumbled.

"You're right. I don't. Besides, there's nothing to say on the subject. I don't date. End of discussion."

"Alexa, there's no reason you shouldn't entertain the idea of having a relationship with someone. It might be good for you. You know it's good to have a work-life balance—not to mention a horizontal workout now and then."

Opening her eyes, Alexa pinned Dyan with an annoyed glance. "Why this sudden interest in my love life?"

Her friend took a sip of her hot chocolate. "You mean besides the fact that you don't have one?"

"I don't have one because I don't *need* one," Alexa

countered. "So quit worrying about me, please. I'm fine—couldn't be better."

"What couldn't be better?"

Both glanced up to see their topic of discussion hovering over their seats. He leaned in as if waiting to hear the punch line of a joke.

"Not what. Who." Dyan smiled sweetly and waited for Alexa to answer.

Letting out an exasperated puff of air that could have leveled a tree, Alexa scowled at Dyan before turning her attention to Clive.

"I was just telling Dyan here that I don't have the time, or the inclination, to date."

"Oh," Clive replied, relaying his disappointment at her news.

Alexa didn't want to, but she couldn't help gazing at Dyan. Her smug look said *I told you so.*

"Yeah, I get that," Clive said, finally rallying to offer a reply. "This line of work is all-consuming."

"Exactly what I've been saying." Alexa nodded in agreement. "We have enough to tackle without worrying about missing date nights or forgetting your significant other's birthday or anniversary. There is no way I'd want to deal with that kind of pressure."

"Unless the man was extraordinary," Dyan remarked.

"He'd have to be."

At that, Clive bowed out under the guise of getting some food.

When he left, Dyan observed Alexa so long that she shifted in her seat.

"What?"

"You've never been in love."

Alexa scoffed. "First of all, that's private."

"And true."

"Okay, I've never been in love in the romantic sense." Alexa stared out of the window. "I've never met a man that

I wanted to get close enough to in order to develop those kinds of feelings. Well, at least not someone I would turn my life upside down for, put him first above everything else and sacrifice my life for."

"Well, at least?" Dyan said, homing in on the statement with zeal. "So, there was someone."

It wasn't a question.

Alexa remained tight-lipped, but Dyan crossed her arms and waited.

"Okay, fine," she replied, admitting defeat. "Yes. There was someone that I was attracted to, but the timing was wrong. I was just starting my career and had a plan to follow—it didn't include a serious relationship."

"Or any relationship from the looks of it," Dyan snickered.

"Exactly."

"Alexa, it's been three years. Dragonfly International is thriving. You're one of the top woman-owned businesses in our field and on the Top 10 Executive Protection Companies list this year. Business is beyond great, and you've garnered respect in what was once a strictly male-dominated field. So I think you can stop and smell a rose or two. Or should I say a man's cologne?"

Reluctantly, Alexa had to laugh at that one. "Dyan, I know you mean well, but I love my life the way it is. So for now, Dragonfly is my top priority and the only thing on my mind."

"It's not your mind that I'm trying to help out."

Shaking her head, Alexa decided to get some sleep. But before she drifted off, Andrew materialized before her eyes. He was smiling at her with his usual self-assured air. Next, she pictured how soft his mouth would feel at the base of her neck.

That thought jolted Alexa upright. Her gaze darted around as if she expected Andrew to be sitting across from her with a smug look on his face.

"No, no," she whispered before wiping her face, simultaneously feeling hot and cold. Why did Dyan have to talk him up? Alexa had been doing well for years without thinking about what could have been. He was a friend and a colleague. Nothing more.

It didn't matter how tall, well-built and incredible he was or what he did to her blood pressure. Andrew Riker was a heartthrob of a distraction Alexa simply couldn't afford.

Chapter 15

Andrew sailed through the air. Seconds later, his back connected with the training mat. The dull thud from his body coming in contact with the thick padding ricocheted around the room.

"Dude, you're not concentrating. Do you want to spar, or don't you?"

Andrew's eyes shut, and his face wrinkled as he tried to work through the pain in his midsection. He could've kicked himself for not being ready to absorb and redirect the energy of that punch.

Slowly getting to his feet, Andrew tightened the belt on his gi. "Sorry, man." He returned to his position. "Let's go again."

This time, Andrew anticipated his friend's moves and did well to counteract them and deliver blows until he got caught with a roundhouse kick.

"Okay, that's it for today."

A bit slower getting up this time, Andrew bent over and took a moment to even out his breathing. "I'm fine."

"Come on, man. Where's your head at today?" Sanjay Kholi groused. "You could've easily dodged both those shots."

"I know." Andrew went to grab a towel. He dried his face and neck and then drained half his water bottle. "Seems I'm a little preoccupied today."

"How many times have you told me that split focus gets you killed or worse—"

"Puts your asset in danger," Andrew finished for him. "You're right. I have no defense for not concentrating."

"I'm not looking for a defense, my friend. More like an explanation."

Sanjay followed Andrew down the hall to the men's locker room. They both stripped and headed for the showers.

"It's Alexa," Andrew finally announced over the loud whooshing of water barreling out of the showerhead.

"What about her?"

"I can't get her off my mind. Especially lately."

"What's that got to do with it?"

It was hard for Andrew to explain something that he didn't understand. On occasion, they ran into each other, and Alexa had always been cordial and happy to see him, but something was off. It was as if they both were waiting for something. He couldn't call it mixed signals, because she had always been clear on not wanting to be anything but friends. Still, there were moments when she'd call to ask his advice about something and they would… Andrew paused to find the right word.

"Linger," he finally said.

"Who's lingering where?" Sanjay roared.

Andrew shut the water off. "It's nothing."

"You aren't making any sense, my friend."

He snatched the towel from the peg outside the shower and dried off before securing it around his middle.

"Tell me about it," Andrew muttered. "I need to forget about it."

Sanjay looked confused. "About lingering?"

"About Alexa," Andrew clarified.

"Oh. If she causes this much dismay, my friend, that would probably be wise."

Sanjay was right. He knew it. It was time to let Alexa go. No more wishing things were different. They weren't, and it was time he stopped wishing things would change and accepted the reality of how things were.

"You're right. Time to quit pining."

Decision made, Andrew felt lighter than he had in

months. He whistled a cheerful tune while he dressed. Then, after bidding his friend goodbye, he went home.

"JJ, I need you," his father called out from his study not even a minute after Andrew came through the front door.

When Andrew poked his head in the doorway, his father motioned to the chair across from his desk.

"Sure, what's up?"

"There's a security consulting assignment for an old client. But, unfortunately, I've got a scheduling conflict that's come up, or I'd go myself."

"No problem."

James glanced up from reviewing the contract when his son didn't continue. He eyed his son curiously. Then, with a slight nod, he sat back in his chair.

"Okay, what's going on?"

Andrew's expression turned quizzical. "I'm not sure what you mean."

"This is the first time you've agreed to cover an assignment for me without asking for a whole heap of details."

"Does it matter? You asked me to help."

"And I appreciate it," his father acknowledged with a wide smile. "But this isn't like you, son. I'm just wondering why the change-up?"

Andrew crossed his leg, resting his ankle on his knee. "Just feeling the need for a change of scenery lately. Something to take my mind off a few things. Besides, we're on a break, so now's a great time to go."

"A few things, or one specific thing?" James inquired. "Or should I say someone?"

"What do you mean?"

"Come on, JJ, I'm your father. And even if I weren't, I'm still a very observant man. You like Alexa, and you've been on a slow burn since you met her. So I say it's time to stop dragging your feet before someone else stakes a claim."

"Dad, first off, I'm not discussing my love life with you—"

"Good, because it's hard to talk about what you don't have."

Andrew shook his head. "Second, stake a claim? I'm not prospecting for gold. Besides, we're just friends. I can't make her interested in more than that. She's been clear since the beginning on how she felt. So there's nothing more to do."

"Balderdash," James replied, then stopped short. "Are people still saying that?"

Andrew snorted. "No one under eighty."

"I've seen you two together. And the fact that she is still in your life tells me that you've gotten past her looking like—"

"Don't say her name," Andrew warned. "It's better if you don't talk natural disasters up."

"I hadn't planned on saying it," James countered. "I was merely going to say that whatever hesitations you seem to have had early on seem to have resolved themselves, no?"

"No. There's still the very big hurdle of Alexa herself. Like I said, she's made herself crystal clear."

"Alexa likes you, son. Regardless of what she says."

"I'm sure she knows her mind, Dad," Andrew countered. "Not that it matters. I will be on assignment, and I'm sure that wherever Alexa is, she's working. So, let's forget it."

"Consider the matter dropped." Then, handing his son the client folder, James waited until Andrew left before relaxing into a smile.

"Molasses may not be the best way to catch this particular dragonfly. Time to shake things up for you and Alexa, my boy, and see what happens."

Five days later...

Andrew adjusted the black bow tie until he was satisfied. He glanced in the mirror before sliding on the midnight blue tuxedo jacket. The black satin lapels provided a subtle contrast between the two. He retrieved his pistol from the nightstand and slid it into his gun holster before buttoning up the jacket.

There was a quick knock at his bedroom door.

"Coming." Andrew strode across the room to open it.

"Good evening, Mr. Riker."

"How are you, Etienne?"

"Very well, sir. Mr. Simms is ready."

He followed the butler downstairs to the group assembled in the foyer.

"There's my security expert," Mr. Simms's voice boomed. "I told a few of my colleagues that you're here to revolutionize my security detail."

"Thank you, sir. I'll do my best."

"Now you're just being modest," Mr. Simms replied. "Phalanx is one of the best in the business, and you know it. That's why you're here." He pulled Andrew to the side.

"I'm sure you heard about that unfortunate mishap a few weeks ago. One of my men got sloppy, and some disgruntled former employee almost caused a scene. Unfortunately, incidents like that tend to have a snowball effect. I can't shake my stakeholders' faith in my abilities to lead or tarnish my company's reputation."

"No, of course not. I intend to observe your team and provide any necessary alterations to processes. You understand that may result in additional training or even staff changes?"

"Whatever you need to do. You have complete operational control, Andrew. I've known your dad for years, so I know I'm in great hands. James didn't even rake me over the coals for not hiring Phalanx in the first place." Mr. Simms chuckled. "I wouldn't have blamed him in the least."

"Don't worry, sir. We'll get things back on track."

He clapped Andrew between the shoulder blades. "I don't doubt it."

Several Range Rovers were on hand to transport the

businessman's entourage to the nearby chalet for a formal charity event. Andrew was there strictly for observation of his client's team.

When they arrived, there was a reception already in progress. Andrew's gaze roamed the luxurious great room, taking in the immaculately dressed guests and uniformed waiters serving drinks and canapés. Before they had come, Andrew sat in on the operations meeting for Mr. Simms's protection officers. The chalet Bruyère was at the foot of the Alps. The residence belonged to one of his client's business partners, and while the view was spectacular, the team was more concerned about entry and exit points, the guests attending and safe houses along the route.

Keeping a low profile, Andrew waved off the flute of champagne a waiter had offered him. He didn't drink while on duty, so he asked for a glass of club soda instead. More to have something in his hand while walking around. When on assignment, Andrew worked hard to blend in. Granted, he was in the Alps and noticed the only people of color at the event were on Mr. Simms's security detail, so there wasn't but so much being a wallflower he could do. That thought made him chuckle.

He was about to take another sip of his drink but stopped. A weird feeling settled into the pit of his stomach. His body's early detection system that something wasn't right.

When Andrew got these hunches, he never ignored them. Instead, he paid close attention to everything happening around him.

That's when he saw it. There was nothing unusual to the untrained eye about the two elegantly dressed people standing there talking, but Andrew could tell the man was upset by his body language. The woman's back was to him, but he saw her leaning into the man to speak with him. Then, when the man tried to step around her, she placed her hand on his biceps and guided him down the corridor.

Before he'd even registered, Andrew was moving to follow them. He set his drink down on the table along the way. He spotted them moving away from the guests and down a flight of stairs. Glancing around, he confirmed that everyone was engaged and enjoying the party.

Silently, he crept down the stairs. At the bottom, Andrew walked into a wood-paneled theater room with two large couches, several plush beanbags and a large projection-screen television. Continuing down the corridor, he poked his head into a sauna and the adjacent steam room.

Where could they have gone? he questioned himself. That's when he heard two muted voices. Silently, Andrew strode toward a room at the end of the hall. He could hear the raised voices and see that the once-agitated man was flat-out belligerent.

"No, I will not calm down. I have every right to talk to her. This is a free country, you know. You can't prohibit me from speaking to whomever I please. Now step aside."

The woman remained planted in front of him. Nothing about her body language seemed excited. Instead, she appeared calm and spoke to the man slowly, soothingly.

"I'm sorry, sir, but Mrs. Crawley is here to enjoy the charity event. If you would like to give me your name, I would be happy to relay any message you have for her tomorrow."

"And I said I'm not doing that. I am going to give her a piece of my mind. I was a good employee. I didn't deserve to get fired over some stupid misunderstanding, which she'd know if you'd let me speak to her. But you know what, why am I wasting my time with you? I don't know who you are, but this conversation is over. Now move."

He reached out to shove the woman out of his way. Andrew watched in growing amusement as she used the man's momentum when he tried to grab her to flip him to the floor by the arm. Before he could utter a word, she hauled him to his feet and grabbed him by the scruff of his collar. When she turned around, and they saw each other, both froze.

Alexa and Andrew were speechless and stood rooted to their spots. Her aggressor tried to use the opportunity to make a run for it, but she was still holding his collar, plus Andrew was blocking their path.

"Andrew?" Alexa said when she'd recovered herself. "What are you doing here?"

He grinned. "You know me. I have a habit of turning up where I'm least expected."

Chapter 16

Alexa crossed her arms. "I'm serious."

"I'm here on business," Andrew explained. "So, how are you, Lexi?"

"I'm doing great—and you?"

Alexa's detainee was incredulous. "Who cares how he is? Let go of my neck."

"Shut up," they both said in unison.

Andrew's gaze returned to Alexa. "Of all the places we could've run into each other."

She nodded. "Who'd have guessed Chamonix, France?"

"Not me." He turned to the man struggling to get free. "I see you're on duty?"

"Yep. I have a client here for a few weeks. And you?" she inquired.

"I'm doing some security consulting."

"Well, that's exciting."

"No, it's not," her captive groused.

"If I have to tell you again to stop talking, you'll be walking home with a limp," she promised.

The man snorted. "And I'll sue that sequined dress off your body."

"How do you stand it?" Andrew asked seriously. "I've only known him two minutes, and I'd love to deck him already."

The man went to say something, but Alexa cut him off. "You've tried to threaten and intimidate my client, and you took a swing at me, so by all means, call your lawyer," she countered.

He grumbled but remained quiet.

Escorting him through the patio door, Alexa guided him

along the wooden deck to the front of the house. Then, spotting one of her employees, she headed his way.

"Is the principal on the go?"

"Yes, Miss King. Dyan took Mrs. Crawley in the lead car. We left car number two here for you."

She nodded. "Escort this gentleman to his vehicle and see that he leaves the premises."

"Yes, Miss King."

When her employee left, physically pulling the protesting man behind, she turned to find Andrew standing with his arms across his chest.

Shaking her head, Alexa went up to him. "Enjoying the show?"

"Oh, yeah," he laughed. "You were impressive, Miss King."

"Thank you, Mr. Riker. Fishing for compliments considering Phalanx taught me everything I know?"

Andrew fell into step beside her. "Not at all. I'm pleased you're doing well and Dragonfly International is thriving. You've made a solid name for yourself in our community, Alexa. That's all my dad and I ever wanted for you."

"Thanks, Andrew. That's high praise coming from you. And it's good to see you."

Their shoes tapped out a staccato beat on the wood decking as they returned to the entrance at the back of the house.

"It's good to see you, too, Alexa."

When they went in, Andrew noticed the slightly blue tinge to her lips and her shivering. Rushing to the couch, he grabbed one of the thick sherpa throw blankets and draped it over Alexa's shoulders.

"Thank you," she said through chattering teeth.

"You're freezing. Why didn't you say something? I could've escorted the whiner outside to your team."

"That's my job, and I'm fine," she retorted.

Andrew studied the floor-length V-neck sequined gown

that she was wearing. The flutter sleeves and slit above her right leg exposed some of her skin to the elements.

"Alexa, your lips almost match the gray of your dress. If you don't warm up soon, I will be forced to escort you to the sauna. Better yet, that might still be a good idea."

"Don't you dare," she cautioned before a shimmer of a smile peeked through a stern frown.

He helped her sit down on the couch closest to the fireplace before he flipped the switch to turn it on. At the same time, Alexa rubbed her shoulders vigorously, trying to warm up. Finally, the gas ignited with an audible whoosh, and flames shot to life.

Andrew sat as close as he could to help with the transference of body heat. He placed an arm around her shoulder and drew her close. Her body wasn't shivering as much as before.

"You'd better not catch pneumonia."

"That's not in the schedule."

His chest shook with delight while he rubbed his hand up and down her blanketed arm. Andrew was startled when Alexa moved closer, resting her head on his shoulder.

The room was eerily quiet save for the occasional muffled voices and footsteps coming from the first floor.

"Always by the book, huh, King?"

"It's easier that way. Everything is predictable—no surprises."

"Yeah," he agreed. "But where's the fun in that?"

It was two days later when Alexa received a text from Andrew. Both got a break in their schedules, so they decided to meet. Dyan was on point as the CPO for the day and took Mrs. Crawley to the spa.

"So, where's he taking you on your date?" Dyan had said when she heard about Alexa's plans.

"It's not a date. We're simply two friends getting reacquainted on our day off."

Dyan pulled out her phone.

"What are you doing?"

"'A date is time spent with another person that is enjoyable and allows you both to grow closer.'"

Alexa's mouth dropped open. "Did you just google that?"

"Yes, I did. And as you can see, by definition, you two are on a date."

Alexa's eyes shot heavenward as she excused herself to go and get ready.

The forecast was for a clear day with a high temperature of forty-seven degrees. Alexa didn't know where they were going. Andrew suggested that she dress comfortably and in layers, so she wore black stretch leggings, hiking boots, a fleece jacket and a long-sleeve Henley shirt. Pleased with her appearance, Alexa grabbed her coat, hat and gloves and headed to the family room to wait.

When the butler announced that Andrew had arrived, Alexa followed him outside.

Several of Alexa's team were walking the perimeter of the house. Each looked surprised when she and Andrew walked by but refrained from comment. The snow was piled high on either side of the shoveled driveway. Andrew's car was toward the entrance of Beauté Majestueuse, so they walked down the road. While they strolled, Alexa took in the snow-covered trees and glorious mountain view. Retrieving her cell phone from her jacket pocket, Alexa took pictures of the snowy scene and a few of Andrew. "How are you this afternoon?" he greeted her, opening the silver Range Rover door and helping her climb up.

"I'm wonderful."

She waited while Andrew walked around to the other side. Then, when he slid behind the wheel, Alexa said, "Okay, so where are we going?"

"Come on. I can't tell you yet. Then it wouldn't be a surprise."

Andrew started the car and entered an address into the

GPS. He used his hand to block the screen from her view, which caused Alexa to arch an eyebrow.

"Yeah, about that. I'm not big on surprises, Andrew. It helps when I'm prepared and—"

"Uh-uh," he interrupted as he pulled off. "You're not working today, so come back off high alert. Besides, you'll like this surprise," he said confidently.

Alexa couldn't argue with his logic. She nodded her agreement and allowed Andrew to continue with their journey while she enjoyed the scenery.

They chatted as he drove. "How are your parents?"

"Doing well. Not happy I'm over four thousand miles away," she explained. "But they're supportive of my career. They always have been."

"That's valuable to have."

"Don't I know it," Alexa agreed. "Our family isn't that large, so it's always special when we get together."

Andrew parked and cut the engine when they pulled outside their destination.

"Where are we? Come on, now is a great time to fill me in."

"Fair enough. We're going skijoring."

Her expression was blank. "What?"

"It's a winter sport that means ski driving, and you're pulled along on skis behind a horse." He stopped. "You can ski, can't you?" Andrew frowned. "I suppose I should've asked before now."

"Yes, I can ski," Alexa responded with a laugh. "This sounds like fun. I'd love to try it."

Thirty minutes later, Alexa was holding on tight as a horse gently galloped through the snowy trails. Her cheeks were hurting, not from the cold but from all the laughing and smiling.

Eventually, their guide led the horses back to the stables. When they turned a corner, Alexa lost her grip and her balance. She went careening off the path and into a snowbank.

"Alexa," Andrew yelled as he let go of the harness. He came to a complete stop before he undid his skis and went after Alexa.

"Hey, are you okay?" he said with concern.

"Fine," she giggled. "Except for the fact that I'm stuck."

"Here, let me help you."

"No, I've got it," she said quickly.

He watched her attempt to stand twice before going over and grabbing her hand to hoist her up. Off-balance, Alexa was stable for a few moments before the skis began to slide.

"Wait, I've got you," he said, trying to keep her steady.

Before either could stop it, Alexa fell backward, taking Andrew with her.

He lay sprawled on top of her in a tangle of limbs. Once Alexa recovered, she started laughing so hard she began hiccuping.

Unable to stop himself, Andrew joined in.

They finally sobered. He gazed down at her. Suddenly, he lifted his gloved hand and moved a wisp of Alexa's hair out of her face.

She stilled.

"Why do you do that?"

A look of confusion crossed her face. "What?"

"Never accept my help? Or, as far as I know, anyone's help?"

"I like doing things myself. It's better that way."

He touched her cheek. "Better or safer?"

All of a sudden, the air between them grew dense with tension. Andrew's face was mere inches away. Alexa could feel his breath mingling with her own, and his eyes were intense, as if he were trying to peer into her soul. She worried that he could hear the hammering of her heart. Alarm bells went off in Alexa's head. Every inch of her warned that this was dangerous. That *he* was dangerous. Her gaze drifted to his lips. His upper lip was a cupid's bow and matched his full lower lip perfectly. There was a bit of razor stubble along his jawline, and the scar from his lip to his chin still mesmerized Alexa. They were so close that all she needed to do was tilt her head up, and their lips would be locked in a kiss.

The moan that drifted between her traitorous lips left her mortified.

She tried to push him off, but his body weight held her firmly in place.

"Andrew, I think we'd better get up," she said, still struggling to free herself.

"Answer me, Lexi."

She blinked several times. She was so affected by his proximity that she had forgotten the question.

"What?" she said, trying to stall.

"Why do you keep me at arm's length?"

"You don't appear to be at the moment, do you?"

"Alexa, what are you afraid of?"

Before she could respond, their guide called out from about one hundred yards away.

It was the proverbial splash of cold water needed to break the connection. Andrew glanced at her a final time before he got up. This time when he held out his hand to help Alexa, she accepted it.

"There you are," the worried man said when he reached them. "Is everything okay?"

Andrew glanced at Alexa with a heated look so intense that it took her breath away. She could only nod her head in response.

Chapter 17

When they returned to the stables, Andrew unsnapped his snow boots from his skis. He turned to help Alexa, but she was already undoing her boots.

One of her buckles was stuck, so Alexa tugged on it sharply.

"Here, let me."

She started to refuse but stopped. Instead, she gave him a demure smile. "Thank you for bringing me. It was a great surprise, Andrew."

The mutual attraction still hummed between them like a powerline, but for now neither acknowledged it.

He grinned. "Glad you liked it," he replied as they returned their gear. "But the day isn't over. How about some lunch?"

"Are you kidding? I'm starving. Lead the way."

Andrew chose Neopolis, an Italian restaurant in the Centre Commercial Alpina in Chamonix city center with an impressive view of Mont Blanc and the banks of the Arve river.

The restaurant was cozy, with wood tables and brown leather chairs. White walls were decorated with paintings, and wood ledges held carafes, baskets and other artifacts from bygone eras.

Alexa ordered the capricciosa pizza while Andrew ordered the spaghetti Bolognese. The restaurant was busy, making intimate conversation difficult, but they enjoyed being there and eating delicious Italian food.

A walk along the river followed lunch, which allowed them a chance for quiet conversation.

"I've enjoyed my day, Drew. Thanks again for suggesting it."

"My pleasure, Lexi," he said, grinning.

Alexa observed the shops as they walked by. Eventually, she said, "To answer your question, it's safer."

Andrew didn't stop walking. After a moment, he said, "You are always safe with me, Alexa. Don't you know that by now?"

Alexa's cell phone chirped. She checked her text message and frowned.

"What's wrong?"

"That's Dyan. We have an issue with the driver in car two. He ate something that didn't agree with him and was forced to make a pit stop."

Andrew nodded and ushered Alexa back to the Range Rover.

"Where's your backup team?" he asked along the way.

Alexa's stride was almost as long as his as they rushed back to their parking space. Andrew's mind was racing with possible scenarios.

"They're en route."

When they got to the SUV, Andrew started the engine and turned to Alexa.

"Where's the lead car?"

Alexa tapped out a message to Dyan and waited.

"On la Mer de Glace," she finally said.

Andrew looked at the navigation system. "That's only four minutes from here. We can intercept them."

Dyan gave Alexa their coordinates, and she added them to Andrew's GPS.

It didn't take long to spot the lead car, but Alexa pointed out a black BMW 7 Series that had pulled up parallel to Dyan's car. They gave it a few moments, but when the other vehicle matched their speed, Alexa turned to Andrew.

"I see them," he said before she could say a word and sped up to intercept the chase car.

Alexa called Dyan's cell phone. "We're right behind you. Have the driver execute maneuver E."

"Will do," Dyan replied before hanging up.

"The driver will speed up so that you can take his place and deal with the other car," Alexa explained.

"Got it," Andrew replied.

Both were all business as they worked together to deal with the immediate threat to Alexa's operation.

He sped up and got behind Dyan's car so that when the driver hit the gas and took off, they quickly slipped in to deal with the BMW. Alexa used the time to write down the license plate number.

The other car sped up to pass, but Andrew's Range Rover connected with the left panel of the vehicle and pushed it to the right. The BMW veered sharply and ran off the road. Andrew shot past to catch up with the principal's car.

"Alexa, are you okay?"

"Yep, I'm fine. Great driving," she replied with a smile.

Andrew caught up to Dyan's car and dropped behind her while Alexa called to check on their second car's driver and let the backup car know that she and Andrew were following the lead.

She ended the call and turned to Andrew. "He has food poisoning."

"Coincidence?"

"Unlikely. He ate the same meal as the other CP officers, and they're all fine. I'll check it out when we get back and my principal's secure."

The two cars pulled into the driveway at Beauté Majestueuse, and Dyan assisted Mrs. Crawley into the house. Alexa and Andrew got out of the car, and he checked the damage on the rental car.

"It's not too bad."

"I'm glad. Thanks for helping me out today."

He grinned. "My pleasure. Never a dull moment, hey, King?"

"That's true," she replied. "Which is one of the things I love about my job."

Andrew nodded. His smile was brilliant. "Thanks for a lively day."

"That it was," she agreed. "I enjoyed the food, skijoring, the walk along the waterfront and the car chase."

Andrew laughed. "Of course."

There was an awkward pause before she said, "I'll see you later?"

He nodded. "I'm headed to Geneva tomorrow, but it'll only be a two-day trip."

Alexa frowned before she caught herself. "Oh. Then safe travels, Drew."

"Thanks. I know you'll hold the fort down, Lexi."

She chuckled. "Always do."

Turning, she strode into the house to find her team waiting in the living room. She returned to all business.

"How's the principal?"

"She's fine," Dyan replied. "Most of the time, she was on her phone conducting business and wasn't paying attention to her surroundings."

Alexa pinched the bridge of her nose. "I'd like an incident report in thirty minutes on what went wrong, how this could've been avoided and what steps we'll take to ensure that things go smoother next time. If Andrew and I hadn't been close, this could've had a different outcome."

Her team agreed and dispersed, giving her time to return to her suite to shower and change clothes. When she returned thirty-five minutes later, everyone was at the dining table waiting.

"Okay," Alexa said, claiming the spot at the head of the table. "Let's begin."

A few nights later, Mrs. Crawley hosted an intimate dinner party for some friends. There were various glass jars and vases filled with water, cranberries, green twigs and floating candles placed as centerpieces on the table and around the room. The warm glow of the candles replaced the bright overhead lighting that illuminated the dining room and complemented the solid custom acacia wood dining table and chairs. There was a runner on the table that included winter touches of evergreens, pine cones and holly. The red and green were a beautiful contrast to the cream-colored china plates with gold chargers and crystal glasses.

Alexa was the CP officer on duty and remained at a distance from her principal for the entire evening. Since they were in a controlled environment and had cleared the guest list, Alexa gave a few of her team the night off. The remaining employees were strategically placed around the chalet to avoid drawing attention. To anyone observing, she was merely one of Mrs. Crawley's employees.

Alexa had her laptop out and appeared to be working, but she observed everyone attending the party to ensure there were no surprises and that the night ran smoothly.

Her cell phone vibrated. Alexa glanced at her principal before she checked it.

How's everything?

She smiled, and her heart fluttered. *Andrew.*

Great. Principal is having a dinner party. Pretty sedate. How's Geneva?

I just finished a training session. Have some paperwork to do, and I owe Dad a call.

I do, too. My parents get antsy if I don't check in often on assignments. You'd think I was still a teenager.

You, too? LOL. How about dinner when I return? I promise it'll be a less hectic day. No car chases or overzealous fans.

Don't make promises you can't keep.

That garnered her a smiley emoji from Andrew.

Fair enough. There might be some chaos and mayhem involved.

That's more like it.

Can I ask you a question?

Sure, Alexa replied.

Did you smile when you saw it was me texting?

Alexa's cheeks flushed with excitement. She pondered if she should be truthful or not. Finally, she typed her answer.

Yes, I was happy to see it was you.

So, you miss me?

Alexa pondered his question. Try as she might, she couldn't deny that she had been thinking about Andrew a lot since he had left. Their ski outing played nightly in her dreams. Each time, they ended up kissing. It was hot and explosive, and always left Alexa wanting more when it was over. Each time she woke up feeling strung tighter than a violin string. It was disconcerting to her. She was placing her toe in water that was sure to burn.

Are you there?

She glanced down at the screen before turning around. Alexa noticed that everyone was enjoying the party and not minding her.

Yes, I miss you. I enjoyed spending time with you, Andrew. It has been a pleasant surprise.

How pleasant? he texted back.

Alexa almost grit her teeth in frustration.

Andrew, why are you fishing for compliments?

I'm not. Merely seeing how truthful you'll be in answering my questions.

I told you that I never lie.

We'll see if that's true when I return and I'm standing right in front of you.

Alexa felt her body growing warmer just recalling the last time Andrew was so close.

Andrew, I have to go. It looks like the guests are leaving.

Duty calls? Fair enough. We will continue this conversation later. Good night, Lexi. Sweet dreams.

There was no doubt that her dreams would be even more intense thanks to him.

Alexa shifted in her chair, suddenly feeling the need for some fresh mountain air. It was time to admit the truth. She was falling and there was no way to stop it.

Good night, Drew.

Chapter 18

Alexa had off the next day, so she went into Chamonix and treated herself to a spa day at one of the luxury resorts. She had received a bamboo deep-tissue massage, followed by a detoxifying body wrap, a eucalyptus steam room session and a few minutes in the hot tub. While she was getting a deluxe pedicure, she called her friend Marena to catch up.

"Alexa, it's been forever since we've spoken. Bring me up to speed. What's been going on with you?"

She watched as the woman sitting on a stool at her feet massaged a cold, blue-green invigorating scrub into her legs. The rhythmic motion lulled Alexa into a further state of relaxation. Alexa leaned back into the soft white leather massage chair and pressed a button to start a combination of rolling and kneading her muscles. A blissful sigh escaped her lips.

"Well, I've been in Chamonix, France, for a few weeks. I leave for home in a few days. Let's just say this assignment has been full of unexpected surprises."

"Really," Dr. Marena Dash-McKendrick remarked. "And what do you mean by surprises?"

"Not all what," Alexa replied, feeling so relaxed that she yawned several times. "Some are a who."

"You don't say? Would one of those whos be Andrew Riker?"

"Yes." Alexa tried not to gush, but it was hard to do with the smile encompassing her whole face. "He tops the list, yes. I mean, figure the odds of us running into each other in France?"

"Seems predestined if you ask me."

Alexa choked on the seltzer water she had been offered. "Predestined? That's laying it on a bit thick, isn't it?"

Marena snickered.

"Oh, stop. It's not all dreamy. We just reconnected, and we're simply getting to know each other better."

"And has this time playing twenty questions changed your opinion of him?"

Alexa paused before she answered that. "No. Quit reading more into this than it is. We're still just friends."

"You're a terrible liar."

"Now you sound like my cousin, Zane."

"He's not wrong. Besides, I can hear what you're still trying to deny in your voice. You *like* him."

"Okay, yes, I do like Andrew. But there's so much going on with work, I can't afford to split my focus," Alexa dismissed. "Before I forget, we have a new client, Ruben Tyndale, who will come in shortly. A very VIP client, I might add."

"Congrats, Lex. I'm glad business is doing so well. Oh, Lucas is here for a visit. He wanted me to make sure I told the 'Amazon' hello."

Alexa laughed. "And how is your brother doing? I knew I shouldn't have told him my nickname when we were on that mission in London."

"Oh, you're never going to hear the end of it. Lucas said it suits you too much. And he's well. He and Coulter have decided to build me a larger workspace in the backyard for all my inventions."

"Speaking of which, anything new that Dragonfly can acquire?"

"Of course," Marena said gleefully. "I'm working on a ring that shoots out a burst of a sleeping agent."

"I know of a few people I'd love to put to sleep," Alexa joked. "If you need someone to test the prototype—"

"Don't worry, I'll send it as soon as it's done. And don't get too excited. It doesn't last that long," Marena added. "Now, back to my original question before you decided to redirect."

The woman doing her feet was rubbing hot stones on

her legs. Alexa sighed blissfully. "I wasn't redirecting," she finally managed to say. "And business has been booming. Dragonfly has had steady repeat business and word-of-mouth recommendations. And now that we're about to sign this new client, we're finally out of the red."

"I'm happy for you," Marena exclaimed. "You deserve it."

"Ruben mentioned the person we would be taking on is an ultra-high net asset. We'll go over the details in our operational meeting when I return home. First, we'll determine why the principal needs protection and how long. Is it because of a digital stalker, angry ex-lover, corporate espionage, or if it's for business travel—"

"You know I'm not applying for a job, right?" Marena laughed.

"Oh, am I boring you?" she countered while accepting a proffered glass of sparkling water with lime.

"To death."

"What? The world of close protection is so exciting," Alexa gushed while adjusting her massage chair. "It's amazing that you never do the same job twice. Every client and operation is different. You know, like when you're making serums in your lab, designing tech gadgets or antidotes to save your husband from certain death by poison."

"Touché," Marena replied. "So what's Zane's take on your latest client?"

Alexa chuckled and pointed to the nail polish swatch that she wanted. "You know Zane. He's betting whatever Ruben Tyndale wants to discuss involves some supermodel with a stalker."

"He would pick the scenario with a supermodel.

"Speaking of people we love to look at, tell me more about Andrew. Has he come to Washington to visit?"

"Uh, segue much?" Alexa teased. "And no, he hasn't come to DC. He's been tied up with work lately, too. He's in Geneva right now but will be returning to Chamonix. I'll get a chance to see him before I go."

"I bet he'd come if you asked him."

"Marena."

"Okay, okay. I'll let it go—for now. But only because I've got to run. Congrats again on landing the new client. Let me know how it goes."

"Thanks, and will do," Alexa promised.

Alexa hung up and had to laugh at her friend. Marena hadn't changed since they met at the retreat years ago. *The one that changed my life. Who would have thought I would decide on this career after going to a transformational retreat that Tanya had suggested?* Her mind drifted to Andrew again. Yes, life did have a way of trying to throw curveballs.

Andrew ended up detained and made it back on Alexa's last night in France. They dined at Le Matafan in the heart of Chamonix. It was a relaxed atmosphere with primarily wood decor with bright red as an accent color used in the tableware, lighting and seating.

Alexa marveled at the hundreds of pieces of wood logs flush on accent walls around the restaurant. It was unique and, paired with the fireplace, added to the romantic flair.

While they dined on pumpkin gnocchis with butternut cream, and octopus cooked in bouillabaisse, they talked about their upcoming assignments.

"It sounds like a wonderful opportunity to showcase Dragonfly. I wish you all the best. Let me know if you need anything."

"I will," she promised. "What about you? Thailand sounds exciting."

"I've been there a few times, so nothing out of the ordinary. Just babysitting a few businessmen for a summit."

"And what's next after that?"

"That would depend on you."

Alexa was about to take a bite of her gnocchi and stopped. "Me?"

"Despite your dire warnings as to why we wouldn't work together, Alexa, I get the feeling that you're not so sure that still rings true."

"Andrew—"

"Before you deny what I know as facts, hear me out. I propose a trial."

Her mouth dropped open. "A what?"

"When our assignments are over, let's schedule some time together. Uninterrupted time to get to know each other better. Without work getting in the way."

"Andrew, I—"

He took her hand, turned it over and kissed the pulse point of her wrist. Instead of releasing it, he held her hand captive, caressing her fingers with the pad of his thumb.

"Don't think. Feel, Alexa."

At the moment, Alexa could barely breathe. She stared at Andrew stroking her hand as if she had just grown the appendage out of thin air.

"That's a good sign."

Alexa felt warm and tingly all over. "What is?"

Andrew leaned in closer. "The fact that I'm not on my knees in a headlock right now." His gaze held a hint of playfulness. "I'd say you're at least amenable to my proposition."

Truthfully, Alexa's answer was yes the moment he suggested it. She'd find a way to deal with those subconscious worries later. For now, there was no way she was refusing anything this man offered.

Alexa leaned in to give him her full attention. His cologne wafted into her nostrils. The woody, masculine scent was heady and lulling her like a seductive siren song.

"Andrew?"

"Yes?"

"I don't like you."

His expression was so intense his gaze could have melted cheese without a fondue set.

"I'm glad. Because I don't like you, either."

Chapter 19

A week later, Alexa was in her office reviewing the operational manager's detailed report on Ruben Tyndale and his company, Tyndale Global Holdings. Their latest annual report was quite impressive. Tyndale had business ties in entertainment, fashion, media and banking.

She was making discussion notes when her administrative assistant buzzed her office to let her know Mr. Tyndale had arrived.

"Thanks, Miranda." Standing, Alexa smoothed her dark gray pantsuit and ran her tongue over her teeth. Seconds later, the door opened, and he was ushered into her plush office.

"Good afternoon, Miss King," Ruben said as he strode across the room.

"Hello, Mr. Tyndale." They shook hands before Alexa motioned for him to be seated.

"Let me start by saying how thrilled I am to meet you finally. Your track record is stellar, Miss King, and I need the best."

"Thank you, Mr. Tyndale. We appreciate your business."

"Please, call me Ruben."

"If you'll call me Alexa," she returned. "Now, how can Dragonfly be of assistance?"

He shifted in his chair. "It's not for me—at least not directly. I have a high-profile business partner and client who needs your company's specialized protection. She's a young lady whose career has taken off. She owns very successful jewelry, makeup line and fashion accessory businesses and recently made the Forbes billionaires list. She will be traveling to several shows in the US and Europe, so I want her safe—especially from her boyfriend."

Alexa sat back in her chair. "Mr. Tyndale, while this isn't outside my company's skill set, I'm curious why you didn't mention to our operational manager that you aren't the principal?"

"Miss King, it's a rather delicate situation, and I didn't—"

Before Ruben could explain, a tall woman burst through the door. She walked in like it was her office. Her winter-white wool pantsuit was adorned with a diamond-and-gold belt. Her bracelets, earrings and necklaces were gold as well. The black suede red-bottomed ankle boots were devoid of adornment, as was the black suede handbag providing an understated anchor to the opulence of her ensemble.

"I'm sorry for the intrusion, Miss King," her assistant, Miranda, said, rushing in behind the woman. "I told her that you were in a meeting, but—"

"It's okay, Miranda," Alexa said, rising out of her chair.

The woman stopped in front of her desk. "Whatever Ruben has arranged, you can forget it. I have no intention of going along with this insanity." She scowled at him. "There is nothing that I'd ever want from this woman."

Before Alexa could reply, the woman removed her black sunglasses and glared back.

The color drained from Alexa's face, and it took several moments for her to recover from seeing her ex–best friend Shelley's baby sister. "Sophia?"

"So, you remember me," she said with a mocking smile. "Good. Then you know that there's nothing I'd ever want from you after what you did to my family."

Sophia spun around and pierced her business partner with a murderous glare. "Ruben, I don't know what you thought coming here, but I don't need *her* help. Nor will I ever need anything from Alexa King. I'm leaving."

"No, you're not," he countered. "You will stay here, and we will work this out."

"How could you?" Sophia accused. "She left my sister to die at the hands of some madman while she saved herself."

"You know that's not true," Alexa shot back. "I went to get Shelley some help. She's here today because of me."

Sophia leaned over Alexa's desk. "You mean she's psychologically damaged because of *you*."

Ruben bolted up and took hold of Sophia's arm. "Okay, let's calm down, ladies. Sophia, this isn't getting us anywhere. I'm sure we can find a way to—"

"Don't you even act like I'm the one being unreasonable when you've blindsided me like this." Sophia yanked her arm away.

"I'm sorry, Mr. Tyndale, but under the circumstances, I don't think this is going to work," Alexa said firmly. "I'll be happy to recommend another—"

"Excuse me, Miss King, can I have a word?" Dyan called from the doorway. "We have a situation regarding a client that I need to speak with you about."

Alexa hesitated.

"It's imperative."

"Certainly, Dyan." Ignoring Sophia, she turned to Ruben. "Please excuse me for a moment."

"There she goes running away again. Typical."

Alexa forced herself to refrain from commenting as she strode to the door. Instead, she turned her attention to Dyan when she got on the other side.

"Okay, what's going on?"

"That's what I'd like to know. So, because of a principal's temper tantrum, you're about to blow a ridiculously lucrative contract for us?"

That brought Alexa up short. "Potential principal. And you interrupted a client meeting for this?"

"He's already paid a retainer fee, and a screaming match was more like it," Dyan retorted. "Alexa, this isn't like you. You can get along with anybody. I've seen you do it."

"This is different," she shot back. "This is Shelley's younger sister. I'll add who is just as vicious now as she was almost fifteen years ago." Alexa stopped talking and sat down at Miranda's desk. She searched through a few drawers before pulling out a bag of chocolate chip cookies from the numerous snacks her assistant kept in her desk. Ripping open the foil bag, Alexa popped a few into her mouth. Closing her eyes, she chewed in blissful silence. Then, almost as an afterthought, her eyes flew open to find Dyan staring at her in stunned silence.

"Stress eating?"

"It's warranted," Alexa countered. "Dyan, you have to understand, there's no reasoning with Sophia about anything. She thinks I'm fully responsible for Shelley's deterioration." She ate a few more snacks before saying, "Maybe she's not wrong."

Dyan leaned against Miranda's desk. "You know that's not true. You told me you were teenagers at the time. I know you did the best you could because you're a fighter, Alexa, and you don't give up. Yet you're ready to throw the towel in now and walk away from a contract with Tyndale Global? Boss, think about it. Anything they touch skyrockets to the top, and regardless of how annoying she is, Sophia Porter has the Midas touch right now. If everything goes well, Tyndale's referrals and possible follow-up work could be phenomenal. It's just the exposure we need."

Leaning back in Miranda's chair, Alexa stared at the ceiling. Her ragged sigh ricocheted around the quiet space like a Ping-Pong ball. "Dyan, this dredges up so much from my past," she said softly.

"You can handle it, Alexa. No one I know is stronger than you when you set your mind to something."

Her friend stood there and waited. Finally, Alexa stood.

"You're right. If Ruben still wants to hire Dragonfly, we will do it. One thing I won't do is let Shelley's sister cost my company a contract. I'll do whatever is necessary to make this work."

Dyan touched her boss's shoulder. "That's the Alexa King I know."

Alexa smiled and threw the empty bag in the trash. She rose and smoothed her suit before turning on her heel to head back to her office. She stopped and glanced over her shoulder. "Dyan?"

"Yes?"

"Can you get a replacement bag of cookies for me? And go find Miranda? She's probably hiding in the break room. Tell her that I'm not mad about Sophia barging into my office. It wasn't her fault. Sophia Porter is like unstable air moving over warm water in September on her best day. At some point, you realize that a hurricane is imminent."

Stifling a chuckle, Dyan agreed and went off to find their younger associate.

When Alexa strode through her office double doors, it was to find Sophia sitting in a chair next to Ruben. The barely controlled anger was emanating from her body like a force field. Alexa ignored the invisible daggers being thrown her way and turned her attention to her client.

"I apologize for the interruption. Unfortunately, it couldn't be helped."

"No problem at all, Miss King. At best, I know this is a tenuous situation, and I apologize for not providing you with advance notice."

"Mr. Tyndale, crisis management is where we excel." Alexa smiled and returned to her desk. "Now, I believe we were discussing why Miss Porter requires protection?"

"That's funny. I thought we were at the point where Ruben and I leave, and you return to your miserable little existence?"

Ruben paled. "Sophia!"

Alexa dug deep to generate a serene demeanor. "But that doesn't solve your security problem, does it?"

"Fine," she capitulated. "But if you ask me, Ruben is being paranoid. I'm in no real danger. Nico likes to be a drama king at times. He and I argued, but it isn't like we don't always kiss and make up."

"Over what?"

"Excuse me?"

"What did the two of you argue about?" Alexa clarified.

"That's none of your business."

Alexa grabbed a pen and Ruben's contract, signed it and then set it aside.

"Now it is. I've been hired to protect you from this day forward. Every move you make is my team's business, Sophia."

She placed her feet up on the coffee table. "Fine. We fought about some stupid investment. Nico wanted me to be a silent partner in some club he's trying to buy with a few friends. I think his friends are useless, and I wasn't about to go along with pouring my money down a bottomless drain, so I told him I wasn't interested. Especially not with the wastrels in tow.

"I've declined business ventures with him before, but this was different. He blew up and threatened that I'd regret my decision. A few days later, one of his friends cornered me at an event and thanked me for changing my mind and bankrolling Nico's portion." She glanced up at the two of them. "I didn't."

Alexa made some notes on her tablet. "What happened next?"

"Nico left for Portugal, and I flew back to the States for a fashion show. I haven't seen him since."

"Do you have arguments often?"

Sophia shrugged.

"Has Nico ever become physical with you?"

"Not if he values breathing."

"Good to hear," Alexa replied, making more notes. "Did you tell him about your conversation with his business partner?"

"No, not yet."

"We'll need to drill down further into your daily schedule, the places you go and the people you meet. The process will take a few hours, so you'll meet with a member of my logistics team."

"Fine. Are we done?"

"For the day, yes."

"I'll be in the limo, Ruben," Sophia replied. She turned to glare at Alexa.

"I'll work with you because I have to, but that doesn't mean I'll ever forgive you for your part in Shelley's issues."

Without another word, Sophia stormed out.

The room was draped in awkward silence.

"I'm sorry about her behavior, Alexa," Ruben said quickly. "Of course she'll never say it, but this latest falling-out with Nico is more significant than Sophia lets on. He's made more than a few missteps concerning business ventures, making me fearful of her getting involved in his harebrained schemes."

"Do they have any joint accounts?"

"Yes, but I don't think it's a significant amount that she keeps in the accounts she shares with Nicholas, but I can't be sure."

"I understand. Dragonfly is on the clock now, Mr. Tyndale—Ruben. We have a team of forensic accountants, so we'll check everything. Rest assured, we'll have a full picture soon."

Her client visibly relaxed. "Thank you, Alexa."

She stood up and walked around her desk to shake his hand. "My assistant, Miranda, will contact you when we have created our operational plan for Miss Porter's protection."

Her client nodded. "I appreciate you continuing with the contract. I know she can be caustic, but I care about Sophia like a daughter. Her father and I are old friends, and with Ralph and Carol wanting to stick close to Shelley, I promised I'd look out for Sophia. Her brand has expanded exponentially, and some might look to exploit her however they can."

"Ruben, I assure you that regardless of our personal history, while in our care, Sophia Porter will have every resource at our disposal to ensure her safety."

Satisfied, he bid Alexa goodbye and left. When her doors shut behind him, she sank to the sofa, flicked off her heels and placed her stocking feet on the coffee table. The surprise encounter left her utterly exhausted. Unable to help herself, Sophia's accusations came to mind. The years had done nothing to temper the sister's animosity. Clearly, she was still to blame for Shelley's plight as far as the Porters were concerned.

There was a lot at stake with this contract, and the earlier bravado about being able to work with Sophia fizzled out like a bottle of sparkling water that sat out too long.

Then, thoughts of her long-lost friend came to mind as if summoned. From Sophia's rant, Alexa surmised that Shelley was still having problems.

That thought didn't sit well with her, and she burst into tears before she could stop herself.

Chapter 20

Nicholas Michaux settled on the black leather sofa in the dimly lit club. The electronic dance music summoned many beautiful people to the dance floor like a beacon. He toyed with the drink in his hand, swirling the amber liquid around in the glass tumbler, but it remained untouched. Usually, he'd be out there dancing and feeding off the crowd's energy, too. Lisbon was famous for its nightlife, and he enjoyed partying with the best of them, but tonight he had more significant problems. Life-and-death problems.

Nicholas shifted uncomfortably. The venue was suddenly too everything. Too hot, claustrophobic and loud. Slamming the glass on the table, he bolted up from his seat. The need for air drove him past the packed space to the second floor. Once he made it down a dark hall, Nicholas turned a corner and headed up another flight of stairs to the club's rooftop. Thankfully, it was empty.

He walked over to the edge and stood there, hungrily inhaling the cool night air while trying to gather his thoughts.

Nothing was going according to plan. Nicholas had suffered countless setbacks, starting with his father's refusal to bankroll his latest project and Sophia pulling out of partnering with him for a nightclub venture with his friends. Both denials were unexpected. He'd made dicey moves to get his portion of the money, and if any of those markers came due before he convinced Sophia or his father to reconsider, he was a dead man.

The picturesque skyline was lost on him as he stared at the brilliantly lit night with unseeing eyes.

"Enjoying the evening?"

Nicholas froze. His jaw clenched in annoyance at the intrusion. "I was."

"She wants to see you."

"She who?"

Turning, he found two well-built men in black suits directly behind him.

"The Siren."

He shook his head. This was not how he envisioned his evening shaking out. "Sorry, fellas, but I don't know who that is."

"She knows you, so let's go."

"I'm not about to go off with two goons I don't know to speak to some woman I've never met."

"When my boss wants to see you, you go."

"Maybe I didn't make myself clear. I don't respond to a summons from some stranger like a trained seal."

The man nodded. "Maybe I didn't make *myself* clear. You, Mr. Michaux, don't have a choice in the matter." He patted his right jacket pocket. "Not if you want to live."

Livid, he motioned for them to proceed. One man took the lead while the other fell into step behind Nicholas.

"I don't need an escort," he snapped. "I'm capable of getting there on my own."

"Our orders were to bring you to Torre de Pérolas, which we're going to do. So quit stalling and get moving."

Nicholas was ushered outside and into a diamond-white Mercedes G 550 SUV.

Torre de Pérolas, the "Pearl Tower," was located in Torres Vedras, a municipality almost an hour's drive from Lisbon. Thankfully, the silence was as luxurious as the vehicle. He was not in the mood to make small talk when his life could be on the line. He hadn't been entirely truthful. He had never met her, but everyone in his circle knew of the Siren.

An arms dealer, a procurer of stolen art and a thief, Siren had several illegal and legitimate enterprises. Not one to be crossed, it was well-known that she had a penchant for setting examples. Nicholas wasn't sure how he had stumbled onto her path, but being known by this dangerous woman was not good.

"We're here," the passenger called from over his shoulder.

Even in the distance, Torre de Pérolas was impressive. The uplighting around the white mansion only added to its stately appearance. Nicholas heard rumors that Siren conducted all her business at the Pearl Tower.

The main house was over ten thousand square feet and sat squarely in the middle of a massive acreage. It was a working farm with stables, a vineyard, several outbuildings, a pool, multiple gardens, a winery and an impressive turret with a wraparound balcony on the back side of the house. It was also well fortified with guards, and word on the street was that the tower was equipped with prison cells.

The car pulled into a circular driveway, stopping at the front door. His escorts got out, with one holding the door open for Nicholas, who didn't bother to thank the man as he exited.

The three men went through the massive wooden door and walked down several corridors. Nicholas checked out the interior on the way. The walls were white except for a great room with a stone fireplace.

Ushered down a floating staircase to a lower level, Nicholas found himself at the entrance to a modern dojo.

"Take off your shoes and follow me," one of the men said.

It was a stark contrast to the warm and homey feel from upstairs. However, the decor was still luxurious, with red-painted accents, rich wood walls and floors with Japanese tatami mats around the room. In addition, there were wall shelves that held swords and other sparring weapons and black lacquer room divider screens. The space exuded controlled power.

At the end were several chairs on a raised dais. The one in the middle was more impressive than the others.

A woman was in the top spot, looking very relaxed and at ease. She was an older white woman with flaming red hair swept into a tight bun. She wore black leather pants, matching knee-high boots, and a long silk balloon-sleeve floral duster in turquoise, gold and black paisley. She sipped a cup of what he assumed was tea with the exaggerated slowness of someone who has the luxury of time.

"Good evening, Mr. Michaux. Welcome to Torre de Pérolas," the woman said.

"I would say thank you, but I don't know why I'm here."

"Have a seat." She signaled for one of her employees to bring a chair.

After sinking into the comfortable black lacquer chair, Nicholas turned to his host.

"Come now, Nico. You can't be oblivious to why you're here?"

He frowned at her use of his nickname. "I don't have a clue. And you have me at a disadvantage, Miss…?"

She chuckled. "Come now, don't pretend you don't know who I am." The Siren sat back and crossed her legs. "Does Gates Budreau ring a bell?"

His jaw ticked. *Yep. You've got a clue now,* he told himself.

"I can tell by your expression that you do indeed know my colleague. Lovely. That saves us some time. Now that your memory has been restored, where is my eighteenth-century Bellasini emerald, ruby and sapphire bracelet?"

Nicholas shrugged. "I'm sorry, but I don't have it. Gates showed it to me one time, but that's it."

"Mr. Michaux, everything you've heard I'm capable of is grossly underestimated. I assure you that I'm much more dangerous than you realize. Now, I want my sixty-three-thousand-dollar bracelet you stole from Gates before I carve you up like a Christmas turkey."

Shifting in his chair, he held her gaze. "I promise you

that I don't have your bracelet. I never stole anything from Gates."

"Your *promises*," she sneered, "are of no consequence to me. He said you have it, and I want my jewelry."

Her bodyguards yanked Nicholas from his seat and forced him to kneel while Siren strode over to the wall and retrieved a katana sword from its holder. She swung it through the air in graceful yet powerful movements.

"Whoa, wait a minute," Nicholas said quickly. He attempted to fight against his captors. "I'm not lying. I didn't steal anything from Budreau. Ask him yourself."

Siren walked toward him. "I'm afraid he won't be talking—or eating solid foods for quite some time. No one steals from me and doesn't face the consequences, Mr. Michaux. It's a lesson you're about to learn. The hard way." She smiled.

Widening her stance, she was about to swing the blade at Nicholas when he screamed, "Stop! I know where to get it."

She paused. "Ah, motivation does work. Tell me where, and I suggest you hurry, because my patience is wearing thin, Nicholas. The next time I swing, my blade won't be halted."

"A friend of my girlfriend, Sophia, has it," he said in a rush. "Gates sold it to them, and I was just the middleman that delivered it. Just give me some time, and I swear I'll get it back to you."

"If you're double-crossing me—"

The burly man released him suddenly, causing Nicholas to pitch forward. His hands flew out to keep from face-planting on the wooden floor. Then he wiped the sweat from his brow with a shaky hand before rising cautiously. "I would never do that," he said hoarsely.

Siren handed the weapon to her bodyguard and then embraced Nicholas. "See that you don't," she whispered before nibbling on his earlobe. "Or I promise you my face will be the last thing you see."

* * *

Andrew was awakened by the vibrating sound of his cell phone. When he was on duty, he never turned it off. He glanced at the time and groaned aloud. It was two in the morning. He had just gotten to sleep two hours before thanks to a six-foot, deliciously sexy protection officer who periodically occupied his waking and now unconscious hours.

Grasping the device, Andrew lay back against the pillows. When he saw the phone number, sleep left him faster than water circling a drain.

It was Alexa. The object of his desire and the disruptor of his sleep.

Got a minute?

Yeah, sure.

Sitting up in bed, Andrew wiped his hand across his face and took a sip of the bottled water on the nightstand before pressing a speed-dial number.

"Hi," Alexa replied after picking up on the first ring. "I'm sorry to disturb you, but I could use a friend."

"No, it's fine. Alexa, what's wrong?" Andrew bolted upright. "Are you crying?"

"Something happened today," she sniffed. "It was unexpected."

"Where are you?"

"At home."

"What's wrong?" Andrew immediately started calculating how fast he could get there.

Alexa relayed her encounter with Sophia. Andrew remained silent while she spoke. Most of the time he spent trying to calm down. Her waking him up in the middle of the night and crying put him on edge. Before he had heard the cause of her distress, Andrew was prepared to land on her doorstep ready to do battle if necessary.

It wasn't a matter of if Alexa King was under his skin; he'd made it clear in Chamonix that she was.

"Well, that's a surprise," he replied when she'd finished.

"Tell me about it," Alexa muttered before blowing her nose. "Andrew, I don't think this is a problem I know how to handle."

He smiled at that. "I disagree. Alexa, you deal with split-second decisions, danger and life-and-death situations daily. This assignment would be no different."

"But it *is* different."

"Alexa, you're trained to compartmentalize your emotions and face them later. I know this is childhood trauma that you're dealing with, but you've learned to categorize your feelings. There are exercises we can go over to reinforce it. Don't worry. You can handle this."

She blew out a breath into the phone. "I don't think I can."

"Why not?"

"Because this is personal. Sophia gets to me, Andrew. I don't know why I ever agreed to do this," she cried. "Nothing good can come of it. She's like a walking day of reckoning that I can't escape."

Andrew swung his legs over the side of the bed.

"Listen to me. I've watched you over the years. I know how you think, how you move, and what you can accomplish when you get your mind, body and soul behind it. Lexi, I know you're scared, but you can do this. I have faith in you."

The line went silent for a few moments before Alexa said, "Why? Why do you have such faith in me when I can't even muster up enough for myself?"

"Because I care about you," Andrew replied simply. "And I'm your friend, remember?"

Alexa's silence tore at Andrew in a way that was unfamiliar to him. It made him feel utterly helpless, and that was something he wasn't used to. He also wished he were there with her in his arms instead of thousands of miles away.

"Alexa, if you need me, say the word and I'm there."

"I know. Drew?" she choked out.

"Yes, Lexi?"

"Thank you." Her voice trembled. "For being here when I needed you."

"You're welcome." For now, Andrew would let Alexa set the pace between them. However long it took, he wouldn't rush her. Now that he had acknowledged wanting their relationship to move forward, he was all in.

"I don't know what I'd do without you in my corner."

He chuckled. "Then I guess it's a good thing you'll never have to find out."

Chapter 21

Alexa climbed up the steps of Ruben Tyndale's private jet. It was a Gulfstream G550 business aircraft that was as elegant as it was functional. The interior had six well-padded cream-colored leather captain's chairs in the front, and a tan suede sofa with cream-and-brown silk accent pillows. The plush rug was off-white in a geometric design. At the far end of the room was a large table with two of the same chairs on each side. The walls were white with the darker cream inlay around the windows and a rich mahogany on the walls separating the seating areas. There was also a bedroom and bathroom.

Handing her bag to the flight attendant, she kept her briefcase with her and headed down the aisle. She greeted several team members before walking to the back of the plane. Then, taking a seat, she secured the seat belt.

"What are you doing?"

Sophia barely glanced up. "What do you mean? I have a flight to Los Angeles, and I'm on it."

"No, *we* have a flight. As in you and your security detail," Alexa replied as calmly as she could.

"Look, they were taking too long. I got tired of waiting around, so I left."

"We've been over this before. You don't get to leave whenever you feel like it. That's not how protection works, Sophia."

"Like I care," the younger woman groused. "I can't help it if your guys can't keep up."

"Can't keep up? You climbed out a bathroom window at the fashion show. But, trust me, if you want us more up close and personal, we will accommodate you."

"Hey, I didn't ask to be here."

"Neither did I," Alexa snapped before she could catch herself. "But for better or worse," she continued, "you are under my company's protection as long as there's a threat. So I need you to cooperate and stay with your detail. Is that clear, Sophia?"

Sophia yawned and lightly nodded. Alexa caught the barely-there agreement, so she let it go. She missed Sophia's smirk.

Alexa reached into her purse and retrieved a pendant. "Here." She handed it to Sophia.

"What's this?"

"It's a dragonfly pendant."

"I can see that, but why are you giving it to me?"

"Because I need you to wear it. It's for security. If there's ever an emergency and you need me, press the wings together for five seconds and release. That activates the emergency beacon, and I'll be able to find you anywhere."

Sophia examined the diamond dragonfly with the emerald wings. "This is so lame," she complained, securing it to her jacket. Her fingers ran over the wings. "Not bad for an imitation."

Alexa shook her head before turning her attention to some briefings she needed to review.

Sophia had several business engagements in Los Angeles and was a guest judge at a contest for aspiring jewelry designers. After landing, Alexa's local team waited to escort them to the Beverly Wilshire hotel. The competition was held in the Burgundy meeting room. Afterward, several fans asked for a picture with Sophia or her autograph. To Alexa's surprise, they stayed until she was done with every fan's request.

"It's time to go," Alexa gently reminded her. "The club opening is soon, and we still need to change."

Sophia was attending a friend of Ruben Tyndale's grand opening for his new nightclub, so they stayed at a guest house in Pacific Palisades that belonged to Alexa's colleague Alejandro "Dro" Reyes. He owned a crisis management company in Chicago. The two often collaborated on assignments with Dr. Marena Dash-McKendrick. Alexa was thrilled to see them working with her. In the field, Dragonfly operatives relied heavily on Marena's tech inventions, while Alejandro's network of global assets provided them with an edge.

Alejandro's house was in a quiet neighborhood, far from the street, and had a fenced backyard that aided in privacy.

Alexa's room was next to Sophia's, making it easy to watch the headstrong young woman. Or so Alexa thought. When it was time to go, Sophia could not be found.

Alexa's team scrambled to locate her and was about to go on a massive search when Alexa's communication manager alerted her that she had spotted a post of Sophia on her social media page from outside by the pool and grotto.

Taking a deep breath, she counted to five. "Go retrieve Miss Porter," she quietly informed one of her officers.

The dance club was packed by the time they arrived. Sophia was ushered to a VIP area at the back of the club that Alexa was happy to see was away from the heavily populated main dance floor. It was a younger crowd, so Alexa chose younger-looking operatives who were easily able to blend in. The club was U-shaped, with bars set up around the perimeter of the room and the dance floor in the middle. Strobe lights danced off every surface, along with the DJ's light show that was synced with the music he played. The repetitious thumping of the club music made it difficult to carry on a conversation without having to yell.

"Stay sharp," she cautioned her team before escorting Sophia to her table.

Sophia didn't take long to announce that she wanted to dance. Alexa allowed it but had several people placed strategically around the dance floor, watching their principal's every move. The man Sophia was dancing with kept putting his hands on her rear end, which she kept moving.

Finally, he got tired of that and attempted to wrap his hands around Sophia's shoulders to pull her close. Alexa saw Sophia struggle against him and rushed to her side. In one fluid motion, she maneuvered herself between her protectee and the dancer.

He reared back in surprise. "Hey, what is this?" he demanded. "I'm dancing with what's her name, not you."

"I'm afraid your time's up," Alexa replied with a smile. "I suggest you find someone else to occupy your time."

"I don't think so."

He went to step around Alexa, but she shifted until she was in front of him again. He was shorter than she was, so he had to glance up when he spoke.

"What are you doing?" he complained. "Look, lady, you're pretty, but I'd have gone outside if I wanted to climb a tree."

Alexa smiled. "Why, thank you. Pick a new dance partner."

He stood his ground. "I don't think so. I like the one I have. This chick is hot."

He tried to force Alexa out of the way, but she grabbed him as if she would hug him. But instead, she grasped his wrists, twisted them around so they were facing upward and applied pressure.

"Ow, that hurts," he roared over the music thumping around them.

Alexa smiled sweetly. "It's supposed to. Now get lost."

She passed him off to another agent and went to Sophia's side. "We're leaving," was all she said.

"But why? The night's still young, and I'm having a good time. Well, I was until that man couldn't take a hint."

"Sophia, that's not likely to improve the longer people drink."

"Well, you handled him, didn't you? So what's wrong

with me staying? You seem to have everything under control."

"Yes, and I'd like it to stay that way."

After escorting Sophia back to the car, Alexa held the door while she got in, then slid onto the seat next to her charge. During the ride, the only thing that could be heard was Sophia's music playing on her cell phone. Eventually, she turned that off and faced Alexa.

"Are you planning to sit and not talk the entire ride home? Is that supposed to punish me? If so, you're falling a little short."

Alexa didn't bother to reply. Instead, she focused on the passing scenery.

Sophia kicked off her shoes and pulled her legs up under her. "I just wanted to enjoy myself without the entourage in tow."

Praying for calm, Alexa said, "You can do that after the threats have ceased. Ruben hired us for a reason—remember?"

Sophia snorted and began to flip through the pictures on her cell phone. "How can I forget? My style has been permanently cramped ever since."

Incredulous, Alexa turned to face her. "And isn't your life worth a little inconvenience?"

That gave her pause. Sophia instantly looked contrite. "You're right," she said grudgingly. "I apologize."

Satisfied, Alexa added, "Make sure you relay that to those officers that you ditched. They're the ones who got reprimanded for your disappearing act."

"Alexa, we have a challenge car." Her driver glanced at his rearview mirror again. "Two cars back on the right. At five o'clock."

Turning around, she spotted the dark sedan. "I see it, Anthony. Where is car number two?"

Dyan got on the radio. "Stuck one light back," she reported after a moment. "ETA five minutes."

She turned back around. "We need some air, Anthony."

"Yes, ma'am."

The twin turbo engine roared to life as the driver sped up to put some distance between them and the other vehicle.

"Who is it?" Sophia kept glancing back over her shoulder.

"We don't know yet," Alexa replied. "Don't worry. We'll lose them."

The BMW 750i cornered well as Anthony maneuvered in and out of traffic.

"Time?" Alexa asked.

"They're coming up now," Dyan confirmed.

Their second car, a Cadillac Escalade ESV, dropped in behind them and stayed at a safe but close distance.

Heading west on Interstate 10, Anthony used the opportunity to whip past a few slower-moving cars. Then he hit the gas, and the powerful sedan roared to life and took off down the highway. Traffic wasn't heavy, so they made it home in twelve minutes.

They drove up the long driveway and parked out front. Team members were waiting to assist. One opened the back door for Alexa. She got out first, then escorted Sophia inside and straight to her room.

"What was that all about?" Sophia inquired.

"Don't worry, we'll find out," Alexa assured her. "Get some rest. I'll see you in the morning."

Returning downstairs, Alexa entered the kitchen and got some hot tea. Dyan was already there.

"The passengers in the sedan following us were some overzealous fans. They were trying to get close enough to get some photos of Sophia."

"They were being reckless and dangerous," Alexa argued. She chose a tea pod, dropped it into the brewing machine and pressed the button. "They could've caused an accident—or worse."

Alexa rubbed her shoulders while she waited for her cup to fill.

"There's something else," Dyan replied, scanning over her notes. "It may not be anything, but one of them had a tattoo on his hand that I've seen before."

Opening the pantry, Alexa glanced around for a snack. "Tattoos are pretty common."

"Not this one. Let me do some research, and I'll let you know."

Finding a pack of Pepperidge Farm Chessmen cookies, Alexa picked up her mug and took a seat at the table across from Dyan.

"Have we found her boyfriend yet?"

"No, but we did a preliminary report and background check on Nicholas Michaux. We're still waiting to hear back from the forensic accountants."

"Thanks, Dyan. Keep me posted."

Alexa's cell phone rang. "Sorry, I've got to take this," she said before answering.

"No problem." Dyan got up and waved goodbye on her way out.

"Hi, Dad."

"Hey, Lex. How's everything? You haven't called in a while, so I wanted to check in to ensure everything is okay?"

"We wanted to check in," Margot corrected over speakerphone.

Picking up her snack, Alexa moved into the living room and sat down. "It's good to hear both your voices. I've missed you."

"We're only a phone call away, honey," her mother replied. "So what's got you so tied up that you can't call home?"

Taking a sip of tea, Alexa closed her eyes and leaned back against the plush cushion. "Not what, who. I've been hired to protect Sophia Porter."

There was a considerable pause before her parents spoke.

"Are you serious? After all that's happened, you've taken Sophia on as a client? Lex, what were you thinking?" her mother hissed. "That family has caused you nothing but pain."

"Mom, I didn't know she was the client when I took the contract."

"Well, now you do, and you can recuse yourself."

She sat forward. "Dad—"

"Alexa, I'm with your mother on this one. Why put yourself through this?"

"Because it's my job," she countered, pinching the bridge of her nose. "Regardless of my feelings, I was hired to protect Sophia. Which I'll do to the best of my ability."

"You're asking for trouble," Margot interjected. "Sophia Porter is selfish and cruel, and tried to make your life a living hell after the attack. And if I know Carol's daughter, she's probably still trying to make you suffer."

Chapter 22

Andrew drove up to the Capital Grille, an upscale steakhouse on Pennsylvania Avenue in Northwest Washington, DC. Across the street from the Federal Trade Commission and the National Gallery of Art, the well-known restaurant was also in view of the United States Capitol and a regular haunt of the District of Columbia's political and business scene. After getting out, Andrew adjusted his suit jacket, handed the keys to the valet parking attendant and went inside. Rich African mahogany paneling and art deco chandeliers were an apropos backdrop to the dark leather chairs and stark white linen. The superlative service was to be expected from a restaurant that was famous for its dry-aged steaks, fresh seafood and worldwide acclaimed wines. While he scanned the interior, he tried to contain his excitement. He would be meeting Alexa for dinner.

The hostess escorted Andrew to a booth at the back of the main dining room. Alexa stood and enveloped him in a hug. His arms encircled her waist as he returned the embrace.

"Welcome to DC, Drew."

"Thanks, Lexi," he replied warmly before sliding into the booth. "I was pleasantly surprised to receive your invitation."

"Why surprised?"

"Well, as busy as you've been with your new client, I thought you'd be tied up until further notice."

She placed the napkin back in her lap and took a sip of her water with lemon.

"Dyan's with Sophia for the next few days at another event."

"She seems to be keeping you busy."

"That's an understatement," Alexa replied. "When we're not arguing over her intense dislike of me, we are working overtime to keep her out of trouble. She enjoys trying to find new ways to ditch her protection detail. I swear sometimes it's like guarding a toddler."

He grinned. "Sophia Porter sounds like the perfect assignment to test your mettle."

"That's an understatement," Alexa shot back.

After the hostess had provided their menus and departed, he turned back to Alexa. "I must admit that I was surprised to get your invitation."

"Well, you did say you wanted us to get together soon."

"True," Andrew agreed. "But a weekend at your parents' house? Won't that send the wrong message?"

"Of course not. They've been briefed," she explained. "And they're fully aware that we're the best of friends without any romantic entanglements."

A humorous expression jetted across his face. He refrained from pointing out that they were way past the "just friends" stage, but he merely said, "Sounds good."

The waiter arrived to take drink and appetizer orders.

Alexa chose the lobster bisque and a glass of chardonnay.

"I'll have an iced tea and the calamari," he said, handing back the menu.

"So, how's work?" she asked when they were alone.

"Busy as usual, but I can't complain. With Dad scaling back on his hours, I've been interviewing for a director of operations at Phalanx."

"Married life must be treating him well if he's reducing his workload."

"I think everyone is shocked at him and Esther deciding to elope. The way he tells it, they didn't have time for a long-drawn-out wedding."

"Hey, there's nothing wrong with wanting the rest of your life to start sooner rather than later after declaring your feelings to the one you love. On the contrary, I think it's romantic."

"At least there were no whispers of a shotgun wedding," Andrew joked.

Alexa almost choked on her water. "Yeah, I think that ship has sailed."

"Seriously, though, I couldn't be happier for them. I'm glad that Dad put himself out there. It's been so long since Mom died. I didn't think he'd find that type of connection again, but Esther is a wonderful woman, and I'm pleased to call her my stepmother."

"She is exceptional. When I was there for training, I remember how warm and welcoming she was to me—to everyone."

"At Phalanx, Esther is everyone's mother. That's one of the things that makes being there special," Andrew pointed out. "She helps keep the trainees from being homesick."

When the waiter delivered their food, they lapsed into companionable silence while they ate.

"Oh, thank you for introducing me to Marena," Andrew said between bites. "Her devices have come in handy on several occasions."

"You're welcome, and I'm glad. She's so talented and has made my job much easier."

"Don't I know it," he agreed. "I've already used one of the cuff links that can be used as an infrared device."

"I've got a compact that does the same thing," she said excitedly. "And I've had to use it twice already."

"I think Marena will never be at a loss for business."

"Don't I know it," Alexa laughed. "But I've already told her she must continue using Dragonfly as her proving ground."

"Oh, she needs to add Phalanx to that list!"

Andrew was interrupted by a cell phone call. It was work, so he excused himself to take it. Alexa watched him walk away. She took a moment to appreciate how good he looked in the dark gray suit and a black shirt unbuttoned at the neck. The cut of his jacket accentuated his broad shoulders. Watching him made Alexa flustered to where she took a healthy sip of ice water.

It was getting difficult for her to deny that thoughts of Andrew had been plaguing her lately. So much so that she'd invited him to DC to her parents' Winter Serve Weekend on a whim. She hadn't thought he'd say yes, and when he did, it filled Alexa with excitement that he was coming and trepidation that her parents might bombard him with questions all weekend.

It was a family tradition they had been doing since her grandfather's time. Friday, guests would arrive and get settled. Saturday, her family would spend an afternoon passing out winter coats and supplies at the homeless shelters, followed by a black-tie fundraiser event at a country club in Upper Marlboro, Maryland. Sunday was church service followed by an afternoon of board games. Alexa's family was competitive, which she'd warned Andrew about in advance. He merely smiled and assured her that he would be fine. *Famous last words*, she thought to herself.

They headed to her parents' house after dinner. Alexa had been dropped at the restaurant by a rideshare service so that she could go back with Andrew. She was excited to use the drive home to spend some alone time with him before her parents swooped in to bombard him with questions and likely embarrassing stories of her childhood. She loved them dearly, but they could go overboard at a moment's notice.

When he got into the car, he grunted. It caught Alexa's attention.

"Are you okay?"

"Yes, for the most part."

She turned in her seat. "What does that mean?" she said warily.

"I hurt my back a few days ago. Sometimes it flares up when I move wrong."

"Oh." Concern for him caused Alexa to reach out and touch the back of his head before resting her hand on the nape of his neck. "Did you get injured during training?"

"No."

"On assignment?"

"Sort of."

She let out a frustrated sigh. "Drew."

"Okay." He chuckled while keeping his eyes on the road. "I was trying to break up a fight, and a large, angry woman decided to use me to break her fall."

Alexa tried to hold in her laugh, but it was pointless. Instead, she dissolved into a fit of giggles.

"I'm glad my hernia amuses you," he said dryly.

She wiped the tears from her eyes with the back of her sleeve.

"I'm sorry, I just… I can see the visual in my mind and can't get rid of it."

Despite his stern expression, Andrew eventually shared in the laughter.

When they arrived, Alexa directed him where to park. After opening her door, he retrieved his bag from the trunk.

"If you'd rather sit out on some festivities, I completely understand."

"No way," he said as he walked with Alexa to the door. "I've carried a wounded, unconscious woman on my back for miles. I think I can handle a little muscle strain."

"Very funny," she shot back. "And it wasn't miles."

"How would you know?" he countered. His eyebrows arched with merriment. "Weren't you passed out?"

Alexa found out after the shooting incident that it was Andrew who'd rushed her to the on-site infirmary after Edgar Jeffries had shot her during the training exercise.

With an indignant huff, Alexa glided past him and went to open the front door, but her father beat her to it.

"Perfect timing," Jake King announced as he stepped aside to allow them to enter. "Everyone just arrived."

Margot joined them in the vestibule. She hugged her daughter.

"Hello, sweetheart."

"Mom, Dad, I'd like to introduce you to Andrew Riker."

"The last time we met, I believe you were seven," Jake replied, shaking his free hand.

Andrew set his bag down. "It's been a while, sir."

"Welcome to our home," Margot enthused before giving him a big hug. "I hope you don't mind, but we're huggers," she explained.

"I don't mind at all." Andrew returned the embrace. "Thank you for having me."

"Of course," she replied before eyeing her daughter. "Any friend of Alexa's is a friend of ours." She turned to her husband. "Jake, this is a precedent, wouldn't you say?"

"Mom," Alexa hissed.

"What?" her mother responded sweetly. "I know you didn't expect us to fall for that 'we're just friends' thing, did you?"

Alexa closed her eyes and tried to remain calm. "It's not a thing. It's the truth."

"Andrew," her father said quickly. "Come on in and make yourself at home. Don't worry about your luggage. We'll take that upstairs later. My brother Curtis, his wife, Ernestine, and my nephew, Zane, arrived not too long ago and are all dying to meet you."

The moment the two men headed down the hall to the family room, Alexa spun around to face her mother.

"Did you have to blindside him two seconds after we stepped through the door?"

"That's not what I did."

"Mom, it's exactly what you did."

"Honey, your boyfriend will be fine. You know it's trial by fire around here. Can I help it if you didn't warn him?"

"He's not my… I already told you both that Andrew and I are just friends."

"I'll reserve my judgment for later," her mother replied before hooking her arm through Alexa's and heading to the family room. "Do you *really* want him to have a separate bedroom, or was that just for show?"

Before Alexa could open her mouth to protest, her mother chuckled. "Did you know that your right eye still twitches when you're about to have a conniption? Oh, Lex, this will be such a fun weekend!"

Chapter 23

"Gates, I don't know where you are, but you need to call me ASAP!" Nicholas snapped before pressing the end-call button on his cell phone.

This is insane, he told himself. *How could Gates set me up like this?* This wasn't just a simple misunderstanding. If he didn't find Siren's bracelet, he was a dead man.

"No luck?" The Siren's henchman snickered. "Personally, I hope you don't find it. I'd love to rearrange your face, pretty boy."

"Will you shut up?" Nicholas groused. "This isn't helping."

The man bolted out of his chair.

"Spare me the flexing," Nicholas said tiredly. "We both know you're not going to hurt me."

"Yet," the man snarled. "Sooner or later, Siren will get tired of this goose chase you're playing and give me the approval to end you."

"Until then," Nicholas stressed in a bravado he didn't feel, "I'm untouchable."

His aggressor patted his jacket pocket. "For now."

Thinking of another number, he turned his back and called another contact.

"Bruce." He sighed with relief when the phone was answered. "I need a favor—"

"Oh no you don't. You haven't paid me for the last favor you owe me. If you were here right now, I'd have you killed."

"Get in line," Nicholas said dryly. He got up and moved to the opposite side of the room to get a modicum of privacy.

"Look, I know I owe you money. I'm good for it. You know that. But right now, I need to know where Gates is at."

"Uh-uh. I don't know anything anymore. Especially not for free."

Nicholas turned and faced the wall. "Come on," he pleaded. "This is life-and-death."

"Not from where I'm standing."

"Bruce, I'm serious. Gates stole something. From the wrong person," he added. "I need to get it back—or else."

"Or else what?"

"The Siren will come looking for anyone that Gates knows or has come in contact with, whether they have her bracelet or not."

"Wait, Gates lifted jewelry from the Siren?"

"Yes."

Nicholas was tapped on the shoulder. He turned around.

"Time's up. Siren wants to see you."

"I gotta go. Think about what I said," he whispered into the phone. "You aren't safe, either."

"I'll see what I can do," his friend replied noncommittally.

"Yeah, you do that—and fast."

"Give me twenty-four hours," Bruce replied, and hung up.

Nicholas didn't know if he had twenty-four minutes, much less hours.

This time he was taken to a garden. He found the Siren pruning a rosebush.

Oh, great. She's a green thumb in addition to being an assassin.

"How's progress, Mr. Michaux?"

He shifted on his feet. "I'm not going to lie. It's slow. I need more time if you want me to locate this bourgeois bracelet of yours."

Siren smiled and removed one of her gloves. "I thought I was clear in my intent," she said with a baffled expression.

Without warning, she walked over to Nicholas and punched him in the solar plexus, followed by an uppercut to the jaw. With a grunt and then a round of violent coughing, he dropped to his knees.

"I have killed men smarter and cuter than you. Your logistical problems are not my problems, Mr. Michaux."

"I get that." The metallic taste of blood in his mouth wasn't the only thing that made him queasy. He was still having difficulty breathing.

Turning to her employee, she said, "Take him to my office. If he doesn't provide Miss Porter's account number the moment after you've arrived, cut off a finger every minute that I don't have what I want."

"No, wait," Nicholas yelled as he was grabbed by the arm and escorted out. He fought every step of the way. "Don't do this!"

The Siren grinned. "Ah, nothing like motivation," she called after him before returning to gardening.

Alexa, her family and Andrew were in the kitchen when she received a telephone call.

"Excuse me, I have to take this," Alexa replied when her phone rang.

"How's everything going?" Dyan asked when Alexa answered.

"Not bad. We're having a great time."

"I'm sorry to disturb you at your parents' house."

"No worries, Dyan. What's up?"

"We heard back from the forensic accountants. I emailed you the report of findings."

"Hang on a sec," she said, rushing up to her bedroom. Sitting at her desk, she opened her laptop and checked her email. After reviewing the document, Alexa leaned back in her chair.

"Well, this likely won't go well."

"I don't doubt it," Dyan agreed. "Do you want me to tell her?"

"No, I'll do it."

"Given your history, Alexa, do you think that's wise?"

"Probably not," she said truthfully, "but it's my responsibility. Can you ask Miranda to call me? I need to speak with her on a few things."

"Sure. Have you spoken to her lately?"

"No, why?"

"Yesterday, I ran into her coming out of the ladies' room and she looked like she'd been crying."

Alexa furrowed her brow. "She hasn't said anything."

"To me, either. I asked her what was wrong, and she tried to brush it off. I think it has something to do with her new boyfriend."

"Apollo?"

"Yep. Miranda is as pleasant and cheerful as lemonade in the summertime. But lately, she seems distracted."

Alexa could've kicked herself for not noticing. It didn't sit well that one of her employees was in distress, and she wasn't aware of it.

"Would you ask her to call me?"

"Will do."

She hung up with her associate and reread the report. Alexa let out a weary sigh before tossing it aside. She did not relish Sophia's reaction to hearing about Nicholas's hidden agenda. "And Mom talks about me having a conniption."

Her thoughts turned back to Miranda. Alexa couldn't recall one day when she wasn't her best. Grabbing her phone, she texted Dyan and asked her to do a preliminary background check on Apollo Hayes. Something was up with him, but Alexa couldn't say what. His not meeting Miranda's friends and her not meeting his didn't sit well. For Miranda's sake, she'd look him over to make sure he was everything he claimed to be.

"Hey, you okay? Your mother asked me to come up and check on you. She said we're leaving in fifteen minutes."

Alexa glanced over her shoulder to see Andrew standing just outside the doorway.

"Yes." She set her phone down. "Just an issue at work that I need to take care of."

When he remained, Alexa said, "You can come in, Andrew."

He eased into the room, peering around as he walked.

Alexa's bedroom looked like she hadn't been in it since leaving for college. Two nightstands flanked a full-size canopy bed against one wall. There were multicolored lights draped around the top, a white comforter set with yellow and green flowers, and a few throw pillows. Three books were stacked on one nightstand with a lamp and an alarm clock.

Across the room was an alcove with a plush white couch and flat-screen television mounted to the wall. A large built-in with a vast collection of books anchored the space.

French doors led out onto a balcony with white wicker furniture and floral-colored cushions. The walls were white, but there were colorful landscapes and pictures of animals hanging around the room. The space was neat, orderly and composed, just like Alexa.

"Finished scoping out my old room?"

A glimmer of amusement sparkled in his eyes. "Not yet."

Andrew walked over and sat on the love seat. "How long has it been since you've slept in here?"

"Usually just holidays."

"That's cool."

Shutting her laptop, Alexa joined him on the couch. "Yep, one of the duties of an only child. Make yourself available for all family functions."

He laughed. "True." He curled a lock of her hair around his fingers.

"It's nice seeing another piece of the Alexa puzzle."

Her eyebrows shot up. "I'm a puzzle?"

"Yes, indeed," he replied. "And I'm enjoying learning how the pieces fit together."

"I'm hardly as exciting as you make me out to be."

He inched closer, regarding Alexa as if he was studying something intriguing. "You are to me."

Alexa found it hard to breathe under the sheer weight of his gaze. Her heartbeat pounded in her ears. She wondered if he could hear it.

Andrew held out his hand. Alexa didn't hesitate to lock her fingers with his. He kissed the back of her hand. "I have to admit, I'm feeling kinda honored right now."

"Why?"

"Because I'm the only man that's been in your inner sanctum."

"How do you know that?" Alexa tossed back. "I've had a man or two in here before."

"Your family doesn't count. Besides, your mother told me."

Alexa closed her eyes and tried to contain her embarrassment. She and her mother were going to have a talk about boundaries.

When she felt the touch of his fingers along her cheek, her eyes flew open.

She wasn't prepared for her reaction to the desire in Andrew's gaze or the way his hand drifted down to her neck.

His fingers touched the pulse point. "Your heartbeat is elevated."

"You don't say?"

Alexa's voice drifted out like an intimate caress. Their eyes locked briefly before he lowered his head and replaced his fingers with his lips.

Her hands closed around his neck and held his head stationary. Leaning into his touch, Alexa didn't protest when Andrew deepened the kiss.

Andrew's weight pinned her back against the cushions.

Her body hummed with excitement as her hands roamed his back, shoulders and the nape of his neck.

"Lexi," Andrew murmured against her lips, trailing kisses down her throat. "You don't know how incredible you feel."

"About as good as you do right now."

Everywhere Alexa caressed, Andrew's skin felt hot to the touch. At that moment, she wanted him with a passion so consuming that it took her several moments to realize he was saying her name.

"What?" she finally managed to say.

He kissed her a final time and said, "Your mother is calling you."

Alexa didn't think. She just reacted.

"Yes?" she yelled so loud that Andrew scrunched up his face in reaction.

"I'm now deaf in one ear."

"Let's go, you two," her mother bellowed.

Alexa moaned. "We have to go."

He smiled at the genuine frown on her face before kissing the tip of her nose.

"Yes, I know."

"I don't want to," she said frankly.

Andrew buried his face in her neck. "And you think I do?"

Alexa took another moment to enjoy the closeness with Andrew before nudging him.

"We'd better go before she comes looking."

He reluctantly got up and helped Alexa to her feet. After she had adjusted her clothing, Andrew reached up and traced the path she had made to guide the few errant strands away from her face. He continued along her neck and down her shoulder.

Not once had their gazes disengaged. They continued to stare at each other in mutual fascination.

Alexa felt her body swaying closer to Andrew.

When did that happen? she wondered. When had she relaxed her "no relationship" policy so completely?

"We should go before your mom sends up a search party," he warned softly.

"Uh, yeah," she replied, clearing her throat. "I wouldn't put it past her."

Alexa moved past Andrew and headed for the door. She didn't need to turn around to check if he was following. The hair tingling at the back of her neck told her all she needed to know.

When they reached the foyer, everyone was putting on their outerwear.

"Perfect timing," her father said gleefully. "We're ready to go."

"Great, I'll go get our coats," she said quickly and bolted to the hall closet. But truthfully, she needed a few moments to gather the wits scattered around her head.

She placed her hand on her heart and felt the rapid staccato beat hammering against her chest. She blew out an exasperated breath.

Get a hold of yourself, Alexa, she chided.

For the first time since Andrew arrived, Alexa started doubting her bright idea to open a box she couldn't close. Now that she had tasted a sample of the fruit, she wanted the entire bowl.

Retrieving their coats, Alexa turned around to find Zane standing right behind her with an amused expression on his face.

"You say one word, and I'll put you in a choke hold," she snapped before shoving past him.

"What?" he countered sweetly before dissolving into a fit of laughter.

Chapter 24

The event ended late, so they hurried home to prepare for the black-tie event across town. When Alexa came downstairs after getting dressed, only Andrew was waiting. She glanced around.

"Where'd everyone go?"

"Since your mother was the event chair, they went on ahead so they wouldn't be too late."

"Oh. Not like I took that long," she muttered, reaching the bottom step.

She finally noticed that Andrew was wearing a black tuxedo with a red bow tie and red silk pocket square. Alexa had to force herself not to gape. He looked more handsome than when she'd seen him in Chamonix, and that was saying something!

Alexa watched him look her over from head to toe before saying, "Lexi, you look breathtaking."

Her face lit up at his praise. It had taken her forever to get dressed, and up until that moment, she had second-guessed every choice. Now she was glad that she had chosen a black satin floor-length gown. It had an hourglass design that was outlined by rhinestones. The arms and low-cut back of the dress were sheer.

"Thank you," Alexa responded as he helped her into a long velvet coat. "You look wonderful, too."

Not releasing her lapels, Andrew backed Alexa up until she was against the wall. Startled, her expression showed her surprise.

"What are you doing?"

"Admiring the view," Andrew quipped before touching her cheek. "You are so beautiful, Alexa King."

She did not get a chance to reply before Andrew kissed her with a heat that could have lit a wet match.

"Drew, we have to go," she whispered against his lips. "Any longer and they'll think we're not coming."

"If the alternative is staying here with you in my arms, I see nothing but upside."

Eventually, he released her coat, but did not let her go. Instead, he rested his forehead against hers.

"Thank you," he whispered against her lips.

"For what?"

"For allowing me to know you better. For a glimpse into your personal life—to *see* you."

Alexa was ready to dissolve into a puddle on her parents' marble floor.

Her line of sight moved from holding his gaze down to his lips. Instead, it lingered on the rapidly beating pulse at his neck.

"Lexi, that's dangerous," he warned.

Her glance traveled back up to his eyes. "I deal with danger every day, remember?"

"Not this kind."

Before she could retort, Andrew held her wrist out of the way before crushing her body against his chest. His mouth claimed hers for a searing kiss. The power of it took Alexa's breath away.

"That wasn't dangerous at all," she murmured against his mouth.

In a flash, Andrew picked Alexa up. Her legs locked around his waist as he backed them up against the closet door. Her gown bunched in yards of silky fabric between them. Before she could react, he kissed a trail from her lips to her neck. He lingered at the spot where her pulse beat out a rapid staccato against her skin.

"Are we just friends, Alexa?"

"Hmm?" she said in a dazed whisper.

Andrew leaned closer. His lips floated just above her

skin and hovered over her ear. His warm breath caressed her as he spoke.

"Tell me that you feel nothing but friendship for me. Say you don't want me as much as I want you, Alexa, and I will never mention it again."

She gravitated toward his touch. A small moan escaped her lips.

"Andrew."

Andrew Riker would run away with her heart if she let him. And right now, Alexa wasn't sure she would stop him, and that scared her to death.

When they arrived, the party had already begun. They picked up name tags at the entrance, where there was a long-stemmed red rose for each lady. A hostess directed them to their family's table, where she found her aunt and uncle sitting.

"Where's everyone?" Alexa asked as Andrew helped her out of her coat.

"Zane and his date are on the dance floor. Your parents are making the rounds," Ernestine replied. "My, don't both of you look gorgeous."

"So do you," Alexa replied with a kiss on her cheek.

Andrew placed a hand on her back and leaned in. "What do you say, Alexa? Will you dance with me?"

"I'd love to." She beamed at Andrew, allowing him to lead her to the floor.

"This is 'Corcovado,'" she informed him as he swept her into his arms. "It's one of my favorites."

"Mine, too."

Andrew guided her into a bossa nova dance. Alexa laughed as they glided together in unison. "You're full of surprises, Mr. Riker."

"So are you, Miss King."

After the dance, Alexa went to the ladies' room to freshen up. As she was coming out, a woman called after her.

"Alexa King, is that you?"

Turning, Alexa's mouth dropped open. "Andi?"

"Yes," the woman cried and, throwing up her arms, rushed across the room to gather Alexa in a loose bear hug. "My goodness, it's wonderful to see you!"

When she finally released her, Alexa stared at Oleander Barlowe, her former roommate, with genuine shock.

"How have you been? Honestly, you haven't changed a bit since college," the woman gushed.

"I hope that's not the case," Alexa retorted. "So, what are you doing here?"

"A client of mine invited me. You know me, always working, and stuffy events like these are the perfect place to land new clients."

Same old ambitious Oleander. She would never let a roomful of rich people go to waste, Alexa noted.

Latching arms with Alexa, Oleander said, "So, what have you been up to?"

She grabbed a glass of champagne off a waiter's serving tray as they walked.

"Still working for your dad's company, married with a slew of kids, a minivan and a quaint Cape Cod in the suburbs?"

"Not exactly." Alexa brought her up to speed on life since college.

"No kidding? How fortuitous that we ran into each other."

Setting her empty glass on a high table, Oleander retrieved a business card from her velvet clutch and handed it to Alexa. "Let's keep in touch, I can definitely send some clients your way—if you return the favor, of course." She winked.

"Oh, uh, sure."

"Thanks, love. You always were dependable."

Alexa glanced around for Andrew so she could introduce them. When their eyes connected across the room, her happiness was crushed by his look of surprise and then pain. A second later, Andrew stormed out of the room.

What just happened? she asked herself.

Disentangling herself from Oleander's arm, Alexa excused herself and rushed out of the room to find Andrew.

Slamming out of the ballroom, Andrew strode down the corridor and out the back door. It was frigid outside, but it didn't register. His emotions were a jumbled mess of broken promises, betrayal and regret.

There, right in front of him, was Alexa talking to the woman who had smashed his heart to pieces before devouring it like chocolates on Valentine's Day. His worst nightmare had just come true. Now he knew why there was a reason Alexa had reminded him of Olee. They were the best of friends!

Bile rose into his throat, and his palms grew sweaty. He hadn't listened to his gut instinct trying to warn him about Alexa King, and now he was paying for it.

Taking a minute to get his anger under control, Andrew eventually went back inside. When he did, he was brought up short by a woman blocking his path.

"Hello, Andrew."

"Olee."

The one word was laced with a perfect balance of surprise at her audacity and hatred. If Oleander was affected at his tone, she did not show it.

She smiled. "I'm surprised you still remember that nickname you gave me."

"I haven't forgotten anything over the years," he said in a barely controlled voice. "What are you doing here?"

"Isn't it obvious? Hobnobbing with the wealthy benefactors, same as you."

"That's not why I'm here."

Her voice grated on his nerves, making him long to get

away. Not willing to bear her presence longer than necessary, Andrew got straight to the point.

"How do you know Alexa King?"

"Alexa?" she shot back with a raised eyebrow. "I could ask you the same question."

Seeing that he was waiting for an answer, Oleander shrugged. "We met in college. We were best friends and roommates. We were inseparable. Can you imagine running into each other again? It's like the years just melted away."

Seeing Andrew frown, Oleander continued. "So, what's your story?"

"We're colleagues," he said, not elaborating.

"Ah. Alexa and I are meeting for lunch in a few days. I have a joint venture I wanted to discuss. It should be very lucrative." She gleamed.

Andrew let out a contemptuous laugh. "You haven't changed a bit, Oleander. Ambition still overrides everything else—except your love of money."

"Neither have you," she shot back. "Still holding grudges. You plan on taking what happened to your grave, I see."

A couple walking by spared the two a curious glance. Andrew took her elbow and guided her down the hall back toward the party.

"I can tell you now that Alexa isn't interested in any proposition you might concoct."

She yanked her arm free of his grasp and stopped walking. "I'd wager that I know Alexa a lot better than you do," Oleander threw back.

His jaw ticked. "Alexa is nothing like you."

Oleander went to slide her hand under his tux jacket. "If you say so," she said smugly. "We couldn't have been besties all those years and not have a few things in common."

Capturing her wrist before she could touch him, Andrew leaned in.

"You know, I don't know what's worse. The fact that

you don't even acknowledge your part in our breakup, or the fact that you're still only interested in using people."

Her once-amiable expression darkened. "People in glass houses should steer clear of stones, lover."

Not bothering to respond, Andrew looked at her disgustedly before leaving. When he rounded a corner, he almost collided with Alexa. His hands instantly reached out to steady her.

"Andrew. I've been looking everywhere for you." She sighed with relief. "What's going on? I looked up, and you'd disappeared."

"Did you invite Oleander Barlowe here?"

Alexa was taken aback by his tone. "No. We went to college together. I haven't seen her in years."

"What did she want?"

Alexa frowned. "She asked to meet with me in a few days to catch up and discuss a business venture.

"Andrew, what is going on with you? You're acting strange."

"Don't do it. Olee can't be trusted and has only ever cared about herself."

"That's not true. We used to be best friends in college."

"So does that mean the two of you are cut from the same cloth?"

Alexa took a step back. His accusation hurt. "Why would you ask that?"

"Because I know her," he snapped. "She'll end up betraying your trust. I'm warning you, don't entertain any business proposition she has for you. You'll jeopardize your reputation fooling around with Oleander Barlowe."

Alexa felt her anger rising. "Andrew, I appreciate your concern, but I don't appreciate you implying I can't handle myself where Andi's concerned."

He threw his hands up in frustration. "Are you that naive? She's a professional grifter, Alexa. She won't hesitate to eat you up and spit out the bones."

"And how would *you* know?"

"Because she did it to me!"

The words shot out of Andrew's mouth like a cannonball.

Alexa's eyebrows shot upward. "Andrew, I—"

He held a hand up to stop her. "I don't need your sympathy. You know what, suit yourself, Alexa. You're going to do what you want anyway. It's obvious you don't need me trying to look out for you, right?"

"You're not being fair, Andrew."

"Just admit it. You don't need anything or anyone. You don't *need*."

The color drained from her face. "That's not true."

"Yeah? You could've fooled me."

Chapter 25

Andrew stared out the hotel room window. A towel was slung low around his middle. His warm body in proximity to the cold window caused it to fog up, but he was oblivious. There was nothing about his evening that had gone according to plan.

Rubbing a hand over his jaw, Andrew retreated from the window. He padded to the bed and fell back onto the fluffy mattress.

He realized that he had overreacted to Alexa's conversation with Oleander, but at the time was powerless to stop it. He would apologize for his behavior, but the fact that Alexa didn't set him straight only reiterated his point that it was Alexa's pride and fear of commitment keeping them apart. Could he be content waiting for her to accept they were perfect for each other? Should he throw in the towel and walk away? That thought didn't sit well. Andrew had never given up on anything in his life. Especially not something he wanted with a passion that kept him up at night and made him restless.

He cared for Alexa unlike anything he had experienced before. Even his relationship with Oleander paled by comparison, and he had thought himself completely in love with her. Alexa was different. His feelings for her had been way past the level of friendly since before she graduated from Phalanx. He was all in the moment Alexa stared at him with a perfect blend of lust and fascination.

"Come on, Riker. You gotta double your efforts to win her over." And he would, but it was hard to overcome Alexa's trust issues and the past. She was complex, stubborn and trapped in a cycle of fear like a spider's prey dangling from its web. But regardless of how long it took, he'd help her break free. The first thing he would do is give her space. As much as it would kill him to distance himself from her, it was necessary. Alexa needed to come to terms with not just their relationship, but the past. Their future happiness depended on it.

Alexa spent the next week at work putting out fire after fire. Several members of her staff were on leave. Either sick or scheduled, it meant they were short-staffed, so Alexa had to fill the gap. She didn't mind. In truth she was glad for the distraction.

It had been two weeks since she had spoken to Andrew. After their argument at the Christmas fundraiser, she returned home to find him gone. He had left a note thanking her parents for their hospitality and wishing everyone happy holidays. Hurt, Alexa had tried to call, but he didn't answer. Unable to deal with the questions from her parents, Alexa pretended that nothing was wrong and Andrew was called away on an unexpected assignment.

She had regretted her words to him, but his behavior had gotten under her skin. Now, he had retreated behind a wall of cool indifference that made her grit her teeth in frustration.

What did you expect? You basically told him you didn't trust him and didn't want a relationship, her inner voice scolded. Plus, pride kept her from setting the record straight on working with Oleander Barlowe. She didn't trust Andi, but she had neglected to tell Andrew that, which in retrospect had only made matters worse. *You got exactly what you wanted, so leave it alone.*

With her relationship with Andrew in tatters, Alexa threw herself into the job. Everyone at work had noticed the change in her mood, and that she had not mentioned Andrew, but no one pressed her on it. Not even Dyan and Miranda.

Her latest assignment was protecting a widowed businessman, Nigel Weatherby, and his young son while they were going to London for a tech conference in Kensington. His company rented out a luxurious seven-bedroom house in Chelsea, an affluent area in central London. It was close to the River Thames, Harrods and Michelin-star dining. In addition to Alexa's team, his nanny accompanied him, as did his assistant. Her principal enjoyed jogging, so they would go out at night after his son went to bed and the house was quiet.

The rental was close to Chelsea Embankment, a road and a walkway along the river's north bank.

While jogging and running weren't two of Alexa's favorites, she did them if it was a client's preference.

They jogged almost two miles in silence before Nigel slowed the pace to cool down. It was cold out, so their walk was brisk.

"So, why does a woman like you get into executive protection?"

She fell into step beside him. "A woman like me?"

"Tall, beautiful and pleasant to be around. From your looks, though, you don't look like you've been in many fights."

"I assure you that I have. It takes more work to avoid physical altercations than to get into them."

"Then you must have a knack for it, because you look like you've been behind a desk all day," Nigel observed. "So, is there a mister bodyguard at home?"

Alexa laughed. The heat from her breath caused a cloud of condensation. Was he flirting? If so, she would firmly shut him down. It was her company policy that employees never got romantically involved with clients. And even if it weren't, Nigel wasn't the one.

Alexa snapped out of her daydream. "No, there's not," she said quickly. "Just a lot of houseplants that keep dying off."

"I know the feeling," he responded. "Luckily for me,

I have a live-in housekeeper who keeps on top of all the greenery."

They continued to chat while they walked. Alexa enjoyed his company, and though relaxed, she was alert. After walking a short distance, she spotted two men approaching, so she stepped in front of her client while continually chatting.

"Pardon me? Do you have a light?" one of the men asked.

"No, sorry, I don't," her client replied.

The stranger glanced over at Alexa. "What about you?"

"What about me?"

"Do you have a light?"

"No," she said sweetly. "I don't."

"How about that watch?" he countered, motioning to her client's wrist.

"If you think I'm—"

Alexa rested her hand on her client's forearm and squeezed lightly. He stopped talking, but his anger was still evident in his stance.

She raised both hands. "We don't want any trouble," Alexa said, keeping her eyes on his hands the entire time.

"Too late," the man in front of her replied with a grin before he lunged.

His hand came up, and Alexa saw the knife. Immediately, she grabbed his wrist and pinned his hand against her leg while rotating with him to get him away from her client. Then she struck him under the chin and didn't wait to see him collapse before turning on the other assailant going after her client.

Grabbing the back of his jacket, Alexa yanked him backward and down to the ground, where she delivered an elbow strike to the stomach. Unfortunately, his coat was thick, so she had to hit him twice.

"Let's go," she commanded, pulling her client along as she broke into a run.

Alexa glanced back twice to ensure they weren't being followed.

"We're clear," she announced at the end of the block.

Two men were running from the house to intercept them.

"Miss King," one of them huffed. "We saw you running. Are you both all right?"

"We're fine, thanks," she said, ushering her principal up the walkway and through the front door.

"Thanks to you." Nigel leaned over to catch his breath. "Your quick thinking kept that situation from being much worse."

"That's what we're here for," she countered.

He reached out for the wall. "I feel a little light-headed."

"That's the adrenaline rush. It'll go back to normal soon."

He nodded. "I'm going to go take a shower and then check on my son. Thanks again, Alexa."

"You're welcome. Good night."

Alexa was surprised to find her bed turned down and a fire roaring in the fireplace when she came into the room.

Decorated in taupe and cream with rose-gold accents, the room was relaxing.

After a shower, Alexa donned a pair of fleece pajamas, climbed into bed and snuggled under the thick comforter. Lying in the luxurious bed wrapped up like a burrito, Alexa's thoughts kept drifting to Andrew. He was the one she always called when she had something on her mind, or after a particularly stressful day or a run-in with a bad guy. Speaking to him made her feel better.

When she heard the indicator for a request for a video chat, Alexa's heart thumped wildly in her chest. *Andrew.*

Alexa grabbed it excitedly. Her elation was dashed when she accepted the call and found Dyan's face on the screen instead. "Oh, hey, Dyan," she said with as much excitement as she could muster in the wake of her intense disappointment.

"Wow," Dyan replied. "I've had more excitement coming from bad guys I've had to beat up than you."

"Oh, I'm sorry. It's not you. I just—"

"Thought I was Andrew?"

"What? No," Alexa countered quickly. "I just had a rough evening. Had a run-in while out with my principal on a late-night jog. Nothing I couldn't handle."

"If that's true, then what caused the rough night?" Dyan countered.

Alexa ignored the knowing grin on her friend's face. Confessing that she missed Andrew with a vengeance and hadn't thought of anything else since he went radio silent wasn't a truth that she was ready to share.

Chapter 26

When Alexa scheduled a meeting with Sophia a few days later, she was exhausted. Jet lag and work were starting to take their toll. To make matters worse, she hadn't connected with her family since returning from London. She had called Andrew and was surprised when she got him. At a loss for what to say, she wished him a happy new year. Andrew had thanked her and wished her the same. He was cordial but distant. After hanging up, Alexa's mood tanked for the rest of the day. Later that afternoon, she had a meeting with Sophia.

As usual, Sophia glided into Alexa's office like she owned it.

When she sat down and finally looked at Alexa, she gasped. "Good grief, you look horrible."

"Thank you," Alexa retorted tiredly. "Sophia, we need to talk."

"Presumably that's why I'm here?"

Ignoring the sarcasm, she retrieved a folder from her desk.

"Are you aware of a joint account with Nicholas in Portugal?"

"What?" Sophia sat forward. "I never opened an account with Nico."

Alexa spun the report around and pushed it across her desk.

Sophia read over the pages before tossing them back. Her face was a mottled red. "This is ridiculous. Clearly, it's a mistake."

"So, you're saying that's not your signature?"

"Uh, what part of forgery isn't coming across? No, that's not my signature. Close, but not exact."

"That's not the only suspicious activity Mr. Michaux has been up to while you've been apart. Didn't he tell you that he was in France?"

Sophia shifted in her chair. "Yes. Why?"

"Well, his cell phone records indicate that he's in Portugal. Just outside of Lisbon."

"So he's not where he said he'd be. He could be hanging out with some friends. We did argue. Likely he's just blowing off some steam."

"Is this one of his friends?" Alexa asked, handing Sophia a photograph.

She scanned the picture of a red-haired woman with Nicholas. Her aloof facade started to slip. "None that I know."

"Her name is Eileen English. Her nickname is the Siren, and she's a dangerous woman. She spent several years in jail for fencing stolen items, extortion and kidnapping. She's been brought up on multiple charges in the last few years, but there was never enough evidence for an arrest. We don't know her connection to Nicholas just yet, but—"

"Why are you investigating my boyfriend? Aren't I the one you're supposed to keep tabs on?"

"Yes," Alexa confirmed. "And those around you who could be potential threats."

"We fought. I'd hardly call him a threat," Sophia scoffed. "You're taking this to the extreme, don't you think?"

"This is what we do, Sophia. We look for suspicious activity that could cause problems for those we protect."

"Well, this has been more intrusive than helpful," Sophia complained. "We've been at this for weeks, and nothing has happened. Clearly, whatever threat I was under is no longer an issue, so it looks like I don't need your services anymore."

"Sophia, we don't know if you're out of danger yet. Therefore, ending your protection is unwise."

"I disagree. I'm done with your team snooping into my

private life. Whatever outstanding balance you have, send me the bill." Sophia jumped up.

"Wait a minute," Alexa replied, rising. "Sophia, I know you're upset about Nicholas, but that's no reason to be reckless and—"

"Oh, *I'm* reckless?" Sophia sputtered. "That's rich coming from you. I knew this was a mistake from the beginning. You haven't changed one bit."

Digging into her purse, Sophia retrieved a checkbook. She filled one out, signed it and slammed it on Alexa's desk.

"Here. I'm sure this more than covers any owed amount."

Alexa didn't bother to take it. "You can't fire me, Sophia. The contract is with Ruben."

"Trust me. He'll side with me when he realizes there's no way we can continue working together. Have a nice life, Alexa King."

Sophia stormed out of the room, almost slamming the door off its hinges.

Alexa bolted out of her chair. "No amount of money is worth this aggravation!"

"Do I even want to know what that was about?" Dyan called from the doorway. Miranda hovered right behind.

"Same Sophia, different day," Alexa muttered. "Just when you think she couldn't act brattier and more entitled, bam! She exceeds your expectations."

"Should I contact Mr. Tyndale for you, Miss King?"

"No, thanks, Miranda. I'll handle this."

Her assistant nodded, then retreated to her desk.

Dyan sat down.

"Alexa, do you—"

"Don't you dare say you think I'm overreacting," Alexa fumed. "*We* are putting our lives on the line for a woman who doesn't appreciate it. And you know what else?"

"You're going to tell me," Dyan said calmly.

"She doesn't waste an opportunity to undermine our efforts." Alexa paced like a caged panther looking for a way out.

"I'll admit that part of the reason I took Sophia on as a client was because I felt guilty about Shelley and wanted to help their family in any way I could, but this is cruel and unusual punishment, Dyan. I'm done putting my employees' lives on the line for someone who doesn't appreciate or deserve the sacrifices we're all making."

"Alexa, I understand. And of course, this is your call. Whatever you want, you know we'll make it happen."

"Thanks, Dyan," Alexa said, plopping onto the couch. "I appreciate the support—and you letting me rant," she added with a smile. "I hope you know how invaluable you are to me."

"Sure I do, Alexa." Dyan came over and hugged her boss and friend. "I'm here if you need me. Oh, by the way. Have you noticed anything off with Miranda?"

"No, like what?"

Dyan shrugged. "I don't know yet. She's just not acting herself. I have to repeat things several times, and she's been jumpy."

"No, I haven't, but I've been meaning to circle back around regarding Apollo Hayes."

"Don't you think you'd better deal with Sophia first?" Dyan reasoned.

"You're not wrong," Alexa agreed before calling Sophia's business partner, Ruben Tyndale, to explain their latest run-in.

"I'm sorry, Alexa. Truly I am," he said ruefully. "I had hoped that Sophia's animosity would have diminished."

"As did I. I gave Sophia some news about Nicholas that she wasn't expecting, and it set her off. I've had time to think about it, and I can understand her lashing out. Even growing up, she was never good with surprises."

Alexa relayed their findings to Ruben.

"What? I can't believe he'd do that to Sophia," Ruben snarled. "I knew he had bad points, but forging documents and possibly embezzling money from her? That's insane—and criminal."

"Sophia is sure there's an explanation for it. So the first order of business is to learn more about why he's hanging out with a dangerous criminal, and how it ties into this new bank account—that is, if we're not fired."

"Earlier, it sounded like you were happy to see her go."

"I was," Alexa admitted. "But that wouldn't solve any of Sophia's problems, would it?"

"No, it wouldn't. And for the record, I was never going to let you go, Alexa. She may not know what's best for her right now, but I do. You and your folks stick by her side. At least until we get all of this mess sorted out."

"How long do you plan to hold me hostage?"

The Siren sat across from Nicholas and waited while one of her servants set a dinner plate in front of her. "Flower Duet" from the French composer Léo Delibes's opera *Lakmé* piped through in-ceiling speakers.

She leaned over and smelled the savory aroma of her chef's latest culinary delight. Her face radiated pleasure as she bit into the medium-rare meat perched on her fork. Siren slowly chewed the food and swallowed before washing it down with a sip of red wine.

"That's a rather harsh word, Nicholas. I'd like to think of you as my guest."

"A guest that isn't allowed to leave of their own volition," he tossed back. "And one that you were more than happy to maim if I didn't provide you with a bank account number. That hardly jibes with my definition of the word."

Nicholas sliced the large rib eye steak and took a hefty bite. It was perfect, but he would never tell his captor that.

Siren motioned to the glass decanter between them. "Wine?"

"No, thank you."

He had no plans to drink anything around the Siren because he'd need his wits about him to come up with a plan to get that bracelet back.

Nicholas wondered about Sophia. Their relationship would be over if she somehow learned about the bank account and him helping the Siren clean her money. He was playing a dangerous game, but his deranged captor had to believe he was on board and getting her bracelet back. She had threatened to chop off his fingers if he didn't.

Desperate for cash to fund his business, he'd done Gates Budreau a favor. Gates had a copy made of the eighteenth-century Bellasini bracelet to sell to some unsuspecting rich man as a gift for his wife. He was mortified to discover the man's wife was Sophia's friend. What if she found out he was involved in the bait and switch? Their relationship would be over.

Nicholas had no idea what his friend had done with the original. He felt like killing Gates himself for involving him in his scheme and putting his life at risk, but how could he blame him? If he'd been the one being tortured instead, he would've said just about anything to save himself.

Gates must've been betting that I'd be able to get back the counterfeit bracelet, Nicholas reasoned. *Why else would he say I had it?*

It was a dangerous move trying to trick Siren. After all, she was bound to realize a fake from the real deal. No. It was too dangerous. He needed the original. If not, he had better be on the other side of the world when the Siren found out she had been duped.

Originally, Nicholas had flat-out refused to help, but changed his tune when one of Siren's goons hung him over the tower railing by his ankles.

At least Sophia is safe, he told himself. Nicholas knew that Siren's threats were far from idle, and the last thing he wanted was to endanger Sophia's life.

This is all your fault, he scolded himself.

Nicholas had been desperate to get his business off the

ground and had no plans to crawl back to his father for more money or involve Sophia. *Now look at me*, he thought bitterly. *That streak of pride may cost me my life. First, I have to find Gates to see who has the original bracelet, and get it back.*

Nicholas didn't know how, but he would convince her to let him go under the guise of getting her precious bracelet. He'd see Gates and force him to give up the whereabouts of the original. If his friend resisted, he'd make him see reason. The first thing he would do if he made it out of the Siren's lair alive would be to contact his father. It was time to put pride aside. He would tell his father that his life was in danger, minus all the details, and pray that his father would assign him a security detail to keep him safe until he located Gates. He was not going to die for anyone.

Chapter 27

"We're here, sir."

Nicholas completed the payment on the ride-sharing app and thanked his driver.

He still couldn't believe that the Siren had let him go. Not that he was under any illusions. He was only free so that he could convince Gates to give him the bracelet and return it to her. It was also likely that he was being followed, and that his life would be in jeopardy once she got what she wanted.

He got out of the car and walked up to the black wrought-iron gate. Next, Nicholas entered the six-digit pass code and stepped aside while the gate opened. Then, before it fully extended, he ran up the stamped concrete driveway and rang the doorbell several times. Finally, after another minute, he walked around to the side of the house. Spotting the large stone planter, Nicholas picked up one of the decorative rocks and twisted it. Then, after shaking the house key into his hand, he returned the faux stone hide-a-key to its place. After unlocking the door, he let himself inside the Spanish-style house.

"Gates?"

Nicholas set the key on the credenza just inside the door. The first floor was completely dark, save for a few lights plugged into outlets. Entering the kitchen, he turned on the light and spotted several dishes on the granite counter and a skillet on the stove. He floated his hand over the pan.

"It's still warm," he said aloud. "I know you're here, Gates," he called as he turned on lights around the house.

The interior was painted white with dark brown wood beams on the ceiling. The home was luxuriously decorated, but Nicholas wasn't paying attention to the open floor plan and decor. Instead, he was zeroed in on the sound of a gun being cocked behind him.

"Don't move."

Nicholas held his hands up and said, "I'm unarmed, Gates. Lower your weapon."

"Nico, what are you doing here?"

"I'm here to talk. That's it. Now, can I turn around without being shot?"

"Okay, but no sudden moves."

He turned around to find a gun pointed at his torso. His friend immediately lowered it but didn't set it down. Nicholas's gaze roamed over his friend. He looked like he had been in a car accident. His right arm was in a sling, his face was bluish yellow in some places from bruising, and he had a black eye and swollen lip.

"Jeez, Gates," Nicholas said in dismay. "You look terrible. Siren's thugs did all this?"

His friend bristled. His expression turned fearful. "What do you know about it?"

"Relax, I'm not here to hurt you. I just want information."

"How do I know that? You break into my home—"

"No, I didn't. I used the spare key. Remember you showed me where it was and gave me the gate code?"

He still looked suspicious. "How did you know I was here?"

"It seemed like a logical place for you to go. You told me once that you come here when you want to disappear for a while."

Gates nodded and relaxed. He sat the gun on an end table before limping outside onto the balcony.

Nicholas followed. The setting sun gave them a breathtaking view of the La Jolla coastline. In addition, his home offered an uninterrupted view of the Pacific Ocean.

Gates gingerly lowered himself to the cushioned sofa. He retrieved a remote from the table and turned on the firepit across from the seating area.

Nicholas sat across from him and leaned back against the plush padding.

"How are you feeling?"

"How do you think?" Gates said bitterly.

"What were you thinking?" Nicholas eyed his friend. "Why would you steal from Siren?"

"Do you honestly think I would've bought that bracelet if I'd known who it belonged to?" Gates snapped. "My contact told me it was in his family for years and was purchased at an estate sale. I had no reason to doubt him. Next thing I know, I'm being picked up at my shop by two of her goons and roughed up because I said I didn't have it anymore."

"Trust me, I know. I've been there."

"She almost killed me, Nico!"

"I'm sorry, Gates. Those same thugs kidnapped me and took me to her villa in Lisbon. The only reason I'm not fish food is that I told her I'd get it back. So I'm going to need that bracelet."

"I wasn't lying, Nico. I don't have it. By the time she darkened my doorstep, I'd already sold it. Who knows where it is now."

"Well, we'd better find out. If I don't, we're both dead."

Gates almost turned apoplectic. "Are you crazy? You brought her men here with you?"

"No," Nicholas assured him. "No one knows I'm here. Her men were tailing me, but I lost them."

Gates was almost hyperventilating. "So you say." He leaned back against the cushions and tried his best to calm down. Wiping his sweaty brow with the back of his hand, he sat forward.

"I'm sorry to bring you into this mess, man. This is not how I expected things to turn out."

"Yeah, well, now we're both screwed." Nicholas stood up and paced around the terrace. "She wasn't just bluster, Gates. Siren will kill everyone standing in the way of her getting that Bellasini bracelet back." He ran his hand shakily over his jaw. "When I did you a favor to get some quick cash, I had no idea it would risk my life—or put Sophia in danger."

Gates's face turned red with embarrassment. "I thought it was a sure thing. We'd make a profit and go. I had no idea things would go south." Gates broke down in tears. "I'm sorry, man."

He sat down next to his friend and gingerly patted him on the hand.

"Look, if we're going to both get out of this alive, we have to work together," Nicholas reasoned. "And the first step is finding the fence that you sold the bracelet to. Our lives depend on it."

Alexa strolled into the office with a decorated box of doughnuts in her hand. She dropped them in the break room and headed to her office.

"Miranda, I've brought your favorite doughnuts in. They're in the break room," Alexa said as she walked past her assistant's desk. Miranda was not there.

Glancing around, Alexa checked her watch. It was after nine. Thinking that she was just away from her desk, Alexa went into her office.

Thirty minutes later, she was working on a briefing when Dyan came in.

"Good morning, Alexa. Where's Miranda? She and I had a meeting fifteen minutes ago. Did you pull her for another assignment?"

"Hey, Dyan. No, I didn't. I came in earlier and she wasn't at her desk. I just assumed she was working on something."

Alexa and Dyan walked out of Alexa's office and over to Miranda's desk. Everything was as pristine as she usually kept it. Right down to the rose-gold monthly planner on her desk with a white pen with a fuzzy tip.

Alexa picked up the desk phone receiver and dialed her

assistant's cell phone. When she didn't answer, Alexa tried again.

"Nothing," she said, hanging up. She turned to Dyan. "Do we have an emergency number for Miranda?"

"Hang on." Dyan called Human Resources and got Miranda's emergency contact.

Alexa dialed Miranda's mother.

"Have you spoken to Miranda today?" Alexa inquired after introducing herself.

"No, I haven't. I was starting to get worried myself," her mother replied. "This isn't like Miranda. Normally, I speak to her twice a day. I haven't spoken to her the entire weekend. I'm very worried, Miss King," her mother said tearfully. "This isn't like her."

"Don't worry, Mrs. Travers. We'll check on Miranda immediately. It's possible she is home sick. I'll contact you the moment I find out."

The second she hung up, she turned to Dyan.

"Let's go."

Miranda lived in Northwest Washington, DC, right off Sixteenth Street, a historic and prestigious road that runs from the White House to the Maryland border and is home to over fifty churches, synagogues, shrines, temples and embassies.

Located on a quiet street, her house was a single-family redbrick home with a black door and shutters and a small, well-manicured yard and a one-car garage. They didn't see anything unusual, so they walked up the steps and rang the doorbell. Dyan pressed the buzzer several times.

"I don't like this."

"Neither do I," Alexa replied.

Retrieving a lockpick and torque wrench from a tool set in her purse, Alexa quickly unlocked the door while Dyan watched out for curious neighbors.

"You ready?" she asked when the door opened.

Dyan nodded and followed Alexa inside.

The house was barren except for a few broken chairs and a lamp on the floor. Paintings hung on the wall askew, and a plant was knocked over.

"Miranda?" Alexa yelled, retrieving her pistol from her purse. She dropped the bag and her coat on the floor so she wouldn't be hindered.

Also armed, Dyan called out as she cautiously moved around the first floor.

Once they had done a sweep, they took the steps to the second floor. There were three bedrooms, so they split up.

"I don't understand," Dyan replied when they met back up in the hallway. "Miranda never said anything about moving."

"My gut tells me that's not what this is."

Alexa retrieved her cell phone and dialed her office.

"I need a trace on Miranda Travers's cell phone—right now."

Dyan rushed down the steps behind Alexa.

"Text me the location when you have it."

Five minutes later, they were heading through Rock Creek Park toward the C&O Canal.

"Thirteen minutes," Dyan said as she maneuvered through traffic. Luckily, it wasn't rush hour so there weren't the usual delays.

The Chesapeake and Ohio Canal operated from 1831 to 1924 along the Potomac River between Washington, DC, and Cumberland, Maryland, to transport coal using mules on a towpath to pull the boats along the canal. It was now a popular running and cycling path, and picnic area for residents and office employees. There were also boat tours during the summer months.

Alexa was on the phone with a member of her operations team as they directed her to Miranda's location.

Parking the car, the two raced down the walkways on one side of the canal. Scanning the area, it was Dyan who spotted her first and pointed.

"There she is."

The two took off running. Their heels tapped out a rhythmic beat on the concrete as they dashed past several restaurants and down the brick-paved walkway that ran across the canal.

"Miranda!" Alexa yelled.

When she didn't turn around, she called out again.

Slowly, she turned to face them. When she did, Alexa stopped and gasped aloud.

Her assistant looked haggard, like she had not slept in days. Her clothes were disheveled, her eyes bloodshot, and her face puffy like she had been crying for just as long.

"Stop," Miranda croaked out. Her voice sounded like gravel being scraped across cement.

"Miranda, what's wrong?" Dyan called out. "Tell us what's happened. Whatever it is, we can fix it."

"You can't fix this," she cried out. "I'm ruined. My life is over."

Alexa held her hands up and moved forward as slowly as she could without being detected.

"Miranda, please talk to me. I want to help you. We both do," she said, nodding toward Dyan. "But we have to know what's wrong."

"I'm wrong. I messed up, and there's no way out."

She inched closer to the railing.

"No, no, no," Alexa called out. "Nothing you could ever do can't be undone, Miranda. I promise you. Just tell me what's happened."

"He's taken everything from me," she sobbed. "My money, everything in my house—things that can't be replaced. And I allowed him to. I fell for all his lies. I let him in and he destroyed me."

She grasped the railing and peered over the edge. Dyan began speaking to Miranda, which gave Alexa precious time to close the distance between them without being detected.

"You know what we do for a living. We can undo anything he's done, Miranda."

"No, you can't," she lamented, not bothering to look up. "My credit is shot, I'm behind on everything. I may even lose my house over this. I was so blind. I thought Apollo loved me, but I was just like all the others, he said. Gullible. Convenient. Easy."

Miranda said the word with contempt.

"I just want it to be over," she whispered.

Hearing his name caused Alexa to pause. Apollo Hayes. The man she had been suspicious about because of his evasiveness at meeting them. She closed her eyes. She was supposed to have looked into his background and got sidetracked by other things. She had dropped the ball. She had failed Miranda. She fought back tears as she moved closer.

"Listen to me, this is not the way, Miranda. Your parents are frantic with worry. I promised I'd call them the moment we found you to let them know you're okay."

"No! They can't know about this! No one knows about this. I can't tell them I've been duped by Apollo and I've had my life stolen from me. I can't hurt them like that. I won't."

In a split second, Miranda hoisted her leg up over the railing and was trying to pull herself up. Alexa sprang into action. She reached her assistant just in time to grab hold of her coat to keep her from falling into the freezing water below.

"No!" Miranda screamed. "Let me go."

Alexa was half over the railing trying her best to hold on to Miranda. Before she could call out, Dyan had reached her side and was helping to pull their distraught friend back to safety. All three landed in a heap on the ground.

"We've got you," Alexa said, breathless from the exertion, but trying her best not to fall apart. "You're going to be okay, Miranda. I promise you'll be okay," she said as her assistant's body shook with despair. Miranda's sobs zeroed in on Alexa's heart and broke it in two.

Chapter 28

Alexa sat on her living room couch engulfed in a loden-green comforter that she'd taken off her bed. She stared at the fireplace, watching the flames greedily devour the wood log she had stacked there. Her doorbell chimed, interrupting the silence like an unwelcome guest. She didn't even bother to look up. When it echoed around the room a second time, she yelled out, "Just leave it at the door." Annoyed that she had to repeat something that she had specified in the instructions when placing her food order.

The firm knocking was the last straw. She groused as she got up and shuffled toward the front door. Unlocking it, she wrenched it open with enough fire in her eyes to go to battle, her blanket draped around her like a medieval cloak.

"I said leave it!" she stormed, but the rest of her tirade died on her lips as she realized it wasn't the delivery person with her dinner order.

Her eyes bulged with shock, an action she instantly regretted because they were puffy and painful.

"Andrew."

"Hello, Alexa. May I come in?" he asked after a few moments of silence between them.

She nodded and shuffled aside. "Watch your step." Plates and glasses lay over every table in her living room. The floor was littered with empty carryout boxes, along with the plastic or paper bags they had been delivered in.

As if the state of the house wasn't alarming enough, Alexa looked like she hadn't slept or showered in a week. She smoothed her hands over her wrinkled clothes.

He motioned toward the couch. "Do you mind if I sit down?"

Shaking her head, she staggered back to the couch and

sat, pulling her blanket around her like a shield. Andrew followed behind, and after removing some magazines and papers from the seat across from her, he sat gingerly on the edge.

She regarded him cautiously. "What are you doing here?"

"I was worried. I haven't spoken to you in weeks. And it's been even longer since I've seen you."

"And now you're worried?" she scoffed. "If memory serves, *you* ghosted me."

"I know. I'm sorry about that. I thought it would be easier for you. Less complicated."

"I thought we were friends. Clearly, I was mistaken."

"Alexa, of course we are. That's why I gave you space. Time to sort things out."

"Well, don't do me any favors," she snapped. "I don't need them. Frankly, I don't know why you're concerned."

"Alexa, no one has seen you for over a week and you haven't been to work. So, yes, that caused me to worry."

"I took some time off."

He glanced around the room. "Yes, I can see that."

"And you can also see that I'm just fine. Who called you? Let me guess: Either Dyan or my parents."

"Both."

"That wasn't necessary." Alexa pulled the blanket closer.

"Alexa—"

She stood. "Thanks for stopping by. You can report back to everybody that I am doing great."

"I'd be happy to, if that were true."

She glared at Andrew with annoyance. "What is it you'd like me to say?"

"How about how you really feel?"

For a second, her face relayed her pain. It was enough to make Andrew feel like he had been gut-punched.

"Please leave," she whispered.

"I'll leave once you level with me, because I know you're not fine."

Something inside Alexa snapped. “Fine, you want to hear the truth? Here it is. I am ripped apart inside! I am devastated!” She started pacing in front of the mantel.

“I can’t sleep, and I can barely keep food down. All I can think about is Miranda. Her face. The fact that she was moments away from trying to end her life! She wanted to die, Andrew. And I could’ve stopped all this. I could have kept her safe and prevented her pain and suffering at the hands of some grifter who saw her as another mark. He took everything from her. And I handed it to him. How does that make me feel? Horrific,” she cried, sinking to the floor.

Andrew came over and joined her on the floor in front of the fireplace. He tried to take her hands in his, but she pulled away.

“Listen to me. What happened to Miranda is not your fault.”

“Yes, it is. My gut told me that something was off about him. So I was going to have my team investigate him. And I didn’t. I was so caught up with Sophia’s histrionics that I forgot. I let the ball drop, Andrew, and it almost cost Miranda her life. Everything that’s happened was my fault.”

“That’s not true, Alexa.”

“It is! I didn’t protect them!” she yelled. “Not Shelley, Tanya or Miranda. I failed them all. They would’ve been better off without me in their lives.”

“You don’t mean that.”

“Yes, I do. I couldn’t even protect my friends. People that I love, Andrew. How in the world am I supposed to protect perfect strangers?”

“By doing the best job you can. By showing up and being present, Alexa. You can’t hide from who you are or what you’ve been called to do. This is a temporary setback. You will find your center again.”

She shook her head. “You should go. You’rc safer not being around me. As a matter of fact, I should just quit the business. I’m no good to anyone.”

Andrew touched her cheek. Encouraged when she didn't pull away this time.

"That's just your pain and grief talking. The Alexa King I know has a heart of steel."

"The Alexa King you know is dead. She died from a thousand cuts."

"No, she's in there," he said, pointing to her chest. "You are a guardian to those you love and the ones you protect. And you always will be. No one is better without you. Do you hear me? Not me or anyone else."

"That's not true. You said some hurtful things at the Christmas party and then left me without a thought. You said I didn't need anything or anyone, remember? So spare me the fake concern and just leave."

"I was wrong," he said flatly. "I was hurt, angry, and should never have pulled away. I'm sorry, Alexa. I thought giving you some time was what you needed."

"What I *needed* was you."

When the tears came, Andrew didn't budge. He sat there with Alexa and held her as she cried. After she fell into an exhausted slumber, he picked her up and took her upstairs and put her to bed. Back downstairs, he took a few minutes to contact her parents and Dyan to give them an update.

"Keep us informed," Jake replied in a worried voice. "If she needs anything, you let us know."

"I will, sir."

Dyan had told Andrew that she would continue taking care of things at Dragonfly.

"I've never seen her this lost before. Any progress she had made since Tanya has just been blown out of the water."

"She needs time and space to heal. She'll get there, Dyan."

When he hung up, Andrew sat on the edge of the coffee table and put his head in his hands. There were so many emotions rushing through him that he couldn't get a handle on just one.

Over the years, Andrew had witnessed many facets of Alexa's emotions. Fear, happiness, desire, anger, love and self-confidence. Never had he seen her bereft of hope. It was devastating. Guilt ate at him for his part in her feeling abandoned.

Angrily, Andrew swiped away the few tears forming in his eyes. He was ready to punch something. If he didn't find a task, he would lose it.

For the next hour, Andrew threw himself into cleaning up Alexa's apartment. When she finally awoke, it was to find him seated in a chair across from her bed. A suitcase at his feet.

"How long have I been out?"

"Two hours."

Sitting up, Alexa leaned back against the headboard. She gingerly tapped at the swollen flesh around her eyes. "I feel like I've been punched a few times."

He went to the bathroom, and returned with a wet washcloth. Sitting next to her, Andrew laid it across her eyes.

"Better?"

She nodded.

After a few minutes, she took it off. She gazed around her now-pristine room.

"You've been busy. And what's with the luggage?"

"You're coming home with me. And before you protest, I'm not taking no for an answer. This isn't a time where you should be by yourself and swimming around in your own head. That's a dangerous place to be, trust me."

"I can't just up and leave everything. Sophia—"

"Dyan has been handling Sophia and everything at Dragonfly for the last week. She'll call you if anything requires your immediate attention."

He touched her cheek before letting his hand drift to her shoulder. He gave it a firm squeeze.

"You need to regroup, Alexa. Let me help you do that."

* * *

She studied every inch of his face. From the brow furrowed with concern to the firm cut of his jaw. Her heart constricted in her chest. She had missed Andrew. Everything about him. He was her best friend and had grown to mean much more. They needed to work some things out. But for now, Alexa sat in the moment with him and soaked up his strength. She allowed it to wash over her and soothe her crushed soul.

In that split second, Alexa realized that she was tired. She was too tired to think, to feel or to come up with reasons why she should turn Andrew down on his offer. Instead of protesting, she merely nodded in agreement.

Alexa spent the next week at Phalanx recuperating. James, Esther and Andrew were perfect hosts and went out of their way to ensure that she had everything she needed to rest, relax and heal. She spent most of her days walking along trails or sitting on the porch while Andrew trained the latest group of students.

"You know that I'd be happy to help."

"You are our guest," he clarified. "One that is in need of some downtime."

"And I've had it. You all have been wonderful to me."

He stopped walking and faced her. "Alexa, you must know by now how much you mean to me—and Dad and Esther."

She reached out a gloved hand and touched his face. "The feeling is mutual. I was in such a bad place after what happened with Miranda. I didn't think there was a way I'd find my way back, but then you arrived—you were my anchor."

Andrew pulled Alexa into his arms. "Correction. I *am* your anchor."

He kissed the bridge of her nose. When he stopped there, Alexa realized that he hesitated in deference to her, so she made the next move and kissed him. She felt him hold back for a split second before he was all in.

It was unlike the previous embraces she had shared with Andrew. This one held a lot more than tentative exploration. It quickly shifted into a heat that threatened to singe Alexa from the inside out.

"Well, that was..." Andrew stopped to search for the right word when they finally came up for air.

"Yeah, it was," she agreed. "This changes some things."

"We're going to be okay," he promised. "We'll figure everything out."

"I know," Alexa said with confidence. "But right now, I feel like I need to cool off."

"You've got a point," he chuckled before sweeping her into his arms.

"Andrew, what are you doing? Put me down!" Alexa shrieked. Her voice echoed off the white-topped trees as he carried her over to a mound of snow.

Wary, Alexa tightened the hold on his neck as she eyed him and the snow suspiciously. "James Andrew Riker II, don't you dare," she warned, inching higher in his arms.

"Oh, I dare," he laughed before depositing her into the flaky heap with a flourish.

She screamed and crawled her way out and got to her feet. She slapped the caked snow off her jeans and winter coat. Alexa's expression promised retribution.

"You're going to pay for that."

"I can think of several ways I'd like to do that," he declared with a wicked grin.

Laughter and taunting were the only sounds heard in the snowy meadow as they engaged in a snowball fight.Andrew gave up after one of her well-thrown missiles hit the tree branches above and dropped a mound of snow on his head.

"Yes!" she exclaimed in victory as she watched him stagger to his feet. "Do you yield, sir?"

"Okay, okay." He howled in laughter while shaking himself vigorously. "I give up. I think I got snow down my shirt."

"Don't expect me to feel sorry for you," she shot back. "Yay, Team King!" Alexa ran around the yard exclaiming victory but tripped on a piece of wood buried under the snow. She yelped in pain as she went down. Andrew was at her side in seconds.

"Lexi, are you okay?"

"Yeah, I'm fine," she assured him. "I just twisted my ankle."

Andrew tried to help her, but she got up alone. Hobbling a bit, Alexa walked around testing her foot.

"You know you don't have to do everything on your own. It's okay to accept help when it's offered."

"You're right," she agreed. "It's been difficult for me, you know? But I'm here, aren't I? So that's proof that I'm trying, right?"

"True," he conceded.

He helped her back to the cabin and had her sit on the kitchen counter while he examined her ankle.

"Looks like it's just a twist. Some ice and elevation should do the trick."

"Thanks for looking at it for me."

"My pleasure."

Andrew pulled a clean dish towel from one of the cabinet drawers and then grabbed a freezer baggie and filled it with ice.

"So, how are your parents?" Andrew finally asked while he wrapped her ankle with the floral towel.

"They're great. Relieved that I'm feeling better and wondering when I'm bringing you back with me to visit."

"Just name it," he replied. "You know I love visiting Washington, DC."

"Be warned. I'm sure Dad will bring up the fact that you caused him to owe Mom twenty bucks."

"Why?"

"After you came to stay, my family had a pool going on if we'd end up together. Dad was doubtful, but Mom never wavered."

His shoulders shook with mirth before he grew serious. "And are we?"

Alexa grasped his hand. "Andrew, I didn't know if I was even capable of having a relationship given my past. But, through it all, you've been patient and allowed me the space to figure things out. I want you to know that I'm grateful for that, Drew. I'm not afraid anymore. I want us to be together. Time isn't promised to any of us, and I don't want to let another day pass without declaring that I care about you, Andrew. Deeply."

He took her face in his hands. "And I care about you—deeply."

Andrew slid her closer to him for a kiss. "Was there an expiration date on that wager?" he murmured against her lips.

Alexa scrunched her face in concentration. "No, I don't think so."

"Good. Then I hope Jake knows that his baby girl caused him to lose."

Alexa poked him in the ribs. "Very funny."

They were still laughing when Alexa got a call.

"It's Dyan," she said after Andrew handed her the phone from her jacket pocket.

"Hi, Dyan. What's up?"

"Hi, Alexa, I'm sorry to disturb you while you're on leave, but we've got a situation."

"Okay. Let's hear it."

"Sophia was abducted."

"What? How was that possible? There should've been two teams guarding her at all times."

"There were, but we were outnumbered. The intel we received was faulty. By the time we arrived at the venue, several teams were waiting. We took on heavy fire. Two of our men didn't make it, Alexa."

Alexa closed her eyes for a moment then slammed her fist on the counter.

"Where was Sophia's last known location?"

"Paris. Not far from her apartment. She was supposed to meet Nicholas Michaux there after her show."

"Why?"

"I don't know, but our advance team said he never showed up."

"I want him found, Dyan. Send the jet to pick me up. After that, I'm going to Paris. I expect the team to have laid out a tactical plan to get her back by the time I arrive."

"There's one more thing, Alexa."

"This isn't bad enough?"

"We know who kidnapped Sophia. One detained man had the same tattoo as the men in Los Angeles. After some painful coercion, he admitted that everyone that works for the Siren has this tattoo."

"Are you certain?"

"Yes. He refused to tell us where Sophia's been taken. He said he'd be killed if he gave up her location. So we contacted the authorities, and he's been taken into custody. Maybe they'll get him to talk."

"Thanks, Dyan. I'll see you soon."

"We'll get her back, Alexa," her friend said firmly.

"I know we will."

After ending the call, Alexa shoved her phone back into her pocket and hopped off the counter. She landed on one foot before gingerly testing the other out.

She could tell by Andrew's expression that she didn't need to elaborate.

"I have to go pack."

"You can't go after Siren, Alexa. She's extremely dangerous."

"She has my asset, Andrew. Which makes *me* extremely dangerous."

He stopped her. "I'm serious."

"So am I." Alexa stared at him in surprise. "I've never seen you look spooked, Andrew. Have you crossed paths with her before?"

"No. I know her only by reputation. She's bad news, Alexa. Bad, deadly news."

"Precisely why I plan on getting Sophia back before she gets hurt."

"Then I'm going with you."

She resumed walking. "No, you're not. This was my operation, Andrew, and it went south. Sophia is Dragonfly's responsibility. My team didn't keep her safe, which means I'm the one who's going to get her back."

Chapter 29

They were still having a heated discussion when Esther and James arrived.

The elderly couple exchanged glances as they set groceries on the counter.

"What's going on?" James asked when he could get a word in.

"Your son doesn't think I'm competent enough to handle a threat," Alexa snapped as she hobbled over and sat at the kitchen table.

Andrew's expression turned incredulous. "Whoa, I said no such thing. Don't put words in my mouth."

"And don't treat me like I'm a child who needs to be rescued!" she shot back.

He threw his hands up in frustration. "Alexa, where is this coming from? I've never once treated you like you couldn't handle yourself."

"Until now."

Andrew's jaw clenched, and an almost painful silence descended. The couple stood glaring at each other so long that James cleared his throat and would've said something, but Andrew turned to his father and Esther and said, "Excuse us."

Without another word, he swept Alexa up in his arms and carried her upstairs to his room.

"I can walk," she groused.

"You need to rest that ankle."

A few moments later, the door shut firmly behind them.

Esther glanced over at her husband. "Well, I've never seen that before."

"Me, either," James replied with a barely disguised smile. "It looks like JJ has finally met his match—and so has Alexa King!"

* * *

Alexa sat at the foot of Andrew's bed, her arms crossed and looking ready for battle. But it was the first time she had seen his bedroom, so despite her mood, she was curious.

His room was spacious, clean and extremely masculine.

"I can tell by your silence that you're still angry."

Alexa turned back to Andrew. "Yeah, I am."

"That makes two of us," he shot back. "Do you know how much I value who you are and what you've accomplished? I've never seen anyone as smart, capable and adaptive as you are. For you to even suggest that I didn't think you could handle yourself is crazy. I'm only worried about you because things are different now, Alexa."

"How?"

"Because it's not you and me anymore. It's *us*." The word shot out of his mouth like it was ejected from a cannon. "We're together now. In a relationship, and I had hoped both committed to seeing where this thing goes."

Some of Alexa's anger ebbed away. Despite her ankle, she hobbled over to him and touched his shoulder.

"Of course we are."

"Then don't go after Siren alone. Being together is hard enough without one of us going off and getting ourselves killed."

"I won't be by myself, Andrew. I'll have operatives with me and—"

"Do you think that gives me one moment of peace or eases the dread that settled into my gut when you said you were going after that lunatic?"

"Andrew, I don't—"

"I can't lose you, Alexa!"

He said the words like they were ripped out of him by force. Andrew ran his hand over his jaw as he struggled with his emotions.

Alexa was stunned. She remained ramrod straight as if her feet were welded to the floor.

Before she could get her bearings, Andrew grabbed Alexa by the shoulders and kissed her as if she'd just asked him for mouth-to-mouth resuscitation. Something uncoiled deep inside Alexa as if Andrew were breathing life into her body. She clung to him like she never wanted their embrace to end.

"Stay with me," he whispered against her lips.

"Drew, I want to, but I have to leave tomorrow. I don't want to make that any harder. For either of us."

"I just want you by my side. That's all, Lexi."

She knew he was telling the truth. Alexa trusted Andrew 100 percent. With her life, if it ever came to that.

Standing on her tiptoes, Alexa kissed him with a newly acquired possessiveness.

Some of the edginess left him. He squeezed her hand and stepped past her to light a fire in the fireplace. Alexa sat on the bench at the end of his bed and watched him. When Andrew was satisfied that it had taken hold, he extended his hand to Alexa. She didn't hesitate. He sat on the chaise longue by the fireplace and pulled Alexa into his lap. They both stretched out and, releasing a collective sigh, watched the fire.

After a few minutes, Alexa said, "Andrew, we both chose our professions for a reason. I temporarily lost sight of why I do what I do, but you helped guide me back from the edge, and for that I'm forever grateful. We want to protect people and keep them safe. We put our lives on the line every day to achieve that goal. So you must know I will do everything possible to protect my assets—and my team."

He stared at the fire as if hypnotized. "I know."

"But," she added, looking up at him, "I promise that I will also do everything in my power to come home—to you."

He touched her cheek and grazed her bottom lip with his thumb before he kissed her.

"And I promise you that I will always do the same."

Eventually, Alexa fell asleep. Carrying her back to his bed, Andrew took off the shoe on her other foot and eased the covers over her. Kicking off his shoes, he got in the bed next to her, but instead he sat up against the headboard and let out a tortured sigh. Nothing about this scenario sat right with him. Sophia being kidnapped and two of Alexa's operatives getting killed were bad enough. But Alexa was walking into the Siren's lair, and that shook him to his core. Andrew leaned over and moved a lock of hair out of her face. There was nothing that he wouldn't do to keep her safe. He had known it for some time, but now that statement truly hit home.

After breakfast the following day, Andrew drove Alexa to the airport to meet her plane. One of the men on her team retrieved her luggage while Andrew walked her across the tarmac to the plane's airstairs.

He hugged her goodbye. "Call me the moment you land," he whispered.

"I will."

"If you need anything—"

"I will let you know," she promised.

He nodded, kissed her a final time and moved away.

Dyan was on board, as was the rest of Alexa's team. Once at her seat and buckled in, she glanced out the window to find Andrew still standing there. Waving, Alexa held eye contact until the pilot announced they were ready to take off. Only when she could no longer see Andrew did Alexa settle back against the seat.

After the plane left, Andrew retrieved his cell phone and dialed a number as he walked back to the Jeep.

"Daniel, it's Andrew Riker. I need to call in a favor, buddy."

* * *

It was a fourteen-hour flight from Colorado to the Humberto Delgado Airport in Lisbon. After landing, Alexa's group was met and taken to a rented house near Torres Vedras. Alexa's dragonfly pendant she'd given Sophia indicated that she was not being held at the Siren's compound, but in a farmhouse nearby.

To ensure the best possible outcome, Alexa contacted her colleague Alejandro Reyes again. Alejandro had painstakingly cultivated a network of allies from around the world. With his help, Alexa had access to resources to ensure they had the best possible extraction plan with minimal collateral damage.

After their briefing, Alexa's team would move out around two o'clock in the morning to get Sophia back.

Though she was tired, Alexa still called Andrew before bed and brought him up to speed.

"Sounds like you have everything fully mapped out."

Yawning, she settled under the covers and tried her best to remain awake.

"Hey, did I lose you?"

"No," Alexa replied, trying not to yawn again. "I'm here."

"Not for long," Andrew teased. "I'm glad you called, but you need some sleep."

"I know," Alexa murmured.

"Be careful, Alexa."

"We will be. Alejandro's men will be on point tomorrow and lead us in. Of course, we'll have the usual complement of body armor and Marena's tech, so don't worry. We'll be ready."

"Sweet dreams, Lexi," he said softly.

Alexa said good-night and hung up. She thought of Andrew and couldn't help the smile that crossed her face.

She thought of her deceased best friend. "You'd have liked him, Tanya," she said before falling asleep.

* * *

Andrew hung up thc phone, but he was wide-awake. He had a meeting scheduled for the next day himself, and if all went well, the Siren would no longer be a threat to Alexa or any members of her team. It was a calculated risk he was taking. One that had the potential to go very wrong, but if it meant Alexa would be safe, it was worth it.

Chapter 30

Dyan rechecked the signal. "It's still strong," she confirmed. "She's in the west wing of the house. It looks like a back bedroom based on the map."

"Okay. Let's move out," Alexa announced.

She grabbed her gear and followed the group outside into the cold night air. It was forty-five degrees in Torres Vedras that morning. Clear skies aided in visibility as they loaded into a van. Dropped a good mile from the location to avoid detection, they went the rest of the way on foot.

Every precaution was taken as they approached the house from the woods. They used thermal imaging to determine that the point of entry would be a back window. From there, they would need to ascend to where Sophia was held, retrieve her and exit the building without alerting anyone of their presence.

Dyan and her team would secure the perimeter and hold off anyone advancing to the house.

Getting inside without incident, Alexa followed Alejandro's men upstairs.

The bedroom had minimal furniture, only a twin bed, a chair and a small table on the other side of the room. The full moon illuminated the area with small pockets of light, helping them navigate. Sophia was asleep, so Alexa knelt down and lightly shook her arm.

"Sophia?"

Her eyes flew open in an instant. Fear and confusion were there in equal measure until her gaze rested on Alexa. She blinked a few times and sat up.

"Alexa?"

"Yes, it's me," she said soothingly. "Come on. We don't have much time."

Sophia nodded before she launched herself into Alexa's arms. Her arms clamped around her neck. "You found me!" she murmured tearfully. "I didn't think you would come."

"Shh. It's okay, but we have to go," Alexa whispered. "Now."

Nodding, Sophia got up and put on her shoes. Her jeans and red shirt were crumpled, but clean. When they were ready, the men motioned for them to follow.

Alexa put Sophia between her and the first man. The other two were behind Alexa, bringing up the rear. They had just reached the top of the stairs when someone opened a door behind them.

Startled, the man yelled, *"Pare!" Stop!* in Portuguese.

"Move," the man behind Alexa commanded. They all rushed down the steps and were met by several of the Siren's men.

Their escorts laid down cover fire and immobilized the assailants while Alexa pulled Sophia behind her to the window.

"Wait, where are we going?" she said frantically.

"Down," Alexa explained.

"On what?" Sophia shrieked.

"We're rappelling down. You'll be okay, Sophia. I'll take the lead, and you follow me."

"No, I won't," she countered quickly. "I can't do this, Alexa. I'm scared of heights."

When a bullet whizzed past Alexa's head, she didn't hesitate to shove Sophia to the floor.

"Sophia, follow me," she commanded. They crawled behind a high-backed chair, and Alexa returned fire.

"Alexa? Are you on the way out?"

"Negative, Dyan. We're pinned down," she whispered, turning toward the earpiece. "The window's no longer an option. Sophia is scared of heights. We'll be target practice trying to get her out the window. The front door is our only option."

"Then you'd better hurry. We'll have company in two minutes."

"Punch a hole," she replied. "I need a clear path."

"Roger that," the team leader replied. "Sixty seconds."

Alejandro's men were back and crouched by Alexa's side. One checked his watch. They had heard the exchange and got into position.

"Fifteen seconds."

"Get ready to run when I say go," Alexa told Sophia. "And don't stop, no matter what."

"Okay," Sophia replied quietly.

Suddenly, the front door exploded, and many pieces of charred wood flew like projectiles into the foyer and around the first floor. Stunned, Alexa's ears were ringing. Still on the ground, everything appeared in slow motion to her. Men who were close to the blast lay either motionless or screaming and writhing in pain.

Rolling over, she checked on Sophia. There were a few cuts on her face, and she was disoriented by the blast.

"Are you ready?" one of the men crouched beside her asked. "It's time to go."

Alexa nodded before turning to her right.

"We have to move." She grabbed Sophia up by the arm.

The five of them sprinted for the gaping hole that seconds earlier was a well-guarded barrier.

Alexa ran ahead with Sophia in the middle, where it was the safest. They had to jump over a few bodies, inside and outdoors, but they met no opposition.

Dyan and her team were waiting near the tree line. Alexa glanced over her shoulder to see the blaze had spread to the second floor.

"Let's go," their team lead called out.

Everyone took off for the waiting van and piled inside. Watching the scenery whiz by, Alexa instructed everyone to check for injuries. Sophia had not said anything during the ride, for which she was grateful. Sometimes she was a bit irritable and nauseous coming down from an adrenaline rush, so she appreciated the quiet.

When they arrived at the safe house, Alexa felt better but tired. Dyan took Sophia upstairs while she debriefed her team. Afterward, Alexa went to her room and showered.

She was too tired to talk, so she grabbed her phone and texted her friend first.

Hey, on a mission. I just wanted to say your dragonfly pendant worked like a charm. The signal remained strong, and we had no incidents. Sophia is safe.

Glad to hear it, Dr. Marena Dash-McKendrick replied. Where are you?

Lisbon.

It's early there, isn't it?

Yep. Haven't gone to sleep yet. I just wanted to say thanks for the tech. I'll call when I get back to DC. Say hello to Coulter for me.

Will do. Talk to you soon, Alexa. Stay safe.

Always am.

Next, Alexa texted Andrew.

Hey, Drew. Op went well. Exhausted.

Good to hear from you. How's Sophia?

Better than I expected. I'll talk to her later after I've slept a few hours. Right now, I'm running on fumes.

I hear you. I'm glad you're all safe. Get some rest, sweetheart. Call me later today.

Will do. How are your dad and Esther?

Well. I'm in the field, so I'll tell them you asked about them when I get back.

Oh? I didn't know you were on assignment.

I know. This just came up. I'll tell you about it later.

Okay. I miss you.

Miss you, too, Lexi.

Alexa set her phone on the nightstand and got under the covers. She was thankful for the dark curtains that would be blocking the sun once it rose.

Closing her eyes, she thought about Andrew. Alexa felt more at peace than she had in a long time. He was the balm that her heart had needed to heal and come to terms with the pain of the past. Shelley and Tanya were losses Alexa never thought she would recover from, and the incident with Miranda, while still fresh, was easing now that Miranda was doing better. Her team was working on locating Apollo Hayes so that he could be brought to justice for his crimes. Whatever it took, she would make Miranda whole again.

Now Alexa wasn't in it alone. This time, she had an ally. She had Andrew.

Despite her initial apprehensions about opening up to someone new, Andrew was constant and dependable, and cared about her in a way that allowed her to drop her guard and be herself.

Suddenly, a sense of dread came out of nowhere, causing her uneasiness. As did the next thought that popped into her head. *Dropping your guard is usually when something goes wrong.*

"Let me get this straight. You two stroll in here with some sob story and expect me to violate my client's trust and anonymity to ask for a bracelet back that Gates sold me weeks ago?"

"More like borrow," Nicholas added.

"How long do you expect me to be in business doing stupid stuff like that?"

"Look at me, man," Gates demanded. "This isn't a game. Our lives are at stake. You bought a stolen Bellasini—"

"Something I do all the time," his associate added.

"But not belonging to the Siren," Nicholas shot back.

The man was thoughtful. "Yeah, that was unexpected."

Gates shifted on his crutches. "Gee, you think?"

"If I help you, what's in it for me?"

"How about your life? You're delusional if you think she'll let us live if we don't give her what she wants. And how long do you think Gates and I will hold out before dropping your name?" Nicholas added.

"And trust me, she has spies and connections everywhere. Who knows, we could be under surveillance right now."

Gates's contact gasped. A look of terror on his face as his gaze zeroed in on the front door of his shop.

"Hey, how'd I know it belonged to her?" he stammered. "In our line of work, it doesn't pay to ask too many questions."

"Then you'll help us track it down?"

Nicholas's cell phone rang. He excused himself and went to answer it.

"Do you have my property yet?"

He paled and shot Gates a worried look. "Not yet. We've run into a few problems and—"

"Your problems don't concern me, Nico. However, you should know that some of my men are babysitting your girlfriend."

"What? Wait, that's not what we discussed," Nicholas roared into the phone. "Where is she?"

"Call it added collateral to ensure you give me what I want—Sophia in exchange for my bracelet."

"How do I know you haven't killed her already? I want to talk to her."

"You're in no position to demand anything. But if you and Gates keep stringing me along, I'll be forced to start mailing your beloved back to you. One lovely piece at a time."

She hung up before he could respond.

Nicholas shoved his phone in his pocket and stomped across the room. Then, grabbing two fists of that man's shirt, he hauled him up so they were eye-to-eye.

"Whoa, what are you doing?" the man sputtered. "Let go of me!"

"Nico, put him down." Gates hobbled over to his friend but didn't get close enough to risk a fall. "What's going on?"

"That psychopath has my girlfriend!" Nicholas thundered before glaring down at the store owner. "Your time is up. You find that bracelet, or I swear, I'll kill you myself."

"Okay," the man cried out. "I promise I'll get it back, but it will take some time. I'll need at least forty-eight hours."

Nicholas shoved him away. "You have twenty-four."

Chapter 31

"Where is she?" the Siren stormed as she threw a tray with her afternoon tea across the room. It hit the wall and shattered. The tea dripped haphazardly down the wood paneling. "When I checked in earlier, you told me everything was under control."

The man sitting across from her shifted on his feet. "It was, but then we had a situation."

"*Your* men are the incompetent fools that couldn't hold on to one tiresome hostage. So I think *you* should be responsible for this excessive lapse in judgment."

"I lost several good men in that break-in, boss," he said defensively.

Siren reclined in her chair, her feet propped up on a small footstool as a servant handed her a new cup of tea. "Well, they can't be that good—they're dead."

The man blanched. "I'm sorry. I won't let you down again, I promise."

"I should hope not. I won't be as forgiving the next time."

Bowing, he rushed out of the room with the remainder of his men in tow. Sipping her tea, Siren turned to one of the employees standing off to her right.

"I don't think he showed the proper amount of remorse. Go explain it to him."

"Yes, Siren. Right away," the man agreed before signaling for a few men to follow.

"Mr. Riker? Mr. Livingston will see you now."

Andrew stood and followed the woman down a dim hallway. She knocked once and opened the office door. Andrew followed her inside.

A large, well-dressed man was sitting at his desk. The

room was elegantly furnished with dark wood paneling. Though it was a long and narrow room, no expense was spared. The oval desk was placed at the end of the space. The window behind it was dressed in floor-to-ceiling black silk drapes.

Above the desk was a large circular wrought-iron chandelier with rows of hanging teardrop oval crystals. Built-in bookcases flanked the desk with recessed can lighting in the paneled ceilings.

To Andrew, it was a luxurious yet claustrophobic space that seemed better suited to be a library than an office of one of the wealthiest landowners in the world.

Randolph Livingston's family was one of the top procurers of stolen art that grossed about six billion worldwide, but Randolph's father began investing in legal businesses decades prior. Eventually, his branch of the Livingstons turned to real estate and managed to triple the size of their fortune. So when his father retired and Randolph took over the company, he made significant gains in keeping their operation legitimate.

"Mr. Riker, it's a pleasure to meet you." He extended his hand. "Though I must say a surprise."

"Thank you, sir. Likewise."

"Please, have a seat."

Andrew unbuttoned his suit jacket and sat opposite the desk in the patterned brown leather chair.

"I won't take up too much of your time."

"When one of my business partners asked for the meeting, I must say, I was intrigued as to why. He said that you worked for him on several occasions."

"Yes, I provided security for him on a few overseas trips to precarious destinations."

"Well, you must be exceptional, because Arthur had nothing but praise when I inquired about you. So, what can I do for you, Mr. Riker?"

Andrew opened the briefcase at his side and retrieved a folder. He slid it across Randolph's desk.

"I found something that I thought would interest you."

Mr. Livingston sighed before he picked it up. "If this is another investment request—" he began.

"No, but it is something valuable to you."

He reclined in his chair to hoist his feet up on the desk. The chair creaked in protest. When Randolph opened the thick folder and started flipping through the pages, he gasped in shock.

The color drained from his face and, after a few moments, was replaced with splotches of red that disappeared below the collar of his crisp white shirt.

"Is this accurate?"

"Yes, sir."

The older man rose from his chair as fast as his large frame could. He eyed Andrew shrewdly. "Why are *you* bringing this to me?"

"Because I now have a vested interest."

"Do you know how long I've had my men on this? And you stroll in here with information I've been trying for years to get?"

Andrew shrugged. "I have a lot of assets at my disposal."

"And I don't?" Randolph stood up and walked over to the window. He stared out at the cold, rainy day. Then, with a loud sigh, he turned around.

Andrew noted that he looked years older.

"I don't care what it takes or how many resources you need. I want you to deliver the Siren to me—alive."

Alexa was exhausted but upbeat as she sprinted down the sidewalk and into her condominium's front door. She retrieved the key from an inside pocket on her exercise pants, unlocked the door and stepped inside.

A few minutes later, Alexa was enjoying the first sip of her favorite smoothie when her doorbell rang.

Disappointed, Alexa set her drink on the counter and strode to the door. Staring through her peephole, she looked surprised.

"Okay," she whispered, and opened it.

"Sophia. This is a surprise."

"Hi, Alexa," she said, standing awkwardly in the hallway. "I hope I'm not disturbing you. Oh, are you about to go out? If so, I can—"

"No, you're fine," Alexa assured her. "I just got home from a run. Come in." She stepped aside and let her enter. Alexa hadn't even been aware that Sophia knew where she lived much less would ever come by to visit.

Taking her coat, she hung it on the freestanding coatrack by the front door. Something told Alexa that she wouldn't be staying long enough to hang it in the closet.

"Would you like something to drink? Hot chocolate, coffee or tea? Unless you want something cold?"

"No, thank you. I'm fine," Sophia replied congenially.

Motioning to the couch, Alexa said, "Have a seat. I'll be right back."

Going into the kitchen to retrieve her smoothie, she took a moment to compose herself. Sophia was not her usual brash, hurried self, which had Alexa feeling wary. When she returned, she sat on the couch next to Sophia.

"This is a surprise," Alexa remarked while sipping her drink. "What brings you to Washington, DC?"

"You."

"Come again?"

Sophia looked like she was in physical pain. She shifted a few seconds and wrung her hands nervously before she finally got to the point.

"My actions placed my team in danger, and I was kidnapped because I didn't listen to anyone when you all were just trying to keep me safe, and I'm sorry," she got out in a rush.

Alexa's mouth dropped open in shock. Whatever she

had been expecting to hear from the younger woman, it wasn't this.

When Alexa didn't immediately reply, Sophia bolted off the couch and began to pace. Tears streaming down her face.

"I've been angry at you for so long, Alexa, that it's been hard to bury the pain and forgive." She took a deep breath. "I was the annoying little sister who was always trying to hang with my big sister and her friends. And then, after the attack, everything changed. I felt like I had a huge part of my childhood ripped from me and I was forced to grow up overnight. We all had to care for Shelley and be there for her. And then weeks turned into months, which turned into years. And I just felt lost—and angry." Sophia glanced at Alexa. "I took that anger out on you, and it wasn't fair. I finally see that."

Alexa was floored by Sophia's acknowledgment. She had not realized that she was holding the smoothie container so tight that her fingers were going numb. She set it down.

For years Alexa had dreamt of a reconciliation with the Porter family. Eventually, she had lost hope of it ever happening. But Sophia was here bearing her soul and explaining how the incident had changed her life, too. Some of the hurt Alexa had carried with her began to lift.

"Sophia, I honestly don't know what to say. I—"

Her client rushed to her side and grabbed her hands. "Please say you'll forgive me for lashing out at you about Shelley, for getting kidnapped, and that you won't terminate Ruben's contract."

"Of course I forgive you, Sophia. I'm not ending Ruben's contract, and I don't want you blaming yourself for being abducted. That wasn't your fault."

"None of this makes sense," Sophia replied with frustration and sat down again. "There were no demands when they grabbed me. I overheard one of the men holding me talking on his cell phone. He said they were supposed to babysit me while the Siren waited for Nicholas to get her bracelet."

"Did he mention details?"

"No. Just that it was priceless to her, and that she'd do anything to get it back."

"She was using you for collateral," Alexa surmised.

Sophia jumped up. "See, this is why you have to help him, Alexa."

Alexa stared at Sophia in shock.

"What?"

"It's obvious he's in over his head. Nico tends not to focus on the big-picture items. He gets lost in the weeds on things sometimes. Whatever he's doing for the Siren, it's obvious that it's dangerous and needs an extraction."

"An extraction?" Now it was Alexa's turn to start pacing around her living room.

"First off, I'm not in the spy business, Sophia. The only people we *extract* are the clients we've been hired to protect. And if we're doing our job properly, this isn't even something we'd need to worry about."

"Alexa, I want to hire you to protect Nicholas."

"Sophia—"

"I'm serious. Granted, he annoys me more times than not, he's fickle and doesn't have a head for business, but I love him, Alexa. I don't want him to end up dead, courtesy of some lunatic woman robbing and killing people to get what she wants. Please, Alexa."

Alexa didn't know what to make of this new development with Sophia, but she was just grateful that they could finally stop being at odds with each other. That they would be able to finally heal the wounds of the past.

She sat sideways to face Sophia.

"I can't, but I have someone in mind for the job."

"You do? Who?"

"Andrew Riker. He trained me a few years ago. He's the

best regarding strategy, tactical, protection and weapons—besides his dad."

Sophia launched herself at Alexa.

"Thank you," she cried.

"It's okay." Alexa patted her back while trying to sit them both upright. "I'll set everything up with Andrew. Nicholas will be in good hands, I promise."

Nodding, Sophia went to stand up, but Alexa stopped her.

"Wait, before you go." Alexa took a deep breath and forged ahead before she got cold feet. "I wanted to ask you how Shelley is doing. I've hesitated to ask because I didn't want to cause you any pain. And I've also been too chicken to inquire," Alexa confessed.

"It's okay, Alexa. I think it's time to talk about it anyway. Shelley has good and bad days." Sophia sighed. "But she is taking care of herself. She is a gardener and landscape designer. Shelley says that she feels most herself when working with the soil and in nature."

"She always loved it," Alexa added. "I'm glad she's doing something that brings her joy."

"It's been hard for her, Alexa. Mom hovering all the time hasn't helped." Sophia's expression turned sad. "What happened put such a drain on our family. I thought my parents would divorce from the strain. But they didn't. It seems like we all turned a corner. Each in our way."

"You don't know how happy I am to hear that Shelley is—doing well. I know it's not perfect, but she's dealing with what happened on her terms. In her way. Shelley is a survivor."

Sophia glanced at Alexa and smiled. "And so are you."

Chapter 32

"Are you sure this is gonna work?"

"Relax, Gates. We have a plan. We stick to it, and we'll be good."

"I don't know if breaking in is the best way to go about this. Why not level with the guy and make him a counter-offer?"

"Do you have sixty-three thousand dollars to give this dude in exchange for the Siren's bracelet? Because I don't."

"I'm sure he doesn't know its true value." Gates rubbed his bearded jaw. "Maybe we could lowball him?"

"Neither one of us has the cash to be waving under his nose nor the time to barter. Have you forgotten about Sophia? The clock is ticking, Gates. I put her in danger, now I have to make this right, and the fastest way to do that is to steal the Bellasini. Now, are you going to help me or not?"

Gates shifted on his feet so long that Nicholas glared at him.

"Okay, okay. Yes, I'm going to help. I almost died once because of this stupid bracelet. I'm not about to make it easy for the Siren to do it again."

"Good." Nicholas lightly punched Gates in the arm. When he instantly grimaced, he apologized.

"Sorry, man. Now, let's get back to work. Shine a light on the lock, please."

Gates reached into the bag he was holding and retrieved a penlight. He turned it on and aimed the beam just above the lock.

"You sure you don't want me to do that?"

Nicholas looked up. "Have you suddenly discovered how to pick a lock with one hand?"

Gates grimaced. "Sorry, I forgot. I'm nervous." His gaze darted behind them and to the left and right.

It took Nicholas several tries, but eventually, the back door opened. Dousing the light, Gates handed his friend the bag and followed him inside.

Several night-lights were plugged into the outlets as they walked through the kitchen and down the hallway, so they didn't need flashlights.

Nicholas turned to Gates and whispered, "Where did your contact tell us to go?"

His friend retrieved a piece of paper out of his pocket. He leaned against the wall for support. Gates beamed the light on the makeshift map and instructions by taking the flashlight out of his bag.

Suddenly, rapid beeping was heard throughout the first floor.

"He's got an alarm." Nicholas scanned the area for the keypad. Then, spotting it, he rushed to the front door. "What's the code to disarm it?"

"Hang on. I'm looking," Gates called out.

"We've got forty-five seconds left. Hurry it up."

Frantically, Nicholas was watching the time count down. "Gates," he called over his shoulder. "Ten seconds."

When his buddy didn't reply, he yelled, "Gates!"

"Five, two, six, one."

Punching the keypad, Nicholas entered the numbers and the disarm button. The beeping ceased, and the pad turned green. He blew a breath out in relief.

Gates came up behind Nicholas. "Man, I just aged about three years." He headed for the steps. "He keeps the valuables in a guest room safe."

Nicholas hurried up the stairs while Gates took his time. Once he'd made the second landing, he turned right and headed down the hallway.

"First door on the left," Gates called up the stairs.

Scanning the room with a penlight, Nicholas spotted a bronze statue on the desk.

"That should be the Greek Spartan King Leonidas," Gates called from the doorway.

"It is. Now what?"

"Rotate the arm with the spear forty-five degrees and then back to its original position. Behind that painting is a wall safe. Key in five, four, six, six. It spells lion."

Nicholas shook his head. "This guy isn't that original."

He did as Gates instructed, and the safe opened without incident. Nicholas grabbed the bracelet and ignored the cash, loose diamonds and other jewelry pieces. Next, he closed the safe and pushed the painting back in place.

"Let's get out of here," Nicholas remarked while placing the Bellasini in a small velvet box.

"You're not going anywhere," a male voice declared.

Nicholas and Gates turned around to find a man holding a pistol blocking their path.

He was tall and was wearing a double-breasted gray suit with a purple silk tie and black dress shoes. He looked like he was going out for a night on the town instead of standing there pointing a gun at them. He was graying at the temples, but everywhere else his hair was black. His face was mottled red with anger.

"Give me one reason I shouldn't kill you both where you stand."

Gates opened his mouth to speak, but Nicholas said, "The Siren."

The man was visibly shaken but didn't lower the gun. Instead, he moved across the room to stand behind his desk. He dropped into the chair heavily but kept the gun trained on Nicholas and Gates. He motioned for them to sit on the couch.

"What does she have to do with this?"

Nicholas shrugged. "Well, she wants the bracelet back that you stole and won't stop until she gets it."

The color drained from his face. “I didn’t steal anything. I purchased that bracelet—”

“From the man that stole it from her,” Nicholas replied. “Do you think she’ll care that you have a receipt?”

“I don’t believe you.” He motioned toward Gates. “Don’t tell me he works for the Siren?”

“No, I’m the guy who had the misfortune of standing next to her when she discovered her eighteenth-century Bellasini bracelet had been stolen,” Gates chimed in. “But I was lucky. The guy who gave up your broker’s name, not so much.”

“What?” The man began to sweat. His gaze darted frantically between them.

“This isn’t what I signed up for. I have a wife and kids.” He reengaged the safety before setting the gun on the desk. “Take it and leave.”

With Nicholas on his heels, Gates hurried on crutches as quickly as he could.

When they returned to the car, Nicholas started the engine but didn’t immediately pull off. Instead, he leaned his head on the steering wheel.

Gates placed a hand on his shoulder. “Nico, are you okay?”

He ran a hand over his face. “That was close,” he exclaimed. His voice shook with emotion. “We could’ve been killed, Gates.”

“Tell me something I don’t know. And for me, it’s been twice!”

Hours later, Nicholas let himself into the loft-style condominium he shared with Sophia. Located near Canal Saint-Martin in the tenth arrondissement, it was in one of the hipper areas in Paris. Sophia had picked it because there were many artisanal boulangeries, or bakeries, coffee shops and fashion designer boutiques nearby.

He loved the exposed wood beams, cherrywood floors, open floor plan and floor-to-ceiling windows in every room.

Opening the door, Nicholas trudged inside, dragging his luggage behind him. After he closed and locked the door, he turned on the hall light to illuminate the way into the kitchen so he could get a glass of water.

He strolled into the dark living room. Groping at the wall, he found the light switch and flicked it on.

"Jeez," he yelled at the sight of a man sitting in a chair by the window. The glass he was holding crashed to the floor.

"Who are you? What are you doing in my apartment?" Nicholas said, overly loud.

"Waiting for you."

"I see that, but who are you? Did the Siren send you?"

Before the stranger could answer, Nicholas ran out of the room. Moments later, he returned with a butcher knife in his hand.

"Start talking," he said, brandishing the meat cleaver in front of him.

"I'm Andrew Riker. Your new guardian angel."

"My what?"

"I've been hired to protect you."

Andrew was about to stand, but Nicholas held the knife out and backed up. "Uh-uh. Not yet. By whom?"

"Your girlfriend, Sophia. She thinks you need safeguarding. Considering the company you've been keeping lately, she's not wrong."

Now that Nicholas was less rattled, he stepped around the broken glass and water and went to sit on the edge of the couch. He ran a shaky hand through his hair.

"I can't take too many more surprises," he muttered. "Start talking, and hurry to the part where I don't call the police or run for my life."

"Trust me. You wouldn't reach the phone—or the door."

Nicholas set the knife down on the coffee table and

stared at Andrew. "And that's supposed to help ease my mind?"

"Sophia knows everything, Nicholas. So now would be a good time to disclose how you got caught up with one of Europe's most notorious criminals."

"Look, I don't mean to be rude— Wait, why am I apologizing? You're the one breaking and entering. So why don't *you* start talking?"

Andrew stood up and began walking around the room. He picked up pictures and other decorative items as he went. "As I said, I was hired by your girlfriend because she found out that you got yourself kidnapped. She also knows that you've been working with the Siren to launder money through a joint account you opened in her name without her consent, which makes it illegal. Alexa King, currently protecting said girlfriend, has extensive information on your whereabouts concerning the Siren. We also know that you connected with a friend of yours, Gates Budreau, who dabbles in stolen goods. Sophia was recently kidnapped and extracted by Alexa's team, which I'm sure you knew by your facial expression. So we can conclude that she was taken to use as collateral to blackmail you into continuing to help the Siren. And by the looks of your buddy Gates, you've been much more helpful than he has. How am I doing so far?"

"On target," Nicholas replied grudgingly. He got up and went into the kitchen. Upon return, he carried a wastebasket, a roll of paper towels, and a small broom and dustpan. Kneeling, he began cleaning the mess.

"Gates asked me to do a favor and give a fake bracelet to a guy who purchased it for his wife," Nicholas explained while sweeping. "My job was to deliver it to the man and collect the payment while the original Bellasini bracelet was sold to a fence, or broker if you will, that Gates knew. But then he sold it to a collector."

"So the collector has it?"

Nicholas hedged. "Not exactly."

"Then what exactly? And I'd be truthful if I were you. Your life depends on my knowing all the facts."

He dumped the glass shards into the trash can. "Gates and I broke into his house to steal it. He caught us, but we convinced him we were working for the Siren and his life was in danger, so he gave it to us without a fuss."

Andrew nodded. "Anything else?"

"No, that about covers it."

"Nobody is safe until she gets that bracelet back."

"I know that. The Siren almost killed Gates over it, and I think she did kill a few of her men over losing it in the first place. Trust me, the last thing I want to do is keep this death trap, but I need to ensure that once she gets it, there are no more threats, kidnappings or retaliation against me, Sophia or Gates."

Andrew picked up his phone and dialed a number.

Nicholas glared at him. "What are you doing? I just came clean about the entire mess, and now is the ideal time you want to be making a phone call?"

"It's a perfect time," Andrew countered. "Sophia is well protected at Dragonfly, and I'm calling in a team to keep you and Gates safe while I go strike a deal with the Siren. Then we'll rendezvous with Alexa when I return."

"I don't think that's wise, dude. I don't know you that well, but you seem like a nice enough guy. I'd hate for you to do something that may get you killed."

"Thank you, Nicholas. I appreciate that, but this is what I do for a living, so relax."

With that, Andrew stepped away to make his phone call.

"Don't worry, man, relax," he mimicked Andrew's voice. "Yeah, I'm sure that's what the Siren's men said before they went headfirst over the Pearl Tower."

Chapter 33

Andrew arrived in Lisbon without incident. A man was holding his name on a sign at Baggage Claim.

"I'm Andrew Riker," he announced as he walked up.

The man nodded. "Follow me."

His guide didn't bother with the pleasantries, which suited Andrew just fine. He didn't want to be here any more than the man wanted to be escorting him around Lisbon.

"Two necessary evils," Andrew said under his breath.

Once they were in the sedan and on their way, Andrew glanced at his watch. He was supposed to check in with Alexa in two hours. He wasn't looking forward to that conversation. Leaning against the plush leather seat, Andrew folded his arms across his chest and closed his eyes. He was tired, hungry and worried about his next conversation with Alexa. She would be livid.

She knew nothing about his plan to make a deal with the Siren. Andrew knew her reputation. She was deadly and wouldn't hesitate to dispose of anyone in her path. But he had a mission to complete, and there was no going back. Soon he'd tell Alexa of his plans, and then all hell would break loose. She'd be angry at him for keeping his operation from her, but it couldn't be helped. He'd sought out Randolph Livingston because of his resources. Andrew couldn't risk Alexa falling prey to the Siren's machinations. Most of them proved deadly, and if anything happened to Alexa…

Andrew stopped. He couldn't even finish his thought. She was too important to him to lose—end of story.

The driver didn't bother announcing that they'd arrived. Instead, he merely drove up the circular driveway and parked the car.

A man immediately stepped up and opened the door.

"Good evening, sir. Welcome to the Hotel Beleza."

Andrew got out of the car and buttoned his suit jacket. "Thank you."

The porter glanced at the trunk.

"Do you have any luggage, sir?"

"No, I don't. I'm just here for a meeting."

"Understood. If you step inside, a staff member can assist you."

Andrew stopped short when he reached the other side of the glass doors.

He could understand why the hotel was named "Beauty." The furnishings were decorated in warm tones of cream and gold. The furniture was cream with Tuscan brown wood for the arms and legs of the sofas and chairs and the tables throughout the reception area. The chandeliers were crystal, and the light bounced off the delicate gold chargers on the tables holding potted plants.

"Good evening, sir. How may I help you?"

"My name is Andrew Riker. I have a meeting with—"

"Of course, Mr. Riker. Please follow me."

The woman took him down a long hallway and through large French doors into a greenhouse. Andrew glanced around at the tropical plants.

He spotted a woman sitting on a stone bench. She was wearing a flowing kimono-style cardigan with a peacock feather design and form-fitting black pants. There was a small table next to her with a tea service and a tray of finger sandwiches and bite-size desserts. Siren was sipping tea when Andrew approached.

"Don't you just love teatime? It's so relaxing and civilized."

"Siren, I presume?"

"Yes." She set her cup down and observed him with mild interest. "What can I do for you, Mr. Riker? Do be seated. I don't like anyone standing over me."

He lowered himself in the chair next to her tea set. He waved away the proffered tea.

"It's what I can do for you that counts," he replied. He reached into his pocket, and out of nowhere, several men appeared with weapons drawn.

"Nice and slow, Mr. Riker. My men don't like sudden movements."

"So I see." Andrew retrieved his cell phone and flipped through several pages before handing it to the Siren.

"You arranged for this meeting to show me what?" she laughed. "A selfie?"

"In a manner of speaking. This picture was taken yesterday."

When she saw the image, the Siren's expression turned from amusement to menacing in seconds. "This is a dangerous game you're playing, Mr. Riker. I don't take kindly to anyone dangling my property over my head like a carrot. Especially someone I don't know."

Andrew retrieved his phone. "From what I've heard, you enjoy a good negotiation. So do I, provided it doesn't end in death."

The Siren tossed her head back and let out a boisterous laugh. "I like you, Riker. You have a sense of humor. That's an asset. Still, it takes extreme guts or stupidity to come here yourself."

He allowed himself a slight smirk. "Who says I'm alone?"

She nodded and then turned to her bodyguard. He retrieved a card from his pocket and handed it to Andrew.

"This is my address. I want my Bellasini in my hand no later than Friday."

"That's in three days."

"Not beyond you, I would think, considering you just showed me a picture of it." The Siren set her cup down and stood. "Don't keep me waiting, Mr. Riker. My patience is not inexhaustible."

Before Andrew could respond, she and her men swept past him and out of the door.

"Three days, huh." He needed to brief Alexa and then arrange to drop off the Siren's bracelet. A moment of discomfort washed over him as he anticipated her reaction to him seeking a known killer out to make a deal.

Andrew retrieved his cell phone from his pocket and made a call.

"It's me," he said, striding out the door and down the hall toward the lobby. "There's been a change in plans. Let the captain know that we're heading to Washington, DC." Ending the call, Andrew got back into the sedan and left.

The Siren observed Andrew's car drive away.

She tapped the headrest in front of her and the driver eased the black sedan out of its parking space and down the long driveway.

"I want someone monitoring Mr. Riker at all times," she told the man sitting next to her. "He's adorable, but I don't trust him. I want him watched 24/7. If he sneezes, I want to know about it. Is that clear?"

"Of course," her bodyguard replied. "I'll see to it personally."

The Siren settled against the buttery soft leather seat and gazed at the lights whizzing by her window. She suddenly looked much older than her forty-five years. Grasping at her head, she pulled the pearl Kanzashi hairpins from the tightly wound bun. Her red hair unraveled and cascaded down her shoulders. She tapped the elegant pin against her thigh. "Fair warning," she said almost as an afterthought. "I'm holding you responsible if anything goes wrong."

Her bodyguard swallowed loudly. "Understood."

Alexa strolled through the glass doors and into the lobby of the Salamander hotel in Washington, DC, and headed straight for Check-In. It was almost eight o'clock at night, and the reception area was buzzing with patrons. Oblivious to the comings and goings and the people chatting away in the elegantly furnished reception area, there was only one thing on Alexa's mind. Andrew.

She had missed him with an intensity that was overwhelming at times and brought her to a major decision. Talking to Andrew on the phone and sharing texts between missions wasn't enough. Tonight, Alexa would show Andrew that she was ready to take their relationship to the next level. She wanted him—all of him.

Alexa had spared no expense getting ready for their date night. She had spent most of the day at a spa getting pampered. There wasn't one inch of her body that hadn't been massaged, buffed and well-oiled. She had also treated herself to a manicure, pedicure, waxing and hairdo. Alexa was so relaxed, she had fallen asleep twice during her services.

"Hello, Miss King," one of the staff replied warmly. "Welcome back. I'll be with you in just a moment."

She waited patiently while the staff member finished up with a customer.

It was cold and overcast outside with a few indications that they might get some snow. Alexa took a few moments to remove her black leather gloves and loosen her black velvet wrap. Her excitement was practically bubbling over. Alexa's foot tapped an absent-minded tune on the marble floor while she waiting for Benny to finish helping a guest.

Benny finally glanced up to give Alexa his full attention. "Wow, you look amazing, Miss King! How can I be of service?"

Alexa smiled at the compliment. "Thank you, Benny. And it's nice to see you again."

"The pleasure is all mine, Miss King," he said warmly. Suddenly, he glanced around. "Are you on duty?"

"Not today," Alexa said with a grin. "I'm meeting my boyfriend here for dinner."

Benny's mouth dropped before he could catch himself. "Pardon me, Miss King, but did you say—"

"Yes, I did." Her smile was as bright as a solar flare as she provided Andrew's name.

Recovering from the shock, Benny checked for his room number and gave it to Alexa. "You know, in all the years I've known you, I've never heard you say that before?"

"Times change, Benny." She winked before heading for the elevator, her strappy black heels clicking on the floor as she walked.

On the ride up in the elevator, Alexa tried to quell her nervous energy. Now that she had decided to make love with Andrew, all the pent-up desire had her pulled as taut as a bowstring. She checked her pulse while waiting to arrive at his floor.

You need to calm down, she mused. *Even your heart rate is elevated.*

When she got there, she knocked twice and nervously shifted her weight from her left to right foot while she waited.

Tonight, everything will change. No going back now, King. You've got this.

Andrew opened the door. Alexa watched the happy smile he was wearing skid off his face. It was replaced with jaw-dropping surprise that made Alexa's insides warm with delight.

When she came inside and Andrew eased the black velvet wrap coat off her shoulders, he let out an audible gasp.

Alexa was wearing a wine velvet Bardot neckline dress. The off-the-shoulder, long-sleeve creation sinfully hugged her body from top to bottom and landed just below her knees. Andrew's gaze drifted lower, taking in her toned legs, and finally to the black crisscross-strap open-toed heels before trailing back up her body. Her hair was smoothed into a chignon bun at the nape of her neck and she wore long dangling gold earrings. Her makeup was minimal, except for the matte wine-colored lipstick.

When his heated gaze connected with hers, Alexa felt

like every nerve ending in her body had fired at the same time. She had to stifle a giggle when he almost dropped her coat to the floor when he took it off.

"Alexa…you are. Wow. Truly breathtaking," Andrew finally managed to get out.

When she leaned in to hug him, his cologne wafted into her nostrils. Closing her eyes, Alexa let herself enjoy the feel of being in his arms after so long apart.

"Thank you," she murmured against his ear. "You look amazing, too."

Andrew had chosen a black suit with a dark gray shirt, black tie and a black-and-gray silk pocket square.

They drifted apart from the hug just enough to kiss. The passionate embrace only stoked the tension circling around them.

Eventually, they moved apart so that Andrew could hang up Alexa's wrap. It gave Alexa time to glance around.

The opulent one-bedroom suite had beige walls and a sizable cream-colored sofa with seafoam-and-gold-patterned pillows. The carpet was also the same color scheme. The glass-and-gold coffee table across from a built-in entertainment unit held a flat-screen television. In the corner by the window were a wooden desk and a fabric chair in the same green color.

In the middle of the floor was an elegantly decorated table with long white taper candles, fresh flowers and covered dinner serving sets.

"I hope you don't mind dining in instead of going to a restaurant," Andrew said as he held out the chair for her and then turned on some soft music. "I found myself not wanting to share you tonight."

Alexa's face pinkened with the hint of a blush. "I'm glad you did. Everything is perfect, Drew."

The personal chef Andrew hired had prepared rack of lamb with an herb crust and plum sauce, along with herb-roasted potatoes and roasted asparagus.

They chatted while they ate, each content to enjoy the other's company.

"Ready for dessert?" he asked some time later when they were done.

Leaning back, Alexa rubbed her stomach. "I'm too full right now."

"I know the perfect thing to help you settle your meal." Andrew stood and helped Alexa up. He led her away from the table and drew her into his arms to dance.

"I'd forgotten how well we dance together," she replied as they moved in time to the lazy jazz tune drifting around the room.

"I haven't. I'll take any excuse I can to get you into my arms, Miss King."

Alexa closed her eyes and leaned her head on his shoulders. "All you have to do is ask, Mr. Riker."

"I've missed you, Lexi," Andrew said seriously. "So much."

"I've missed you, too, Andrew."

He spun her around and then dipped her. Andrew continued to lean over until he kissed her lips. "Have I mentioned how incredibly sexy you are?" he asked when he pulled her upright.

"I'd rather you show me, Drew."

Before he could respond, Alexa's hand drifted up between them and unbuttoned his suit jacket and eased it down his broad shoulders before tossing it on the chair. Next, she ran her hands across his chest and then up to his head to pull him down for another kiss before leading him over to the couch. When she guided him down, she straddled his lap.

"What are you doing?" he breathed against her lips as his hands came up to either side of her waist.

"Something we should've done a long time ago."

"Alexa," he said raggedly. The shred of control that Andrew was trying his best to exert was splintering by the minute. "I need to talk to you."

She began to unbutton his shirt. Next, she kissed a trail down his firm chest. She leaned forward and playfully bit his bottom lip. "It can wait until morning."

Andrew grasped Alexa's wrists to halt her progress before easing her off his lap.

"I'm afraid this can't. Alexa, I went to see the Siren."

Chapter 34

"You what?"

A bucket of cold water couldn't have had a faster effect on squelching Alexa's libido.

Andrew repeated himself.

She smoothed her dress down. "I heard what you said. What I'm not clear on is what possessed you to do that?"

"The centuries-old gem bracelet stolen from the Siren was worth about sixty-three thousand dollars."

"That's a hefty price tag. But what does that have to do with us right now?"

"She kidnapped Sophia to use as an incentive for Nicholas to return it. Plus, a husband of one of Sophia's friends purchased a replica of the stolen piece. He bought it from Gates Budreau, a fence, or dealer in stolen goods, and friend of Nicholas. Gates talked him into delivering the fake to the man. Unfortunately, Nicholas didn't know about the original being stolen from the Siren until she had him kidnapped and brought to Torre de Pérolas."

"So, when did you find all this out?"

"After Sophia hired me to protect Nicholas, I insisted on full disclosure. So he told me everything, including him and his friend Gates breaking into the house of the guy that purchased the original."

"He did *what*?"

"Yeah. Luckily for them, Nicholas is quick on his toes and convinced the guy the Siren sent him. That was all he needed to hear, and he gave up the bracelet."

"So where is it now?"

"I have it."

Alexa frowned. "Why?"

"That's what I went to see her about. I struck a deal that

I'd give her the bracelet in exchange for her not coming after anyone else."

Andrew watched as Alexa's expression changed from avid interest to growing anger.

"You went to see the Siren without telling me about your plan first?"

"Yes."

"Andrew, why would you deliberately keep this from me? You know how dangerous she is—everyone knows—and yet you felt it was a good idea to negotiate with her or try to make deals with a known killer? The police have tried to get something to stick to the Siren for years, but she never directly gets her hands dirty. Instead, she uses her minions for all the scare tactics and shakedowns. Did you know they call her Lady Teflon?"

"That's exactly why I did it, Alexa. I wanted you as far away from the Siren as possible. This woman kidnaps, kills or has people beaten within an inch of their lives for the slightest provocation. I wasn't going to risk you getting on her radar."

"Oh, *you* weren't going to risk it?" Alexa snapped before jumping up from the couch. "How could you go behind my back? I deserved to know what you were planning. This affects my protectee, too."

"I had a call to make. Nicholas is under my protection, and I did what was necessary to keep him safe. Telling you beforehand had no upside."

Andrew regretted his word choice the second it left his lips. He closed his eyes and prepared himself for the retaliation, which was swift.

She sucked in a breath. Her eyes narrowed. "What did you just say to me?"

"Alexa, I—"

She held up her hand. "Uh-uh. Don't backpedal now, Drew. You said it, and you meant it. And for the record, I don't need you swooping in with your shiny red cape to save the day. I'm not some weakling who can't take care of herself."

"I never said that."

"I have a global company specializing in close protection and security," she continued as though he hadn't said anything. "Which qualifies me to fight my own battles—and those of my clients," she snapped.

Too angry to sit still, Andrew also bounded off the couch. They faced each other like it was a cage match.

"I'm aware of your credentials, Alexa. I'm the one who trained you, remember?"

"And you think that qualifies you to protect me when I don't need it?"

"No, but my being your boyfriend does. And before you try to disagree, you should know I stand by my decision. Nicholas and Gates are in danger every second they have that bracelet. I'm glad that Sophia had the foresight to ask me to protect him because at the rate those two were going, they'd eventually be found by the Siren's detail and killed. Sophia was captured once, Alexa. How long would it have been before she was retaken?"

Alexa was about to turn away, but he stopped her.

"Do you think I would stand by and risk that happening? If Sophia was in danger, I knew that would entail you putting yourself in harm's way to keep her safe—that wasn't a scenario I was willing to risk."

"I risk my life every day, Andrew. You know that. I don't interfere in your ops. You had no right injecting yourself into mine. When I need a guardian, I'll ask for one."

Agitated, Andrew paced the floor. "So, you're not going to try to see this from my side? You're going to ignore that I did what I had to because I care about you?"

"That doesn't give you the right to try to coddle me, Andrew."

"I will always protect you, Alexa, no matter what—and

that's with or without your permission. You do that for the people you love."

Alexa stopped for a moment. She was stunned at Andrew's declaration, but then she shook her head. "That's not love, Andrew. That's control. And if you think I'm giving anyone control over me, you're mistaken."

Andrew crossed his arms over his chest. "And there it is. I knew sooner or later that we'd get to the crux of the matter. This argument isn't about me keeping you in the dark about the Siren or your accusation that I'm trying to control you. It's about *your* need to control everything that happens in and around you because you're scared of feeling helpless."

Alexa recoiled as if she'd been struck. "That's not true."

"Isn't it?"

"No. It's about being in a relationship with someone you can communicate with and trust—someone that has your back."

"When have I not had your back, Alexa?" Andrew roared. "Everything I have done since we met was my attempt to protect and keep you safe. I had every intention of telling you about my meeting, and yes, I was dreading it because I knew you'd be upset, but I did it anyway. And before we made love," he added. "Because I never want anything standing between us."

"Really? Well, if that were the case," she shot back, "you would've told me about it before it happened, not after."

She brushed past him and went to the closet to get her coat.

"Where are you going?"

"Isn't it obvious? I'm leaving."

"Just like that? We haven't resolved anything, and you're just going to up and leave?"

"Yes, because if I stay, I'll say something that I can't take back."

"Alexa, if you head out that door, I can't guarantee I'll be here when you get back."

She wrapped her coat around her like a shield before she turned around. Their angry gazes connected from across the room.

"Goodbye, Andrew."

Storming out of his suite, Alexa was so angry that she was shaking. Once at the elevator lobby, she jammed her gloved finger on the down button and waited impatiently for it to arrive. She glanced over her shoulder a few times, but the corridor was empty. By the time she'd reached her car, she still hadn't calmed down.

Alexa drove straight from the hotel to her parents' house. When she entered the house, she found her parents in the family room playing cards.

Her mother glanced up in surprise. "Alexa? Hi, honey. What a wonderful surprise," Margot said. "Wow, you look beautiful! How'd your date with Andrew go?" She glanced at her watch. "Ended a bit early, didn't it?"

"Thanks, and yes, it did. Sorry to just pop in unannounced."

"Nonsense," her father replied. "This is your home, too, sweetheart. You know you're welcome anytime."

"Thanks." She plopped onto the couch, removed her heels and put her feet on the ottoman. "I didn't feel like going home."

Margot studied her daughter for a few moments before she said, "Alexa, what's wrong?"

"It's Andrew," she confessed, not bothering to deny there was a problem. "He and I just had a huge fight. Huge."

Her parents turned around in their chairs and gave their daughter their undivided attention.

"About what?" her father inquired.

Reaching for the unfinished bowl of chocolate-drizzled popcorn, she stopped.

"Hold that thought. I'm going to wash my hands." Alexa rushed from the room.

Jake turned to his wife in question.

"Don't ask me," she replied as if he'd spoken aloud.

"I guess we'll find out soon enough."

Alexa returned and resumed her seat. She picked up the bowl and dived into the chocolaty treat.

While she ate, she recapped her argument with Andrew. Then, when she was done, she turned to her parents.

"Well?"

"Well, what?" her mother countered.

"Was I wrong to get angry at his high-handedness?"

"Alexa, we're not getting into the middle of your disagreement with Andrew."

"Mom, I'm merely asking if you think I overreacted or if what I said was founded."

"I'm going to agree with your mother on this," Jake chimed in. "We'll leave you to work around your impasse with your boyfriend. But I will say that he has a point, honey."

Alexa stopped munching. "Dad?"

"Ever since the Great Falls park incident, you have been hypersensitive in a few areas."

"Your father is trying to say yes," her mother added. "You have a problem when you think you're not in control of a situation. I'm not saying I agree with how Andrew went about meeting with what's-her-name, but I agree with him wanting to keep you safe."

"I don't need him for that," she said grudgingly.

"Alexa, you are in a relationship now," Jake pointed out. "He cares about you. Andrew wanting to protect you is ingrained in him whether you want it to be or not. And the same for you. You'd protect him if the need arose, wouldn't you?"

"Dad, of course I would. But I don't need him keeping information from me."

"Of course you don't," he agreed. "And I agree with you on that. I'm merely pointing out that his motives didn't sound like he believed you incapable of protecting yourself."

She mulled over her parents' words while they returned to their game. Finally, when they were done and getting ready for bed, Alexa said, "Do you mind if I stay here tonight? I'm wiped out."

"Of course not." Margot went over to hug and kiss her daughter. "We'll see you in the morning."

"Good night, kiddo." Jake also did the same. "Turn everything off before you come up."

"Okay, Dad. Good night."

Alexa retrieved her bowl and resumed eating while she stared at the dwindling fire in the hearth. She was exhausted, and her mind was a jumble. Their fight was the first since becoming a couple, and it was a bad one. And considering that she had walked out on Andrew, possibly a game changer.

Pulling a throw blanket from the back of the couch, Alexa stretched out on the sofa and stared at the glowing embers in the fireplace. She pondered what Andrew and her parents had said about her need to control her surroundings. Her past was still tainting her view of the present. Deep down, Alexa knew they were right and that it was a problem she would have to acknowledge.

The fight with Andrew replayed in her mind's eye. The realization that she could lose him caused her stomach to ball up in knots and her heart to hammer in her chest. Alexa curled up into a ball. "My God, what have I done?"

Chapter 35

"Sweetheart, wake up."

Feeling a gentle nudge on her shoulder, Alexa opened her eyes.

"Good morning, Lex," her mother replied, sitting on the coffee table adjacent to the sofa.

"What time is it?" Alexa murmured.

"It's a little after ten."

"Seriously? I can't believe I slept so long." She sat up and stretched. "Or that I didn't make it upstairs."

"Your dad made breakfast this morning. We saved you a plate."

Standing, Alexa folded up the blanket and laid it on the couch. "Thanks, Mom. I'm going to go up, shower and get dressed."

When she got upstairs, Alexa peered in the mirror in her bathroom. She wrinkled her face at her bloodshot and puffy eyes. "You look horrible," she said aloud.

Later, Alexa assessed the clothes she'd left in her closet. First, she retrieved a pair of jeans and a red wool turtleneck sweater. Next, she searched a few shoeboxes and found navy blue sneakers. Brushing her hair into a top bun, Alexa was almost done when her cell phone rang. Picking it up from her bed, she was disappointed that it was Dyan, not Andrew.

"Hey, Dyan. What's up?"

"What's wrong?" Her friend and employee sounded worried.

"Nothing," Alexa answered.

"Mmm, okay. I'm sorry to bother you on your day off, but Sophia is in an uproar. She spoke with Nicholas yesterday, and he was freaking out because he can't reach Andrew."

"What do you mean he can't reach him?"

"He said Andrew had an appointment and his team came in to guard Nicholas. Andrew was supposed to check in after the meeting, but that was yesterday, and there's still no word."

"He's here in DC. I met up with him yesterday, and we—"

"Fought?" Dyan asked.

Alexa sat on the edge of the bed. "Why would you say that?"

"Because you sound out of sorts."

"Yes, we did," she confessed. "And it was big."

"So where is he now?"

"I don't know." She got up and started throwing on clothes. "Andrew was at his hotel last night, and I haven't heard from him today. Hang on."

Alexa placed Dyan on hold and called Andrew's phone number. It rang several times before going to voice mail. Then, ending the call, she transferred back to Dyan.

"He's not answering, but his cell phone isn't turned off."

"Maybe he's in Portugal? Nico told Sophia about the Bellasini bracelet and Andrew's deal to return it to the Siren. The deadline was today."

"He wouldn't have left without saying goodbye," Alexa countered.

"Yeah, but you just said you had a huge fight. Maybe he did."

"Regardless of what happened, Andrew wouldn't do that. I'm going back to the hotel. In the meantime, I want his cell phone tracked and an update from his team on his flight plan."

"I'm on it," Dyan replied, and hung up.

Running down the stairs, Alexa went into the kitchen.

"I've got to go," she said. "Andrew missed a check-in with his team. He'd never do that, so I'm going to find him."

"I'll go with you," her father replied.

"No need, Dad, I'll be fine. I'll let you know if I need anything."

Margot hugged her daughter. "Be careful, Lex."

"Always, Mom."

The Salamander turned up nothing. Andrew had not checked out yet and no one had seen him leave that morning. One of the managers escorted Alexa to his room. There were no signs of a forced entry, and nothing seemed out of place. He was just gone.

Alexa went home. As she was parking, she received a call from Dyan.

"Hey, what do you have?"

"GPS shows that Andrew's cell phone is at your condo, Alexa."

She took a moment to lean against the steering wheel in relief. Andrew was safe and waiting for her at her place.

"Thanks for tracking him down, Dyan."

"My pleasure, Alexa. Can you—"

"Yes, I'll have him call Nicholas and his team," she agreed.

Ending the call, Alexa took the elevator upstairs. Turning the key in the lock, she realized that the bolt wasn't engaged. Opening the door, Alexa wasn't prepared for the scene inside.

Andrew was fighting for his life against three men. He was thrown into her entertainment center and crashed to the floor in a heap. Pictures and books that were on it followed him to the floor.

"Andrew!"

Alexa didn't think. She just reacted. Dropping her purse, she ran across the room and attacked the first man she reached.

Punching him in the gut, Alexa followed through with an uppercut. He stumbled but did not go down, so she grabbed a statue from her end table and whacked him. Then, she rushed to jump in front of Andrew, not bothering to watch the attacker go down.

While he struggled to his feet, Alexa bought him time by blocking a punch from the closest man. He brandished a Taser, but she knocked that out of his hand with a well-placed kick. She recovered and swept his legs out from under him before delivering an elbow strike to his mid-section.

Andrew hit his opponent in the nose, breaking it. The man screamed and dropped to his knees, blood gushing through his hands.

She turned to check on Andrew. "Are you okay?"

He wiped a trickle of blood from his mouth. "I've been better."

Before they could catch their breath, three additional men burst through Alexa's front door.

She didn't wait for them to get close to Andrew. Instead, she ran across the room and launched herself at the group. The first to recover, she delivered a blow to the carotid artery in one man's neck, rendering him unconscious. The second rushed past her. Before she could pursue him, another assailant grabbed her and shoved her into the wall and then the glass foyer table. It collapsed under her weight.

"Alexa!" she heard Andrew call out.

Breathing heavily, she scrambled to her feet. Two men held Andrew down. She went to move, but she was grabbed from behind. An arm snaked around her neck. While she struggled, she watched the third man rush up and stab Andrew.

"No!" she screamed as Andrew doubled over in a heap.

Alexa balled up her fist and hit the man holding her in the groin. Then, as he dropped to his knees, she delivered an uppercut to his jaw.

"Andrew," she yelled out, and ran to his side. She stopped halfway when she saw one of the men hold up a weapon.

She heard a muffled sound and then felt something pierce the skin on her neck.

Reaching up, Alexa retrieved a dart. She stared at it, but her vision grew blurry, and her steps faltered.

"No," she said in a voice that sounded foreign to her ears. Dropping to her knees, she struggled to move, but it was fruitless. Her body would not cooperate. The last thing Alexa saw was Andrew's still body sprawled out on her hardwood floor.

"Alexa? Lex, wake up!"

The darkness slowly receded. Her name was being called repeatedly, but it sounded to her like it was through a far-off tunnel.

"Is it raining?" she slurred.

Eventually, the haze cleared, and her parents and cousin, Zane, loomed overhead. Her face was wet to the touch. She glanced down and saw a washcloth in her mother's hand.

"Andrew?" Alexa bolted upright, her head spinning in protest of the sudden movement.

"Easy," her cousin warned. "Go slow, Alexa."

Zane helped Alexa to her feet. She weaved a few times as he lowered her on the couch.

"Drink this." Her father held a glass of water in front of her lips.

After taking several sips of the cool liquid, her throat felt better, but her body ached like she had been in a cage fight.

Gazing around the room, the events were beginning to return. Broken vases, a ruined entertainment center, glass everywhere, and several turned-over plants and pictures. Everywhere she looked relayed the remnants of the fight.

She checked her watch. Twelve hours had elapsed.

Alexa shook her head and instantly regretted it when pain grabbed a hold of her.

"That can't be right." She turned to her father.

"Dad, where's Andrew?"

Jake looked worried.

"He's not here, sweetheart. When we arrived, you were on the floor unconscious, and your apartment was empty."

Her worst nightmare realized, panic coursed through her, trying its best to incapacitate her, but Alexa tamped it down. She'd fall to pieces later. Andrew needed her now.

"They took him." She jumped to her feet but then swayed. Everyone reached out to steady her.

"I have to find him."

"Who's they? And you can't go anywhere just yet," her father reasoned.

Margot returned with a first aid kit she had found in Alexa's bathroom. Taking a Band-Aid and ointment out of the case, she bandaged her daughter's head.

"We need to take you to the hospital," her mother reasoned. "Who knows what those goons injected into you."

"She's not wrong," Zane replied while sweeping up debris and dumping it into the trash can he had retrieved from Alexa's kitchen while Jake assisted.

"There's no time," she said dismissively before turning to her father. "The Siren took him, and I'm going to get him back. But first, I need to go to Andrew's suite at the Salamander. I need the Bellasini. That's why he was taken."

"What?" Jake replied.

She got up. "I'll explain when I get back."

"No, you'll explain now, and we're all going with you," her mother countered.

"We don't have time," Alexa said tersely. "Plus, it will be dangerous, Mom. I'm not putting my family at risk."

"We're not asking," her father remarked.

"Fine," Alexa agreed. "Wait here."

She hurried up the stairs. When she returned, Alexa was wearing all-black tactical clothing with a backpack in her hand.

"Let's go."

While Jake drove, Alexa explained.

"Andrew has a centuries-old bracelet that was stolen from the Siren. A woman that is a criminal and killer. Sophia Porter's boyfriend, Nicholas, and his friend Gates were involved in its disappearance. Andrew promised to get it back in exchange for her leaving us all alone. Unfortunately, he didn't make the deadline, and now he's been taken for collateral."

When they arrived at the hotel, Benny escorted them to Andrew's room. Her family helped search.

"I found it," Margot exclaimed, coming out of the bedroom.

She held it up in the light. The sapphires, rubies and emeralds shone brilliantly.

Margot laid it against her skin. "Wow, this thing is something."

"Yes, and right now, it's the only thing keeping Andrew alive."

Alexa's phone rang. Not recognizing the number, she answered it anyway.

"Hello?"

"Hello, Alexa. I won't bother introducing myself. You have something I want, and I have something you want. I propose we make an exchange. Unless you don't want your boyfriend back?"

It took everything in her to remain calm. "Of course I want Andrew back—unharmed."

Her family stopped and zeroed in on the conversation.

"And I want my bracelet. So do we have a deal?"

"We do."

"And the girl, of course."

"I don't understand."

"Sure you do. Bring my bracelet and Miss Porter."

"I will do no such thing," Alexa said vehemently. "I'm not about to deliver my client to you."

"You will if you want to see Andrew again—alive, that is."

Chapter 36

Terror ripped through Alexa, but she fought to remain calm.

"I'm doing what you asked. You wanted your bracelet, and I'm delivering it to you. Sophia has nothing to do with this."

"Oh, but she does, Miss King. She's the love of Nicholas Michaux's life and, therefore, essential to me. Besides, I have a bone to pick with Nico. He made me wait and caused me great inconvenience. So now, either bring the girl to me, or I start killing people, starting with your beloved parents, Jake and Margot. They have a lovely house, by the way. It's your call, Alexa."

Alexa's hand tightened on the cell phone. She glanced over at her father. "If you harm anyone I love," she whispered, "I promise I'll kill you."

"Aw, brave words. And while I appreciate your spunk, time is ticking, Miss King. You have the power to save everyone or kill them all. I don't care which you choose. I'm fine either way. I'm sure you'll be able to find the Pearl Tower. So don't keep me waiting."

"I want to speak with Andrew. I need to hear that he's still alive."

"Can't you just take my word for it?"

"No."

There was some shuffling on the Siren's line before she heard the one voice that mattered most.

"Hey, Lexi."

She closed her eyes and said a silent prayer. Andrew sounded tired, but it was still wonderful to hear his voice. "Drew," she breathed. "How are you?"

"Suffering from a minor knife wound, but I'll survive. Are you okay?"

She fought back tears. "I'm fine. Promise me that you'll keep yourself alive until I get there."

"No," he replied firmly. "Don't give her what she wants, Alexa. Stop worrying about me. I'll be fine."

There was a shuffle, and then she heard, "No, he won't unless you give me what I want. If you don't, your lover will die."

"He's injured and needs medical attention."

"You aren't in a position to demand anything."

"Yes, I am. I don't care how many threats you make. If anything happens to Andrew, the deal is off."

There was a long silence before the Siren said, "Fair enough. I suppose a dead hostage isn't much of an incentive, is it?"

She hung up before Alexa could respond.

Placing her phone back in her pocket, Alexa and her family rushed back to the car. Her father drove while Alexa gazed out the passenger window, struggling to pull herself together while she filled them in on the conversation.

"None of you can go home. It's not safe. She knows where you live and likely has her men watching the house." Tears flowed down her face, and her hands shook so badly that she crossed them.

"Don't worry about us," her father replied. "Getting Andrew back safely is the priority."

"I can't lose him," she said softly.

Jake squeezed her hand. "Everything will be okay, sweetheart."

"No, it won't. The last time Andrew and I were together, we fought, and I told him I didn't want to see him again. I didn't mean it," she cried. "I would give anything to take back what I said."

"Andrew knows that, sweetheart."

"How do you know, Dad?" she said tearfully.

"Because he knows your heart."

"Love is powerful and can heal all things," Margot replied from the back seat. She squeezed her daughter's shoulder. "It can survive even the most difficult of tests."

"I do love him," Alexa finally admitted. "I've wasted so much time being afraid, and now Andrew might die without knowing that."

"Alexa, you will save Andrew and defeat this crazy woman," Zane chimed in. "I know it."

She spun around. "How do you know?"

Zane flashed her a reassuring smile. "Because you're the best at what you do, Alexa. Trust that."

When they arrived at her condo, Alexa called her office to make arrangements for her team. Next, she phoned her friends Alejandro and Marena for help, along with Andrew's father, James, to bring him up to speed on the situation.

"I'll meet you in Lisbon," he stated.

There was no way that Alexa would try to talk James out of being involved in helping his son. So instead, she thanked him for the help and got to work.

Thirty minutes later, Jake pulled up at Ronald Reagan Washington National Airport. He retrieved her bags while Alexa said goodbye to her mother and cousin.

"Promise me that you'll go somewhere safe."

"They will," her cousin promised.

"Be careful, Alexa."

"I will, Mom."

Margot hugged her tight. "Okay. Then go get your man."

Alexa smiled and kissed her on the cheek. "That's the plan."

Zane enveloped her in a fierce hug. "I'm so proud of you. Now, go sweep the floor with this psychopath!"

"I will."

Jake was waiting behind them.

"You call me if you need anything, Lex," he said gruffly. "You hear me?"

Alexa went into his arms. "I will, Dad. I promise."

Taking her luggage, she waved goodbye to her family and headed to the jet. When she got on board, the flight attendant took her bags while Alexa spoke briefly to the captain. Then she trudged to her seat. However, she stopped short when she saw Dyan, her driver, Valerie, her assistant, Miranda, and Sophia waiting.

"What's going on? Why are you all here?"

"We're here to help," Dyan replied.

"You are helping by keeping Sophia safe," Alexa remarked sternly. She turned to her assistant. "Miranda, you should be at home resting."

"I'm fine, Alexa. And after all you've done for me there's no way I'm not helping, too."

"I heard about the Siren taking Andrew and her demands," Sophia chimed in. "I'm going with you."

"No, you're not," Alexa countered. "It's too dangerous to have you anywhere near her, Sophia. She wants to use you to make Nicholas suffer. I'm not giving you over to her—even to save Andrew. You're under my protection, which supersedes everything else."

"This is Andrew's life at stake, Alexa," Sophia countered.

"I'm aware, but I still won't risk your safety. He wouldn't want me to."

Sophia sat forward. "Well, it's not your call to make."

Alexa's eyebrows shot up. "The last time I checked, I'm still the CEO of Dragonfly. And my decision is final."

Sophia turned to Dyan and smiled. "Tell her."

"Alexa, Ruben canceled his contract. As a result, Sophia is no longer under Dragonfly's protection."

Alexa glared at Sophia. "What did you do?"

"I overheard you speaking with Dyan. That's how I learned the Siren demanded that you bring me, and you said no. I can't allow you to sacrifice the man you love for me. I've been horrible to you for years, Alexa. I've blamed you for things that weren't your fault. This is my chance to make amends for how I've treated you. You've lost a lot, too, and I won't be the cause of more heartbreak for you."

The captain announced that they had been cleared for departure. Seeing the resolute expressions of her staff and Sophia, Alexa shook her head and took a seat.

Exhaustion poured over her like rainwater, so Alexa took a quick nap before briefing her team on their operational plan. When she awoke, Dyan was on her computer, Sophia was watching something on her phone, and Miranda and Valerie were talking.

Realizing that she hadn't eaten all day, Alexa buzzed the flight attendant and requested some food.

Once she had slaked her hunger, she opened her laptop and got everyone's attention to go over the plan.

"We have three teams on the ground—Dragonfly's operatives, Andrew's men, and James and his officers. But I'll have operational control. While I'm meeting with the Siren, all teams will move in to surround the main house. James's men will cut the tower's main power and access to the backup generators while our team takes out their transportation. His men will move in and will be responsible for ensuring we retrieve Andrew and get back out safely."

"And what will I be doing?" Sophia inquired.

"Staying safe with the backup team."

"That's not going to work. You heard the Siren's demands. She wants you to deliver me as well, Alexa."

"Sophia—"

"Look, I've listened to your plan, and I think it's lacking one major thing."

Alexa looked up. "What's that?"

"Leverage."

"We have it. The Bellasini is what she wants most. We

keep that until everyone is out safely, and then I hand it over."

"That's not enough," Sophia persisted. "We need another carrot to dangle over her head, and that's where I can help."

"How?" Dyan queried.

"We hit her where it hurts—her wallet. Remember those accounts she forced Nicholas to open in his and my name so she could launder her money? Well, thanks to Nico, I've got access to them. We transfer those funds and use them as leverage to secure our safety."

Alexa shook her head and grinned. "Sophia, that's genius."

"Thank you." She beamed. "I'm sure her millions are worth more to her than that bracelet."

"Okay, ladies," Alexa said excitedly. "Let's go to work."

Chapter 37

When they arrived at the Humberto Delgado Airport in Lisbon several hours later, Alexa felt secure that their plan would succeed. And thanks to Sophia, they had a wild card that the Siren would not anticipate.

A black Mercedes-Benz Sprinter van was waiting to escort them to their rental villa about forty minutes from the Siren's compound.

Their rental home was a majestic two-story casa of white stone with bright lights and mature trees and flowers. It was dark, and she was tired, so Alexa didn't pay too much attention to the exterior.

There were guards strategically placed outside. Several stepped up to retrieve their luggage when they left the van.

"Good evening, Miss King," a matronly woman said as they walked into the entryway. It was bright, with white walls and dark brown baseboards and doors. The tan and brown tiles were in a checkerboard pattern, and there was a grandfather clock and a table with two armchairs nearby. Tapestries and paintings were strategically placed around the space, as were statues, planters and mirrors.

The steps to the second floor looked centuries old, as did the wrought-iron railing.

"Welcome to Casa Encantada. My name is Senhora D'Sousa."

"Olá," Alexa replied, and then switched to English. She introduced Sophia and her staff.

"Everything is in order. We have light refreshments in each bedroom, and every room has an en suite bathroom."

"Thank you, Senhora D'Sousa."

They followed the housekeeper upstairs. The older woman was short and shapely, and wore her salt-and-pepper hair pulled back into a chignon. She wore a navy blue dress with white trim and comfortable black shoes. She reminded Alexa of her aunt Ernestine.

Alexa walked in and glanced around the charming room.

One of the men set her bags at the foot of the bed and left. Across the room was a sofa and coffee table with a food tray and a glass water bottle. Though exhausted, Alexa nibbled on some nuts and dried fruit and drank a small glass of water. Next, she took a quick shower. Then, not up to putting her clothes away, she only retrieved a pair of cotton pajamas and socks.

After dressing, Alexa climbed into the bed and turned off the light. She turned on her side and stared out the window. For the first time all day, Alexa was alone, and it was quiet. She took a moment to think about Andrew. Her heart ached at what he must be going through. Her newfound love expanded in her chest and fueled her desire to rescue him. She would do whatever it took and bring all her expertise and resources to bear to save the man she loved and to keep Sophia safe.

"Please hang in there, Drew. I'm coming," she murmured before falling asleep.

Andrew tried several times to find a comfortable position in which to sleep. His stab wound in his midsection was giving him a hard time. True to her word, the Siren had sent a doctor in to assess his injury. He was happy to hear that it wasn't fatal, but it required stitches.

He couldn't forgive himself for being so careless. But after his fight with Alexa, he hadn't slept well, tossing and turning all night before finally giving up on sleep. By daybreak, Andrew had decided to see Alexa and sort everything out. She had said goodbye, but it didn't occur to him for one minute that their relationship was in danger of being over.

He arrived at her condo, and when she didn't answer,

he turned to leave but heard a noise inside. Bracing the door, Andrew rotated the knob as quietly as he could and inched the door open.

Seeing two men moving around Alexa's apartment made him furious. He was then flooded with fear. Was she there? Was she hurt?

That thought prompted him to action. He barreled into Alexa's living room and began pounding on the intruders. Unfortunately, when a third man arrived, they were able to do him harm. When he looked up and saw Alexa rush into the mix, his first reaction was that he would kill her for being so reckless. The second was that he'd never seen her more beautiful. Watching her defend him made his heart swell with love and pride. Andrew had known before that he was in love with Alexa, but seeing her take on those men to keep him safe was his undoing. He fell even harder.

"Good night, my love," he whispered, and closed his eyes.

Alexa found James sitting in the dining room when she came down for breakfast the next day. She rushed right over and into his arms when she spotted him.

"I'm so glad you're here," she murmured against his chest.

"Where else would I be but here helping you bring JJ home?" he said, hugging her tightly.

"I'm sorry I couldn't stop them from taking Andrew."

"Uh-uh. None of that, Alexa. I know you did everything you could to defend him. So don't despair, kiddo. We are going to get him back. Our plan will work."

They were moving out that evening, so the entire team gathered to go over the plan until everyone was briefed and ready to go.

When Sophia saw Nicholas enter the room, she ran over and flung herself into his arms. He caught her and held her tight.

"Are you okay?" he whispered into her hair.

"Yes," Sophia confirmed. "I'm fine."

"I'm sorry," Nicholas confessed. "For all of it. When I heard you'd been taken..." He stopped and struggled to speak for a few seconds. "My entire world turned dark."

"I know," she agreed. "I'm sorry, too, Nico."

Nicholas leaned down and kissed Sophia with a passion that relayed his feelings as clear as if he'd spoken them aloud.

He searched her face. "Are you ready?"

"Yes," Sophia said with conviction. "Let's take her down."

Alexa's team moved out at two o'clock in the morning. Valerie drove one of the four black armored Mercedes-AMG G 63 SUVs that Alejandro Reyes supplied while the other teams were spread out between the other three and the Mercedes-Benz Sprinter vans. Everyone was dressed in black tactical gear with body armor, except Alexa.

"Are you okay?" she asked Sophia.

"Yes," she replied confidently. "I'm good."

A few moments later, she turned to Alexa. "But, if—"

"It won't," she replied, reading Sophia's mind. "You're going to be fine. We all are."

Per their usual procedure, the teams were dropped a mile off and continued the rest of the way on foot. All except Alexa's vehicle, which continued up to the house. Equipped with night-vision goggles, the groups splintered off when they reached the Siren's compound. Each team with a specific job to do.

Adjusting her communication device in her ear, Alexa said, "We've arrived. Bluebird and I are heading in."

"Roger that, Guardian. We're in position and awaiting your signal."

Valerie drove up to the door and stopped. Men immediately headed toward the car. Each took one side and swept it for explosives. Then, satisfied, they opened the back door.

"Watch yourself," Alexa warned Valerie.

"I will. You, too."

Opening the door, one of the Siren's men stepped aside to let Alexa and Sophia get out.

"Your driver can park around the—"

"She stays right where she is," Alexa said firmly. "I don't plan on being long."

He didn't reply but turned and headed to the house. Alexa and Sophia followed behind.

As they entered, they were patted down before being led to meet the Siren. Sophia was carrying a laptop bag that was searched as well. The man checked Alexa's pockets, but they only produced a penlight, lip balm, a key chain and the velvet bag holding the Siren's bracelet.

"They're clean," the man announced.

"This way," another replied.

Alexa took a mental note of every window, exit and person they passed.

They were led down the floating staircase into the Siren's dojo. She spotted the woman sitting across the room on a raised dais. Her red hair was braided into a single plait that rested on one shoulder. She was wearing black leather pants and a black top, and a red-and-black open-front cardigan that fell just above her ankles.

"You must be Alexa."

"Siren," Alexa replied.

"I see you brought the girl after all."

"Where's Andrew?"

The Siren waved to one of the men across the room, who left and returned with Andrew in tow. Alexa noted that he was disheveled and moved with difficulty because his hands were bound behind his back. By the thin line of his lips and gray pallor, Alexa suspected his injury was causing him pain.

He was given a chair to sit on between Alexa and the Siren.

"As you can see, I kept my end of the bargain. Now, where is my property?"

Alexa reached into her jacket and retrieved the velvet bag. She handed it to the closest man, who took it to his boss.

When she opened the pouch, her eyes lit up with excitement as she studied the bracelet. Then, satisfied, she nodded to one of her employees, who went over and cut the ties binding Andrew's hands.

Andrew sagged in relief and rubbed his wrists.

"Now, the girl."

"What about another trade, Siren?"

The older woman was intrigued. "I'm listening."

"Let Andrew and Sophia go in exchange for me."

"No," Andrew said, getting up. "You have what you wanted. Let Alexa and Sophia go and keep me."

Alexa shook her head. "Andrew and Sophia go."

"I have a counteroffer. How about I kill all of you and be done with it?"

"You could, but then you'd lose millions of newly laundered dollars—or did you forget that?"

The amused smile slid off the Siren's face like oil on a slick surface.

"Looks like you did forget." Alexa turned to Sophia and nodded.

Sophia walked over to a table, opened her laptop bag and retrieved her computer.

"Wait, what is she doing? Why wasn't she checked?" the Siren demanded.

"She was," one of her men replied. "She's not carrying any weapons."

Sophia logged in to her bank account and set up a transfer. Then logged in to the following account and repeated the action. Finally, she spun the PC around to face the Siren.

"If they don't leave, I hit this button, and your money goes poof."

The Siren's face remained calm. "Foolish girl, you can't press anything if you're dead."

"That's true, but if I don't text the branch manager an abort code in fifteen minutes, he will complete the transfer for me." Sophia smiled triumphantly. "What's it going to be, Siren?"

The Siren's expression turned furious. She let out a roar of anger, threw off her cardigan and charged at Sophia.

Alexa tapped her ear as she moved to intercept her foe. "Ten minutes," she whispered.

"Roger that," came the reply over her earpiece.

"Alexa," Andrew called out. He went to move, but one of the Siren's men grabbed his shoulder and forcefully shoved him into the seat, causing him to grimace in pain.

Placing herself in front of Sophia, Alexa evaded several of the Siren's hits, but one caught her square on the jaw, and she struggled to maintain her balance. When the Siren tried to sweep Alexa's legs out from under her, she nimbly avoided the move and countered with several body strikes, knocking the Siren to the ground.

Several of her men rushed to defend her, but she ordered them to stop.

"She's mine," the Siren announced, spitting out blood.

The two continued sparring, with neither gaining the advantage.

"She's tiring," Andrew called from across the room.

"Shut up," the man guarding him warned.

Andrew switched to German to instruct Alexa on a defensive move.

"Danke," Alexa called out before implementing his suggestions.

She began hitting the Siren with combination moves that she couldn't defend.

Finally, realizing that Alexa was gaining the advantage in hand-to-hand combat, the Siren took it to the mat and tried to best Alexa with jujitsu. She tried a rear choke hold, but Alexa was trained on how to break it, and her response was automatic.

Tucking her head, Alexa grabbed the Siren's arm and pulled it down hard. Then, quickly, she wrapped her leg behind the Siren's calf, dropped her base, and spun around before pushing against her blocked leg. The Siren immediately lost balance and crashed to the floor. Alexa mounted her and delivered several blows.

Eventually, the Siren was able to push Alexa off and make it to the side wall. She retrieved a katana sword from its sheath.

Alexa yanked another of the ancient swords from the wall in the nick of time to defend herself against the Siren's attack.

Steel collided with steel as the two women fought. Each moved around the dojo mat with skilled precision as they engaged each other in battle. The Siren had more skill and thus the advantage in using the katana, but Alexa was calmer, providing her an edge.

Suddenly, a loud pop sounded, and the room went pitch-black.

"What's going on?" the Siren called out.

"I don't know, boss."

"Then go find out, you imbecile," she snapped.

Alexa silently dropped her sword and got low to the ground.

"Sophia?"

The younger woman flicked her miniature flashlight on and off once like Alexa instructed and remained quiet.

They heard a man moan, and then a loud thud.

"Andrew?" Alexa exclaimed, trying to determine the direction of the sound.

"I'm okay. One down," Andrew confirmed, breathing heavily. "Who knows how many more to go."

Suddenly, an arm snaked around Alexa's neck.

"I can play in the dark, too," the Siren whispered in Alexa's ear.

Bending over, Alexa flipped her and followed through with a hit to her solar plexus when she landed on the mat.

Gunshots rang out in the distance.

She retrieved her penlight from her pocket, turned it on and moved it in a sweeping motion around the room. "Andrew, Sophia, we've got to move."

"Okay," Andrew replied.

Alexa turned and flashed the light on the other side of the dojo.

"Sophia?"

"I'm here."

Seconds later, one of the men grabbed Sophia around the waist. Remaining calm, she fished her lipstick out of her pocket. Sophia twisted the barrel to the left and right before touching it to the man's arm around her neck.

He started shaking violently and then dropped to the floor.

Free, Sophia turned off the mini Taser, grabbed her bag and headed to the steps.

"Not so fast." The Siren slammed into Alexa, knocking her to the ground.

"Andrew, you two get out of here," she called out. "You'll have help."

As if on cue, the lights were restored, and James and his team rushed down the stairs.

The Siren used the distraction to pin Alexa to the ground. Then she retrieved a knife from her boot and slashed Alexa's arm. Next, she raised it to her face.

"I'm going to leave you with something you'll always remember," she threatened.

Grabbing the Siren's wrists, Alexa struggled to get the blade away from her face. When she was successful, Alexa placed her knee to her opponent's chest and launched the Siren over her head, giving herself time to get up.

Finding her sword, the Siren swung wide and would have seriously injured Alexa had she not jumped back.

Spotting her sword, Alexa dived to get it. When she got to her feet, she brandished it to keep the Siren at bay.

The clashing of steel against steel was deafening.

"Eileen, stop!"

The loud, deep voice boomed from across the room. Startled, the Siren whipped around. When she saw the man standing there, the color drained from her face, and her sword clattered to the floor.

"Dad?"

James was helping his son while his men disarmed the Siren's remaining bodyguards. When Andrew glanced up and saw who it was, he smiled.

"Good to see you again, Mr. Livingston."

"Likewise, Riker. Though I have to admit that you look terrible."

"Thank you," Andrew said tiredly.

"A member of your team contacted me with the coordinates. Thank you for that. You held up your end of our deal and found her. I'll do the same."

The Siren glanced at Andrew and then at her father. "What do you mean?"

Randolph regarded his daughter. "It's time we end this, Eileen."

Her face contorted with anger. "Stop calling me that," she said vehemently. "My name is Siren."

"You are Eileen Livingston, my daughter. And it's time you came home."

"I'm not going anywhere with you. And it's English. I'm using Mom's maiden name now," she spat. "And you can't just barge in here, throw your weight around and interfere with my plans. How'd you even find me?"

He didn't respond. Instead, Randolph touched her wrist.

She yanked her arm away. "What are you doing?"

"That's your mother's bracelet. I gave it to her before she died."

The Siren jutted her chin out. "And she gave it to me. It's all I have left of her."

"That's not true," her father replied. "There are many things I have saved that belonged to her that now belong to you. But this—" he pointed to her hand "—was always your favorite, so I knew if it went missing, you'd move heaven and earth to get it back."

She backed up several paces. "You had it stolen?"

"Yes," Randolph replied. "It was the only way I could find you, to draw you out. I'm just sorry men had to die in your quest to get it back."

"You tricked me?" Her eyes grew bright with tears. She glared at Andrew. "You led him to me," she spat. "This is your fault." She tried to lunge at Andrew, but Alexa blocked her path.

"Don't try it," Alexa warned.

"Your reign of terror ends now, Eileen. You're coming with me, and I'll get you the help you need."

"No, I'm not. And stop calling me that. I'm a grown woman. If you think I'm going to give up my life of independence to be under your thumb again, you're mistaken, Father," she said as if the word were a curse. "I have a very lucrative business that I built from nothing. I worked hard to get where I am."

"No, you killed and intimidated people to get where you are. You're sick, and you need help," he said gently. "Please, let me help you."

The Siren continued to back up. "No." Her voice shook, and she looked confused. "You're just trying to trip me up. I ran away from that mausoleum for a reason, and I'm not returning."

Randolph signaled his men. The Siren spun around to look for her bodyguards, but they were gone. She ran to grab her sword, but they beat her to it.

"Don't touch me," she yelled when two men took her by the arms and ushered her up the stairs. "No, you can't do this. I'm the Siren. Do you hear me? I promise I'll kill every last one of you when I get the chance. I'm the Siren!"

The echoes of her screaming eventually faded away.

Randolph sank into a chair. He sighed loudly. "I'm sorry for all the trouble my daughter has caused. Unfortunately, she has a delusional disorder, just as her mother did. I took Eileen to the top mental health professionals. Her treatments worked for a while, but she refused to continue her sessions. Then, while I was on a business trip, Eileen got free of my staff and ran away."

His eyes were saturated with pain. "You can't imagine the helplessness of having a child run away and not being able to find them. I had my men searching everywhere, but my efforts were useless. By the time I heard about the Siren—" His voice was racked with grief. "I was too late to help my wife before she…died, but I have found a facility that can provide Eileen with the help she needs. One where I can visit her and help in the healing process."

"What about the people hurt or that died because of her?" Alexa asked.

"She isn't well enough to face prosecution, Miss King. And honestly, with my legal team, it's unlikely that she would. But this is my cross to bear, and I will do whatever it takes to ensure my daughter isn't a threat to anyone again."

Randolph got up and left with his men, looking decades older than when he first arrived.

Alexa held Andrew's hand. "It's over."

He squeezed it back. "Thanks to you."

"It was a group effort." She smiled and then grimaced at the cut on her lip. "Andrew, about the things I said—"

"Forgiven," he finished for her. "I went to your condo that morning to apologize and humbly ask you to reconsider leaving me. Alexa, I never meant for you to feel like I doubt how capable you are of protecting yourself, me or whomever you're hired to guard. You're my world, Alexa. You have been since you stepped into my life. And I will do anything to keep you safe from harm. It's who I am. I'm just sorry I went about it in a way that caused you to doubt my true intentions."

Alexa shook her head. "Forgiven. And you should know that I went back to the hotel that morning to tell you I was sorry for what I said. I'm truly grateful to you, Andrew, for how you've protected, cared about and supported my endeavors since we met. Because of your hard work, dedication and commitment, I found a career that I love and a passion for serving others in a way that keeps them safe."

"And *you* whole."

She smiled. "And me whole." She laced her fingers through his. "I'm not scared anymore. I know what we have is real. You were right. We can't live in a bubble worrying about losing those closest to us. I can finally let go of my past and direct that energy to my future."

He touched her cheek. "Our future," he corrected.

Alexa beamed with happiness. "Our future."

Andrew lowered his head and kissed her. Alexa's hands came up to rest on either side of his face. A few moments later, she pulled back.

"Do you know the first stop on our new journey?"

He grinned lasciviously. "Do tell."

"The hospital," she said lovingly.

Andrew chuckled and wrapped his arm around her waist.

"Lead the way, Miss King."

Chapter 38

"Here, is this better?"

Alexa took a pillow from the couch and adjusted it behind Andrew's head.

"Much." He sighed happily. "You know, I don't think I ever told you how proud I am of you. You were willing to let me die to save Sophia. That shows that you take your job seriously."

She burst out laughing. "Well, I'm glad you approve. Though I had no intention of letting you die, Mr. Riker. In truth, I would've been devastated if something had happened to you."

"Because you realized you loved me?"

"Yes, after our fight and you were taken, it hit me square between my eyes that I loved you and didn't want to lose you."

Andrew touched her cheek. "You are never going to lose me, Lexi."

She settled next to him on the couch. "You can't promise that, Andrew. None of us is in control. Our lives could be over in the blink of an eye."

"True, but when you love someone, you give it your best shot and do what you can to keep each other safe."

She leaned in and kissed him. "I love you, too. But honestly, Drew, because of what we do for a living, sometimes it does worry me." She snuggled closer, careful not to lean on him too heavily.

They watched the fire blazing in the hearth in silence for a few minutes before Andrew said, "You know I'm not made of glass, right?"

"I know, but the doctor said it'll be another week before

you can get your stitches out. And until then, no strenuous activity—of any kind."

Andrew leaned over and kissed Alexa's lips, then a trail down her neck.

She immediately gravitated toward his touch. "You're not playing fair." Her words drifted out of her mouth like a soft caress.

"You know, there are a few things that I can think of that are not necessarily categorized as strenuous."

"No, sir," she laughed, pulling back. "You promised you'd be back to one hundred percent before the next group of trainees arrived. I love you, Andrew Riker, but those sparring sessions with overeager students can be a bit much."

"And I will," Andrew said, chuckling, before picking up her hand and kissing her palm. "And on that note, lunchtime is over. Back to work we go."

"Ugh," she protested. "I'd much rather be snuggling on the couch here with you."

"That prospect is just as exciting for me, but you know if we're late, Dad will come looking for us."

Alexa bolted off the sofa. "You've got a point. Let's go. Phalanx is calling."

They rode the ATV from the guest cabin back to the main building for their next class. Alexa enjoyed helping Andrew and his father with the training sessions. She had taken a leave of absence from fieldwork at Dragonfly to stay in Pagosa Springs for an extended period until Andrew was fully recovered. She was still acting CEO and conducted most of her business by video conference while Dyan handled meetings with new clients and Alexa's duties as the principal chief protection officer.

"There you two are," James said when they returned to the training room. "I thought I would have to send up a flare signal."

"You know Alexa wouldn't miss jujitsu training. She loves grappling with the students."

"I'd rather be grappling with you," she whispered in Andrew's ear.

His gaze could have scorched a block of ice.

"Anytime you want to try those nonstrenuous activities, just let me know."

She laughed and playfully pushed him away. Then, after taking off her coat, Alexa warmed up to prepare for their next class. When the students trickled in a few minutes later, Andrew took the lead, instructing the students on which grappling techniques they'd learn during the class.

While he explained, Alexa used a volunteer to execute the motions that Andrew relayed. Unfortunately, the student didn't understand the technique at one point, so Andrew stepped in to demonstrate.

"Be careful," Alexa warned.

"Always am." He winked.

As Andrew explained, he placed his hands on Alexa to show the trainees how their bodies should rotate in and out of a position. Next, he demonstrated how to flip an opponent using the attacker's body weight, not their own.

He flipped Alexa, and she landed on the mat.

"Sorry, my love," he said sweetly as she lay there staring up at the ceiling.

"No problem, my love," she responded with a saucy grin.

Rolling over, Alexa pushed herself up.

"You dropped something, Miss King," one of the students remarked.

"Oh?" Alexa was wearing a karate uniform called a gi, which didn't have pockets. "Thank you," she said, automatically looking down.

There was a black velvet ring box sitting on the mat. She stared at it for a few more seconds before gazing, bewildered, at Andrew.

"What in the world?" she said as she knelt to retrieve

the box. When she opened it, all the air left Alexa's lungs. She remained frozen in her spot, speechless as she stared at the square-cut diamond engagement ring with stair-step diamonds flanking the main one.

When she looked up, Andrew was down on one knee in front of her. Her hand covered her heart as she stared at him through unshed tears.

"Alexa Yvonne King, I have loved you since I carried you back after getting shot in the chest during training."

The group let out a collective gasp, each looking around worriedly.

"I had a bulletproof vest on," Alexa said, trying to ease the horrified students' minds.

"You are intelligent, caring, funny and sexy," he continued. "Plus, you truly make me the best version of myself. I would be elated to spend the rest of my life loving, working with and coming home to you. Will you do me the honor of becoming my wife?"

Alexa leaned forward. "James Andrew Riker II, I have admittedly been stubborn and have run from relationships, but you have shown me that love can be constant, and I don't have to fear it, nor does it have to end in sorrow or tragedy. Because of you, I know that love is patient, kind, understanding and long-lasting. Being vulnerable enough to give another person a chance to share your life is the greatest gift of all. I love you, Drew, and yes, I will marry you, and I can't wait to be your wife."

Beaming proudly, Andrew leaned over and kissed Alexa. She wrapped her arms around him and cried tears of joy as she returned the kiss. Everyone clapped as he placed the ring on the third finger of her left hand. Alexa peered at the brilliant diamond ring for several moments, in awe at the surprise proposal. Then she spotted her family standing off to the side. Alexa was so shocked that she yelped before rushing over to greet her parents, cousin, aunt and uncle. Next, James and Esther stepped up to offer their congratulations. James dismissed the class early so their families could return to the house and honor the newly engaged couple.

While they were celebrating, Alexa received a video call from Sophia. She and Nicholas wished her and Andrew congratulations.

"Thank you and Andrew for protecting us both," Nicholas stated. "And for keeping us, you know, from being dead."

Alexa's eyebrows rose. "Oh, you're welcome, Nico."

"You know, we worked so well together that anytime you and Andrew need operatives, Nico and I would be happy to lend a hand."

"Wow," Alexa said with genuine surprise. "If the need arises, we'll let you know."

"Cool. I have a special engagement gift for you, Alexa." Sophia grinned. "Just a moment."

She and Nicholas moved out of the way, and another woman moved into view.

Alexa was stupefied. "Oh my gosh. Shelley?"

"Yes," her old friend confirmed. "It's wonderful to see you, Alexa."

"Likewise," she said between tears. "I can't believe it's you. You look amazing," she cried.

"So do you. Sophia's told me so much about your life now. I'm so happy for you."

"Sophia has kept me in the loop, too. I'm glad you're living life to the fullest, Shelley."

They chatted for a few more minutes before Shelley had to go, but she promised to keep in touch.

"I'd love to as well," Alexa confirmed.

When they ended the call, Alexa found her fiancé and wrapped her arms around his middle. She told him about her video call with the Porters.

"Thank you," she said sincerely. "This was a perfect proposal, and I love you so much."

"I love you, too, soon-to-be Mrs. Riker."

"I love the sound of that."

* * * * *

Don't miss Lisa Dodson's other thrilling title:
Six Days to Live
available from Harlequin Romantic Suspense!

COMING NEXT MONTH FROM

HARLEQUIN

ROMANTIC SUSPENSE

#2267 COLTON'S DANGEROUS COVER

The Coltons of Owl Creek • by Lisa Childs

For Fletcher Colton's first case as lead detective of Owl Creek Police Department, he'll pose as Kiki Shelton's assistant. But keeping the famous DJ safe from the serial attacker The Slasher doesn't threaten his professional cover as much as Kiki herself does.

#2268 OPERATION RAFE'S REDEMPTION

Cutter's Code • by Justine Davis

Financial guru Charlie Foxworth has a score to settle for her family. And teaming up with military operative Rafe Crawford—and her brother's too-cute, too-clever canine, Cutter—to bring a traitor to justice is her sole option. If only Rafe hadn't shattered her heart years ago...

#2269 PERIL IN THE SHALLOWS

New York Harbor Patrol • by Addison Fox

Seasoned detective Arlo Prescott is the best in his field—and determined to uncover the source of Brooklyn's newest crime syndicate. Partnering with Officer Kerrigan Doyle will expose them not only to the dangerous underbelly of New York...but to feelings that threaten their whole operation.

#2270 THE SUSPECT NEXT DOOR

by Rachel Astor

Mystery author Petra Jackson's solution to her writer's block is to surveil her handsome neighbor Ryan Kent. Unbeknownst to her, he's a private investigator trying to solve a murder case. Soon her amateur sleuthing—and undeniable attraction to Ryan—leads to more than she bargained for!

HRSCNM0124